ROWDY ARMSTRONG
Wrestling's New Golden Boy

David Monster

Facebook.com/RowdyArmstrong
Facebook.com/RowdyArmstrongWrestlingBook
Twitter.com/RowdyArmstrong
DavidMonster.com

ISBN-10: 1515379051
ISBN-13: 978-1515379058

DEDICATION

To Eric Pedersen, Brad Armstrong, The Warlord, Arn Anderson, Chick Donovan, Buddy Rogers, Tommy Rogers, Reggie Parks, Mark Lewin, Steve Austin, Eddie Graham, Tyler Black, Dolph Ziggler, Nikita Kiloff, Sheamus O'Shaunessy, Chris Candido, Mike Enos, Tom Magee, Scotty Young, Tyler Nitro, Al Perez, Pete Kuzak, Mike Tolbert, Dale Veasey, Darren Young, Rene Dupree, Robert Duranton, Ivan Putski, Rocky Johnson, Rene Lasartesse, Evan Bourne, Cody Rhodes, Randy Orton, Bruno Sammartino, Gronda, Paul Roma, Tom Zenk, Don Muraco, Anthony Bravado, Mike Barton, Tony Garea, Bob Emory, Bill Melby, Rob Terry, Matt Walsh, Mike Awesome, Nathan Jones, Steve Strong, Thunder, Brian Cage, Jay Cutler, Jon Anderson, Jeff Farmer, The Patriot, Prince Devitt, Jessie Godderz, Lashley, Big E Langston, Romeo Roselli, Alex Wright, Dave Draper, Kevin Von Erich, Kevin Kelly, Matt Murphy, Steven Walters, Roderick Strong, Brock Lesnar, & Chris Masters, not to mention the wrestlers of BG East & Can-Am, & all the others who inspired me & made me love Pro Wrestling.

Forgive me if I left you out. There are so many I can't remember them all.

CONTENTS

ACKNOWLEDGMENTS

If you were a dude who discovered his inclination for other dudes, before the inception of the internet, Pro Wrestling was your first porn. There was no where else you could see hot dudes, almost naked, going at it.

But, Pro Wrestling is about a little bit more than just plain old sex.

The best Pro Wrestlers maintain exceptional physiques while exposing themselves to the highest possibility of injury and pain. They act out the proverbial struggle between good and evil and every man's desire to dominate, or be dominated. With their oiled muscles and revealing trunks they also give a satirical wink of acknowledgment to the homo-erotic nature of the sport. It's Humor & Sex, Comedy & Tragedy all rolled up in a hot, sweaty, swollen, worked-out package.

Pro Wrestling is more than a sport. It's a fetish.

1 THE BEGINNING

It all started, for Rory Pedersen, the same as any man. The year was 2025, he was 13, and saw something that woke him up, erotically speaking. To call it a "sexual awakening" would be a cliché and an understatement. Like any other teenage boy, it became more of a sexual obsession.

He was watching Professional Wrestling in the Virtual TV Room with his 11 year-old brother, Reed. Both boys were excited, and Rory quickly realized it was for very different reasons. Reed became animated & involved, while Rory sat still and pulled a pillow over his lap.

DYER ANDERSON vs. THE GOLDEN BOY

The match they came upon was already in progress. Big, brawny Dyer Anderson, the current World Heavyweight Champ, was being worked over in the corner by a smaller, beautiful, buff Blond man.

Rory was obviously aroused, but something happened that pulled the *entire* focus of his world on to this match, and Pro wrestling. The Blond man grabbed the front of Dyer's trunks, wrapped his fingers around his entire bulge and yanked down. Dyer's face contorted into a grimace, and Rory thought he saw the faintest glimmer of pleasure. The Champ held on to the ropes, and his knees trembled.

The Ref smacked the Blond man's shoulders, and warned him to take the action out of the corner. The cunning blond beauty pointed at something across the ring, and when the Ref looked away, he squeezed and yanked Dyer's bulge, again. He, then, backed away with his hands up, showing the Ref he was a completely clean wrestler.

Dyer cupped his pained groin, and dropped to his knees.

Rory swore he saw Dyer's bulge tented out in his trunks. He blushed, fully excited under his pillow.

Rory identified with the Challenger. He, himself, was blond, and hoped to be as muscular and good-looking as this beautiful bad boy. He already started working out, was on the swim team, and had been studying karate since he was 6. At 13, he was 5'9", and weighed 155 tight pounds. Between swimming and running, his face and body were almost always tanned, which set off his light gold hair, and blue eyes. His little brother looked a lot like him, but there was a touch of red in his hair. He was thicker and seemed that he'd be a bit broader as he grew up.

Rory liked Dyer Anderson, the presently helpless Champ. He was a ring veteran, about 40 years old, and was billed as 6 feet, 265lbs. He had thickly muscled arms, chest, back, shoulders, legs, and a bit of a belly. He was manly, tough, and hairy, with light brown hair. Something about his thickness held Rory's interest, especially the way his big butt jiggled when he was slammed in his beer belly.

Dyer's opponent was quickly becoming Rory's favorite,

though. He desperately wanted to know everything about him: his name, where he was from, how tall he was, how much he weighed, and how he could be so beautiful and yet so mean in the ring.

The Blond man backed away from Dyer Anderson, with his hands up, as the Ref bent down to ask The Champ if he was ok to continue.

The crowd also loved this new Blond heel. Cheers exploded when he posed and wiped down his muscles.

Dyer used the ropes to pull himself up. He rubbed his aching balls.

The Blond man came up beside the Ref, tapped his shoulder, and when the Ref turned away from The Champ, the Blond was able to   whack Anderson's bulge with an open-handed slap.

Dyer howled and leaned over the ropes. The Ref checked him, and Blondie's hands were up, again, proclaiming his innocence. The announcer finally said the Blond man's name, "Chris Enos", and hailed him as "The Sports New Golden Boy". He was the current U.S.A CHAMP. Rory repeated his name, "Chris Enos".

Dyer Anderson struggled on the ropes and Rory actually felt tense for him. He loved the new guy, but knew Dyer would be humiliated to lose. Chris wiped down his muscles, again, then sauntered over to The Champ, who was still grimacing and holding on to the ropes for dear life. Chris stepped in front of Dyer and opened his arms up, in a pose of ultimate dominance.

BAM! Dyer hit him with a quick, HARD right to the abs. The

Champ was playing possum, not nearly as hurt as he pretended.

Chris's eyes bulged and he lost his breath. His hands cradled his abs. Dyer grabbed Enos's right wrist with his left hand. WHAM! He buried another right into the challenger's stomach. Chris's butt jerked back, as he doubled over.

Anderson grabbed a handful of Chris Enos' blond hair and pulled his head back. Enos held on to his stomach and groaned. Dyer CHOPPED him across his chest with a SMACK! He did a pained little dance as his perfectly muscled pecs bounced. Dyer licked his lips, and couldn't resist. He grabbed those sweaty muscle pecs and clawed them. Chris howled and teetered on his tiptoes. He pulled backward and ended up with his back against the ring post.

The Ref slapped Dyer's shoulder and called for a break. Dyer dropped the claw and gave Enos's pecs a backhand CHOP. The Challenger expelled his lungs with a loud "OOOF". His red chest bounced, again, and he held the ropes as hard as he could.

Anderson leaned in, his big meaty, hairy chest up against Chris's smooth, tight pecs, and whispered something into Chris's ear, with a sneer. The Champ's thick paws were wrapped around The Challenger's wrist, and in a split second, Enos was whipped across the ring, where his back hit the opposite ring post with a THUD!

"Ungh!" Chris was dazed and winded, again. He slumped, and his elbows hooked over the top rope, keeping him almost on his feet.

Again Dyer pressed his brawny torso against Chris's shiny, chiseled physique. Rory saw Anderson's big butt flex slowly, twice, and imagined that he was grinding his bulge into Enos's. Rory's mind was spinning, and he ached to be alone with these two wrestlers, in the ring.

The Champ stepped back, and whipped the Challenger across the ring into the opposite post. THUD!

Dyer backed away, almost to the opposite corner. He ran, with all his might, toward The Challenger. In another show of his greater experience in the ring, he was able to stop about six feet in front of Chris, just out of range of the boot that Chris kicked up to try and nail The Champ in the breadbasket. It was just an inch from making contact. Dyer smiled, and pointed at the wily challenger, then laughed, because he saw the kick coming a mile away.

Enos was still recovering in the corner. He shook his head as Dyer powered in with an uppercut to the gut that was so hard Chris's legs flew up. Spittle flew out of his mouth, along with a howling groan. He slumped down lower, sitting on the middle rope, wildly trying to catch his breath.

The Champ pulled him out of the corner by his hair, once more. Chris tried to stop him with a jab to his stomach, but it was too weak. Dyer responded with another uppercut to the gut, as he kept a hold of The Challenger's hair. Chris's jaw went slack, and his eyes closed as he grimaced and held his aching abs.

Dyer scooped him up in a crotch and shoulder lift. The Blond's abs were now against Anderson's upper chest. He carried the muscle boy center ring, and SLAMMED him down on his back. The Challenger arched up, and cried out.

Dyer leaned down and pulled the hurting blond boy up to his

feet, by his golden locks. He was so dazed, desperate, and reckless that he made another grab for Dyer's bulge.

The Champ kept a hold of Chris's hair, and pulled him backwards into the ropes. His big butt flexed, again.

The Ref called for the break, "Off the ropes!"

"Unhh. I can't." Anderson looked down to his groin that was being roughed up at the moment.

The Ref smacked Chris's arm, "Break it!" but he didn't release. The Ref then pulled Chris's arm with a YANK, and Dyer screamed out as Chris's claw was ripped from his bouncing cock and balls.

Rory was transfixed. This time was able to see long enough to be sure that Dyer had indeed started to get an erection.

Dyer Anderson cupped his bulge with both hands. Rory didn't even blink. He was transfixed on the Champ's crotch. He had to see that hard-on, again.

The Ref pushed Chris away, scolding him, but he just argued back, pointing at The tormented Champion.

The ref shook his head, saying "NO" to whatever Chris was arguing about. BAM! Dyer's fist came out of nowhere. Chris's head shot up, and back, and he hit the mat, back first. He groggily looked up into the lights, and saw stars.

Dyer was right there, pulling Chris to his feet, by his hair. Once more, he scooped Chris up in another crotch and shoulder lift. He flipped Mr. Enos upside-down, and secured him in a belly-to-belly bear hug. The crowd went crazy. This was the set-up for

Dyer's finishing move: "The Wrecking Ball Pile Driver". Dyer buried his face between Chris's legs and his head moved around, as he walked his prey to center ring.

Rory squinted and wished he could see what Anderson was doing with his mouth.

Dyer hopped up and dropped down, pile-driving Chris Enos's beautiful head into the canvas. He immediately fell limp, staring up at the lights, again. The Champ rested for a second, in his kneeling position, with The Challenger's dazed head between his knees.

He lowered himself on top of Enos, and pushed his face into the front of the Challenger's trunks, then slowly ground his own bulge into Chris Enos's handsome face.

The Ref dropped down and pounded the mat, "ONE...TWO...THREE!!!" The victory bell sounded. "DING! DING!"

Dyer rested on top of his beaten opponent for a drawn-out moment too long. He burst out screaming, and rolled off, over to the ropes, holding his bulge. Apparently, Enos had bitten him.

The Champ yelled and threatened the defeated Challenger, pulling himself to one knee. He rubbed slowly between his legs. Enos rolled the other way, out of the ring. He slowly wiped off his muscles, flexed, and posed for the crowd, as if he was the victor.

Anderson watched with an incredulous, angry expression.

Rory was going insane. He swore he detected an erection in the front of Dyer's trunks, again. The Show cut away to the announcer, as he awaited an interview with the Champ.

"Gotta go to the bathroom!" Rory excused himself. He ran to his room, and locked the door. In no time, his holographic monitor was on, and he searched for anything he could find about Chris Enos. For hours he obsessed over the Golden Boy.

He watched Professional Wrestling religiously after that, alone as much as possible.

The All World Pro Wrestling Federation

In 2025, it was "discovered" that several government agencies had records of detected radio waves originated by a non-human source, since the early 2000's. They had been working on deciphering them, and although none would release the content of the messages, they claimed they were "non-threatening". Most people didn't believe their authenticity, and "alien transmissions" became a joke for the rest of the decade. Religious organizations panicked and protested JPL, NASA, the US Government, Science, and anything else they could scream at. Every religion and philosophy lost followers, in droves.

Plans to colonize Mars were also being realized. Teams were organized and launch dates were already set.

Companies and corporations, large and small, rebranded, renamed, and reorganized to include the rest of the universe as possible commercial avenues. The ALL WORLD PRO WRESTLING Federation, or The A.W.P.W., became ALL WORLDS PRO WRESTLING - an easy fix. They used the slogan, "All WorldS Pro Wrestling: IT'S THE S!" for years after, even though other companies, in different fields, had used it decades earlier.

Rory Starts Wrestling

Rory started a collegiate wrestling class. It wasn't the same as Pro, but he loved the feel of the struggle, the power, using his muscles against an opponent, the body contact, the rivalry, and the camaraderie.

He learned the basics pretty quickly, and did well against all the guys his age. He joined a local extracurricular wrestling team, as his junior high didn't have one. By the time he was 15, and a freshman in high school, he'd already won a few local tournaments. He started sparring and lifting weights with a teammate, Todd James, who was 20lbs heavier and 1-½ years older. They became good friends. Todd was almost 17 years old, 6', 195lbs. Rory had become a 5'11" 175 muscular 15 year-old, and the only freshman to make the Junior Varsity team in High school.

Todd shared Rory's passion for every style of wrestling. He had no intention of competing in Pro, but was Rory's biggest supporter. They even practiced pro holds and moves.

Rory kept up with Pro matches from all around the world, and would search for any digital recording or live holographic show he could find... alone in his room.

He became obsessed with Chris Enos and his road to the belt. Enos made no secret of his goal. Unfortunately, after his failed attempt, he slid down the list of contenders.

Next in line was the French Champion, Rene Sebastian, who had been chomping at the bit for months. Some countries previously displayed active disinterest in the World Title, preferring to wrestle exclusively for the fans of the own country, but that was changing.

RENE SEBASTIAN –France's Champ

Rene Sebastian was 5'10", 225lbs, muscular, and although he was smaller, and lean, his butt was just as big as Dyer Anderson's. That big bubble butt made him world-famous to wrestling fans. He had chestnut colored hair, hazel-green eyes, and always wrestled in powder pink bikini pro trunks. His hair was short on the sides, but long on top, and during the match was forever falling down, obscuring one eye.

His hands always made their way into his opponent's trunks. Many considered him the dirtiest wrestler in the business, although Chris Enos's reputation was building. Rene was also notorious for having a semi, or full erection, for the majority of a match. He was never embarrassed by it, and whether he won or lost, he loved his job.

He would even rub his erection in his rival's face, which always brought him physical pleasure. Rumor had it that he would wrestle nude, in his practice matches. Rory searched endlessly for any kind of recording of them.

Sebastian began every match by air-kissing both of his opponent's cheeks. It was never a ruse for a sneak attack, just a sincere gesture. He would often end matches the same way, which was interesting, considering the way he dealt with his opponents during the match.

After circling, and locking up, Rene would begin his sensually sadistic assault on his opponent's testicles, nipples, penis, and midsection, all the while, with an erection. Sometimes, that erection would sneak up and poke up out of the waistband, or leg hole of his small wrestling trunks. Every so often it would be completely revealed by all the tugging, ripping, and clawing from an opponent who would fight fire with fire.

Rene was a fan favorite. The crowd loved seeing him manhandle an undeserving clean-cut rookie, but they were in heaven when he was on the receiving end of dirty tricks. He had groupies, and even other wrestlers, from all over the world throwing themselves at him.

Rene Sebastian held on to the Title of Mr. Paris for three years as he battled the All France Champion, Edouard Du Jardin, every time unsuccessfully. He wanted that title as much as Chris Enos wanted the All Worlds Heavyweight Belt.

Edouard Du Jardin, known as "Le Taureau" in France, or "The French Bull", in the rest of the World, held the title for many years, undefeated. At 5' 10", he was a thick, brawny 255 pounds, and was a former strength trainer and power lifter.

He was the type of Frenchman who thought the world revolved around France, and never cared much about challenging champions from other countries.

Known to be a complete gentleman outside the ring, he openly detested Rene's dirty style of wrestling. Rene's tactics would only work on Edouard for so long, until one ball-grab too many would enrage the French Bull, and he would flatten

Monsieur Sebastian.

When Edouard turned 45, he retired, undefeated, and declined all challenges, including from Rene, to whom he had already given 10 title matches. Sebastian wasn't the slightest bit ashamed of his losses to Edouard, and he publicly begged Du Jardin for an 11th chance. No dice.

A tournament was held in which the top ten wrestlers in France competed. Rene became the new champ, but just barely. Two rivals came very close to defeating him – one bigger, and one much smaller.

Rene Sebastian vs. Frederick Souris

The smaller one was Frederick Souris, also known as "Freddie The Mighty Mouse". He was a 21 year-old, tiny muscle boy, 5'2" tall, 160 lbs. He was just as sexually sadistic as Rene, maybe even more so. Their match became a "Battle of the Boners", and they both inflicted very visible pleasure and pain on each other.

At one point, Frederick had Rene in the ropes. He pulled Rene's hard-on through the leg hole of his trunks, and was pinching the head of his erection. Rene's body trembled, and it looked like he was holding back an orgasm.

Freddie was then able to flip Mr. France on his back, and pin him, with his own hard-on pressing down on Monsieur Sebastian's face.

Rene kicked out just before the Ref's hand came down for the 3rd count. He was scared. How could a younger man, who was

60lbs lighter, knock him out of the tournament?

The little muscle boy used Rene's chin to drag him up to his feet, easily lifted him up, and slammed him back-first into canvas.

Rene was a hot, sweaty spectacle, arching his back, which hoisted his hips up and showed off the erection poking out the leg of his trunks.

Souris showboated for the crowd. He looked down at Rene, who was rubbing his back, that boner was still exposed. Souris had to push his own erection down. It felt good.

Freddie ran to the ropes, rebounded, jumped high, and went for a big splash on Mr. Sebastian. As Freddie came down Rene caught him in both arms, squeezed him in a bear hug and rolled him over for the pin. Souris was stunned, but managed to push the bigger man onto his side, and escape the bear hug before the 3 count.

Freddie sat up with big eyes, his mouth hanging open. Rene swung his legs up and caught Freddie's head in a leg scissor, and *squeeeezed*. Freddie grabbed on to Rene's thigh muscles and tried to pull them apart, his fingers an inch away from that erection, still sticking out of his trunks.

Rene flexed his big, shiny quads, which pushed his manhood into Mr. Souris' cheek. Freddie was very strong for his size, and he worked to get Rene onto his back. He almost succeeded, but Rene pulled on Freddie's hair, and flopped Mighty Mouse back down to the mat.

Rene's hard-on throbbed into Freddie's face, as he flexed

and re-flexed his thighs. Freddie couldn't take it anymore. He grabbed it and pulled HARD. Rene's eyes squinted and his mouth opened wide. He said, in French, "Oh yes! PULL HARDER!" Freddie certainly tried to, and Rene moaned louder. Souris worked to get a better grip, and pulled harder. Rene moaned, again, and whispered, "If you do it again, I'm going to cum."

Freddie wondered, if he could make Rene cum, maybe that would distract him. But, while Freddie was thinking about that, Rene grabbed Freddie's hand and flipped him onto his back. He launched himself up so he was straddling Freddie's neck, his knees pinning Freddie's arms. Rene smiled, and pushed his hard-on into Freddie's open mouth.

Freddie was pinned. He kicked and flailed. He tried to hook Rene's arms with his legs, but the bigger man easily caught and hooked them.

Rene had Freddie all rolled up.

"UN! DEUX! TROIS!" The ref pounded the mat, and Rene Sebastian got the three count. He remained on top of Freddie Souris, pushing his erection in and out of the little muscleman's mouth. Freddie was mad, humiliated and defeated, but also enormously aroused.

The Ref lifted Rene up off the smaller man, with his right arm and kept it raised in victory. Sebastian's erect penis was still poking straight out the leg hole of his stretched-out, powder-pink trunks.

He made his way to the ropes, with his hands on his hips. He turned to lean on them, and looked back at Freddie, now on his knees, sporting his own erection. Rene put a knee on the middle rope and pushed it down. He motioned Freddie over. The little Muscle Mouse sprang up, and exited through the gap Rene made for him. They walked up the aisle to the locker room, together, boners bobbing.

Rene Sebastian vs. Alexandre Sauvage

The bigger man, who almost beat Rene, was Alexandre Sauvage. He was trained by, none other than, Edouard Du Jardin, himself. At 6'2", 245lbs, Alex was amazingly thick for a French man, and surprisingly agile for a big man. He was a great athlete, but hadn't mastered his sadistic side, which gave Sebastian the edge. In fact, Mr. Sauvage was just as much a gentleman as his trainer, but hadn't learned how to tap into his rage, like "The Bull" did so easily. He was basically a big, handsome jock boy, with dark brown hair and hazel eyes.

Early on in the match, Alexandre was able to take control with a chain of moves that had Rene Sebastian looking like a dazed jobber, who had never had a match before.

Edouard Du Jardin sat ringside, with a huge smile on his face.

After kicking out of a pin, for the second time, Rene scrambled to the ropes, and held on. The Ref backed Alexandre away.

Rene pulled himself to his feet, humiliated, shaken, but also surprised that he was already sporting an erection. He tried to shake out the cobwebs and get mad, but this sudden arousal had gotten the better of him. Alexandre was a very muscular specimen of extreme masculinity. Sebastian was relieved that Sauvage was straight, and never attacked the trunk region of other men. He was hugely attracted to him, and wasn't sure what would happen if he had to defend himself sexually.

Alexandre came in quickly and dodged to Rene's left just as Rene tried for a kick to his midsection. Rene was impressed by how well Edouard had trained his protégé.

Alex threw an elbow, clocking Rene dead on, in the jaw, then easily applied a very hard full nelson. A dazed Rene wondered how he was being worked so easily.

After a few moments, Monsieur Sebastian was able to walk them both over to the ropes. The crowd could see his very prominent erection, and for the first time, Rene was a bit self-conscious about it. He tried to hook a leg over the bottom rope, but Alexandre yanked him back away from the ropes, and cranked the nelson harder.

Rene was sweating. This was the second time in the tournament he was actually worried he might be beaten. He was desperate. Alexandre was a big, strong, strapping Ox, and his nelson was unbreakable. Rene couldn't make a dent in it. He tried to flex and grind his butt into Alex's bulge, hoping to distract him.

Alex responded by laughing and saying, in French, "Nice try, buddy."

At no point did his nelson weaken, even slightly. Rene worked on walking them back to the ropes, and almost managed to get his leg hooked, when Alex yanked him back, again.

The Ref asked Rene if he wanted to submit.

He spat back, "Are you FUCKING crazy?" Rene was limp and tired, but his hard-on wagged, as his opponent manhandled him.

Alexandre was becoming very confident. He told the Ref, "Ask him, again! He's not getting out of this!"

Rene slammed his butt back, into Alex's crotch.

Alex just clamped the nelson tighter, but as he concentrated on that, Rene finally managed to get them to the ropes, and hook a leg.

The Ref called for the break. Alex gave a clean break, but he was annoyed. He smacked Rene's chest as he moved back, "You know I would have gotten the submission, eventually!"

"Yeah, right, you dreamer!" Rene sneered at Alex, but he knew it was true. He could never have broken out of the hold without the Ref's help. He held on to the ropes for a while, rubbing his neck and shoulders, and moving his head from side to side. When he finally did unhook his leg, and let go of the ropes, Alex was back on him. He wrapped Rene up in a bear hug, trapping his arms to his side. He squeezed Monsieur Sebastian, and leaned back, lifting his victim's feet off the ground.

Alex had just made a huge mistake, although he could never have known. When he trapped Rene's arms inside his own, Rene's right hand ended up just an inch from the front of his trunks. Rene gasped for breath as his hand immediately made it's way in. Rene relished the mix of fear and surprise he saw on his *captor's* face.

Edouard had neglected this part of student's training. In a

similar situation, Rene would have seen Ed's eyes flash with anger, and if he continued to molest Mr. Du Jardin's privates, he'd turn him into an unstoppable raging bull. Maybe it was because Alex was a rookie, or because he hadn't yet completely come to terms with his own sexuality, but Rene's fingers, wrapped around his cock AND balls, threw him completely off his game.

Alex held on to the bear hug, but called out in French, "WHAT THE HELL? REF! HE'S GRABBING MY FUCKING DICK!"

The Ref shrugged. There wasn't a territory left in Pro Wrestling that prohibited manhandling of an opponent's manhood, in fact it was highly encouraged. If there wasn't a certain amount of molestation in a show, the fans would protest.

Rene pulled up on his rival's genitals and Alex couldn't take it. He relinquished the bear hug and grabbed his tormentor's wrists, trying to pull his hands away.

Edouard Du Jardin settled back in his seat and frowned, partly annoyed with Rene's antics, but also somewhat entertained that he got to watch Rene Sebastian do this to someone else.

Rene quickly pulled up and down on Alex's jewels, and Alex stood, petrified, howling. Rene then grabbed Alex's wrist and propelled him into the ropes. He threw up an arm, ready to catch Alex with a clothesline.

Instead, Alex rebounded, then dropped down, and lunged a big elbow into Rene's midsection.

"OOO-Uhnnn!" Rene doubled up, holding his gut.

Alex took a moment to rub his still aching bulge.

Rene stepped back to the ropes, and faced his opponent. He couldn't help but smile when he noticed that Alex's bulge was a bit bigger and stiffer. That energized his sexual sadism. He pushed himself back, into the ropes, then propelled himself forward and jumped up, hitting Alex in the chest with a standing drop kick.

The baby bull stumbled back a few feet, but managed to stay standing. He charged, and dropped down, again, aiming another elbow at Rene's stomach. Rene saw it coming and was able to pull to the side, out of range. Alex had to grab the ropes to stop himself, and ended up on his knees with his torso sticking through.

Rene was behind Alex. He wrapped an arm around his neck, in a kind of one-armed headlock, pulled him down on the mat, and, of course, his other hand made it's way into Alex's trunks. Sauvage grimaced, and it became apparent that Sebastian was fingering and squeezing something.

Alex undulated back and forth, kicking his legs like a dolphin, while focusing all his attention on trying to get Rene's hand out of his trunks. He yelled, "ARRET! ARRET!" which means "STOP!" in French.

Rene couldn't stop smiling. As good a wrestler as Alex was, he had lost his concentration. He wasn't wrestling anymore. He had been knocked off his game, and was now just reacting to dirty tactics.

Rene kept a hold of his opponent's privates and swung his legs over so he was covering Sauvage. The ref dropped down for the count, but Alex was able to easily buck Rene off of him before the 1st slap of the mat.

Rene rolled up to his feet quickly, while Alex held his privates and struggled to his knees. The Ref asked him if he was OK to continue. He snarled, "OUI!"

Monsieur Sebastian was now back to his old cocky self. He got behind Alex, again, and pulled him up to his feet by his hair. Alex yelled out, still preoccupied by his aching genitals, which he was still holding on to.

Rene wrapped his arms around Alex's waist and hoisted him up. He dropped backwards, and crashed Sauvage's shoulders into the canvas, in a German Suplex. He held on, and had Alex in another pinning predicament. The Ref dropped down, but Alex easily kicked out, again.

This time, both wrestlers rolled up to their feet, and faced each other. Rene's smile grew when he saw the look on his rival's face. Alex was furious, but there was also trepidation in his eyes. That was never present in Edouard's.

Mr. Sauvage knew he was a better technical wrestler, and that he was stronger, but he had no idea how to compete against Sebastian's dirty tactics. He raised his hands, challenging Sebastian to a test of strength.

Rene pretended to be worried, and approached The Baby Bull slowly, to show him that he knew who was stronger. He meekly raised one hand, and as Alex clamped down on it, Rene's free hand clamped down on Alex's balls. He had to laugh. He couldn't believe Sauvage could be such a good wrestler, but so dumb.

Alex grabbed Rene's wrist with both of his hands. He was at Mr. Sebastian's mercy. He scrambled backwards, trying to free himself, but Rene kept that claw on his nuts. They wound up in the corner, Alex's back to the ring post.

Rene pulled them back out.

Alex yelled, in French, "REF! MAKE HIM STOP".

The Ref laughed, "Stop him from doing what? If you didn't want your penis and testicles molested, you never should have wrestled Rene Sebastian."

Rene flashed a great big proud grin. He looked Alex straight in the eye and laughed.

Sauvage appealed to the Ref. Surely there was something he could do.

Rene reared back and buried a big right fist into his opponent's gut. WHAM!

Alex doubled up.

Rene didn't waste one second. He dropped down behind Alex, hooked an arm up through his legs, and rolled him down on his back for another pin. One hand thrust itself into Alex's trunks from the front, the other was wrapped around Alex's leg and found its way into the back of his trunks. Sebastian leaned his back across Sauvage's chest, and had his legs up in the air.

Alex floundered like a caught fish, his big, muscular legs kicking spastically and independently.

Rene bit his lower lip and concentrated on what he was doing in Sauvage's trunks.

The kicking stopped. Alex's face turned red and started

trembling, "No! No! No! No!..." Whatever Sebastian was doing in those trunks seemed to immobilize the big guy. He begged, again, "No! No! No!..." only in a lower, strained voice.

The Ref dropped to the canvas. SLAP! SLAP! SLAP! "UN! DEUX! TROIS!"

Rene got the three-count easily. Alex was so traumatized, he hardly even knew he was pinned.

Sebastian shot up to his feet. He bent down to offer a hand to the defeated Challenger, but he backed away, and cautiously rose to his feet at a safe distance. Rene was all smiles, but Alex was humiliated, holding the bulging front of his trunks.

The bell rang out and the Ref raised Rene Sebastian's right hand in victory, while Alex fumed.

Rene stepped forward with an extended hand, and congratulated his opponent on a hard-fought battle. He said, in French, "That was a good match. You're a tough..."

But, Alex slapped his hand away, "And YOU are a dirty cheater!"

Rene smirked. He became more aroused seeing Alex's hard-on as he turned to storm out of the ring.

Sauvage looked down when he got to the ropes and saw his mentor, Edouard Du Jardin sitting in the front row, with his arms crossed. He immediately turned around, and walked back to Rene, center ring. He extended his own hand, for a shake, "You are, indeed, a formidable competitor".

Rene smiled, and vigorously shook Alex's hand, "Thank

you. I look forward to our next match".

There was a flash of fear in Alex's eyes, as he gave Rene a slight nod, then exited the ring.

Rene posed for the crowd, which was on its feet.

When he went to exit, he also spotted Edouard Du Jardin. They made eye contact. Rene admired Du Jardin immensely, but was always very intimidated. He was surprised to see Edouard's lips slightly curling up at the edges, forming the tiniest smile.

Rene, in turn, gave Du Jardin a salute.

DYER ANDERSON vs. RENE SEBASTIAN

All Worlds Pro Champ vs. All France Pro Champ

Dyer Anderson was very confident he could easily beat the Frenchman. He had survived a sexual onslaught from the master of Sadism, Chris Enos, and while he would never admit it publicly, he rather enjoyed it. This upcoming match with Rene Sebastian wouldn't be anywhere near as genitally demanding... he hoped. Anderson joked in interviews that he would match his boner against Mr. France any day of the week. He also stated that he'd put his big butt on the line against Mr. Sebastian, and went on to say that he couldn't wait to get his hands on Rene's.

A special interview was set up where they were on camera together. Even though they had just met, they came across more like old buddies than bitter rivals. They laughed, joked, and smiled while trading threats.

Dyer Anderson squeezed Rene Sebastian's shoulder when

he said, "You know I'm going to own your ass, right Frenchie? Grab my dick all you want. You're gonna end the match on your back, with your legs in the air!"

Rene loved that. He answered back, in French, "After I win, you'll be sucking my dick in the locker room!"

Anderson didn't know the words he said, but he understood the meaning clearly enough. The interview ended with them hugging and Rene's trademark kiss to both of Dyer's cheeks. Anderson loudly whispered in Sebastian's ear, "You'll be kissing my other cheeks after our match"

He was surprised when Sebastian replied, in English, "Gladly!"

AWPW World Heavyweight Pro Champion DYER ANDERSON vs.
AWPW Heavyweight Champion of France RENE SEBATIAN TITLE MATCH

Announcer: "LADIES AND GENTLEMEN, INTRODUCING THE CHALLENGER, IN HIS SIGNATURE POWDER PINK TRUNKS, STANDING 5 FEET, 10 INCHES TALL, AND WEIGHING 225 POUNDS, THE CURRENT ALL WORLDS PRO WRESTLING HEAVYWEIGHT CHAMPION OF FRANCE, RENE SEBASTIAN!!!"

Rene Sebastian posed like no other wrestler. He turned his back to the audience, so they could see his big, muscular bubble butt. Over his shoulder a wink and a naughty smile told the fans that he came to play, just as he always did.

"AND, MAKING HIS WAY DOWN THE AISLE, THE CURRENT AWPW HEAVYWEIGHT WORLD CHAMPION, IN THE ROYAL BLUE TRUNKS, STANDING 6 FEET TALL, AND WEIGHING 265 POUNDS, DYER ANDERSON!!!"

His fans were there in force. If there was anyone booing, it was completely drowned out by thunderous ovation. Dyer stomped his way down to the ring like a prize Clydesdale. His huge smile was genuine, as he waved and stopped to shake and slap hands.

After all the fanfare, the Ref called them to center ring, and had their attendants take their Championship belts away. He began his inspection with Mr. Sebastian.

Dyer Anderson poked the front of Rene's trunks, and the boner, already present. Anderson said, "He's got that *thing* in every match. I wanna make sure it's for real, and not something he's smuggling into the ring!"

Rene put his hands behind his head and smiled, "Take a look for yourself!"

Dyer hooked a finger into the waistband of Rene's trunks and pulled it back to expose Rene's erect penis pointing to the side, resting on his balls, which were pushed up by his tight, pink trunks.

Dyer smiled. He and the Ref gawked at it for one full minute. Rene adjusted, to give them a better view. Dyer released Rene's trunks, which snapped against his waist. "This is gonna be a fun match."

Rene noticed that Dyer's trunks had gotten a bit tighter, as well, while he was examining the boner. Rene nodded, "Mais oui."

The match started pretty typically, as matches do between opponents who respect each other. Dyer got the first move: a headlock leading to a hip toss. Rene rallied back with an arm drag. It went back and forth like that until Dyer was able to overpower Rene and body slam him. Rene held his back, grimacing. Dyer pulled him up to his feet, by his hair, and clamped on a tight headlock. He loved having his big arms bulging around another man's neck and red face. Rene gripped his bigger opponent's wrists and tried to pry himself out.

Sebastian employed every clean wrestling technique he knew and couldn't escape. Nothing worked, until he reached into his trusty old bag of dirty tricks, and also into Dyer Anderson's trunks. He squeezed and fondled the Champ's genitals.

Dyer held on to his headlock and even flexed it harder, while his body convulsed with pain and pleasure.

The crowd went crazy. They were wondering why the sexual assault hadn't happened earlier, as there was so much sexy trash talk leading up to this match. Some fans even speculated whether there would be any real wrestling, at all.

Dyer's face showed a man who was struggling, but also experiencing his fair share of bliss.

Rene PULLED down on The Champ's erection.

Anderson threw his head back, "ANGHHH!" but didn't loosen up on the headlock. Rene then worked on Dyer's balls, YANKING them down. Dyer screamed out, but CRANKED even HARDER causing Rene to gurgle and flail his arms.

Dyer thought he might be able to get a submission with the headlock. He was in complete control, even with the Frenchman's sensual manipulations.

Rene wasn't going anywhere, his face was now purple, and he had sunk down to one knee. Anderson was becoming pretty cocky. Every time Sebastian got to his feet, Dyers big, huge arms were able to choke a little more air out of the Frenchie and force him back down, as he proudly withstood the sexual onslaught.

Monsieur Sebastian pulled Anderson's hard-on out through one of the leg holes of his trunks, and his balls through the other. Everyone in the audience was on their feet, and some were using virtual viewers to get a close up look at the Champ's tortured privates.

Dyer's balls were in agony, but that only fueled his anger up to a point above his pain threshold. Of course, the excitement he was deriving from being in control and worked over, at the same time, helped a great deal.

Had he been in a private match, with no belt on the line, and no cameras recording the outcome, he might have surrendered to the Frenchmen, and his pleasurable tactics... repeatedly.

Rene withdrew his grip on Anderson's penis, which was completely red, but immediately bounced back to attention. His hand made its way behind Dyer's big beefy butt.

Dyer sighed, and relaxed, thinking that Rene was weakening. That was a stupid conclusion. A shocked expression flashed across his face. He started doing an awkward dance, scurried forward and pushed Sebastian's hands away.

The Ref didn't see what happened.

Dyer was in the corner, pulling his trunks out of his ass.

Rene was free. He massaged his neck.

Dyer stepped forward, holding his butt cheeks. He complained to the Ref, "His finger went up my ass!!!"

The Ref held up his hands and suppressed a laugh. "Yeah? And?"

Anderson should have known better than to waste time complaining. He had control, and it would have been wise to keep it going.

Rene struck suddenly. He instantly had Dyer's balls in his grip, again, and sent a hard hammer-fist into Anderson's gut. Dyer spit out, and doubled up, his eyes bulging out.

Rene kept his grip, and another fist pounded Dyer's steel gut, sending them both back a couple of feet. Dyer was wobbly and Rene was hot to see the Champ on his knees. BAM! Another punch had Dyer doubled and shaky, but not down. He stumbled back, into the corner, with Rene still clamped on his nuts. Anderson gripped the ropes, his face now white.

Rene was awfully proud of himself. He gingerly put his fingers under Dyer's balls, which were still hanging out the leg-hole of his trunks. He lightly lifted them up, and said, "Voila!" The whole world saw Dyer Anderson's exposed, reddened balls. His big, swollen penis was still erect, sticking out the other hole. Rene pointed at The Champ's erection and yelled, in accented English, "Zees eez zee World Shampee-ohn!"

Something about being aroused and publicly exposed, excited Dyer even more, but the thought of a man from France taking his title began fuelling the fire in his belly.

Rene had taken the head of Dyer's hard penis between his middle and index fingers and was now finger-scissoring it, to Dyer's excruciating delight. The Champ felt the fight slipping away. He shook his head, trying to get his mind back in the game. He kicked his legs up, while holding on to the ropes, in an attempt to wrap them around Rene. In doing so, he caused his penis to be ripped out from between Rene's clenched fingers. He yelled out. It was very painful, but almost orgasmic at the same time.

Rene wagged his finger in Dyer's face, as if he was a naughty boy. He grabbed Dyer's penis, again, while he sunk another fist into the Champ's gut. WHAM! Dyer's head flew back, and he slumped in the ropes.

The Ref slapped Rene's shoulder, and pulled him back. "OUT of the corner!"

Rene turned to the Ref, "Why? 'Ee loves eet! Look at 'eem!" He pointed to Dyer's big, crimson erection, but as he turned back toward the Champ, Dyer was able to get his boots up, successfully plant his soles on Rene's chest, and PUSH!

Rene went flying, past the Ref, and landed on his ass, center ring.

Dyer ignored the pain as best he could and started to adjust his trunks, in an effort to hide his erection. When he saw Rene on his ass, he realized he shouldn't waste a second. He charged out of the corner, jumped with his legs spread wide. Monsieur Sebastian looked up just in time to see the big man's crotch coming at him. It slammed him in the face, and knocked him back on the canvas. Dyer was now sitting on Rene's neck, his exposed cock and balls rubbing against Rene's face.

Rene was too stunned to react. He slowly moved his head back and forth, and The Champ's balls made contact with his lips.

Dyer loved the way it felt, so he pressed his testicles into Rene Sebastian's mouth. At first Sebastian squirmed under the Champ, but then he looked up with a smile, and let Dyer's balls drop in. Dyer flexed, like a Champ, dominant in the match once again.

The Ref dropped down for the count, "ONE! TWO!"

"AYE-YAAAAH!!!" Dyer jumped off Rene, and stumbled over to the ropes, holding his balls.

Rene rolled up and made his way over to the Champ, who had one hand on his balls and the other up, pointing at the Challenger. "HE FUCKING BIT MY BALLS!!! WHY DOES EVERYONE FUCKING BITE MY BALLS?!!"

Dyer held on to the ropes and yelled to the Ref, "KEEP HIM AWAY FROM ME!!!"

The Ref warned Rene about biting. He just shrugged and sauntered up to Anderson, who put his hand on the French man's chest to push him back. Rene knocked Anderson's arm away and gently wrapped his arm around the Champ's head. THUNK! He sent a quick jab to the Champ's throat.

"GLGhhh!" Anderson's eyes clamped shut.

The Ref got between them, and asked the Champ if he was

OK to continue. Dyer didn't say anything, but nodded his head.

Rene moved back in, pushing the Ref aside, with his body. Dyer stuck his upper body through the ropes, with his hand up, "Keep him away from me!!!"

Rene moved around the other side of the Ref, and there was Dyer Anderson's big, meaty butt, sticking out of the ropes. Rene dug his fingers under the bottom of Dyer's butt cheeks, and YANKED his trunks up, wedging them into his ass crack.

Anderson yelled out, "HEY!"

Sebastian smacked Dyer's rear-end, "Zees beeg, beautiful butt!" Then, he bit it.

Dyer howled, again, and the Ref pushed Rene back. The Challenger sauntered around the ring, both arms up, while the crowd screamed and hollered.

Dyer stood up, next to the ropes, looking ridiculously like a big, thick, jobber boy. His erection and balls were still hanging out in front, and his red butt cheeks were exposed in the back.

His anger was rising, but he was also flustered, and looked like a man who had been really worked over. He held on to the ropes, trying to buy some time. The Ref stayed by him, telling him to either "Wrestle, or throw in the towel!"

Rene walked back, and grabbed a handful of Dyer's hair to pull him away from the ropes, but the Ref was between them, and pushed the French man back.

Rene let go, but gave The Champ a big, humiliating slap across the face, and sneered, "Come on Shamp, geev eet up!"

Dyer's blood was now boiling. That smack in the face was not a good idea... until Rene snuck back around the Ref and smacked Dyer's exposed butt cheeks, again. Dyer was once more reduced to looking like a rookie. He stomped his feet and yelled at the Ref, "Keep him away from me!!!"

The Ref answered back, "Just wrestle!!", and Dyer started arguing with him.

Rene snuck up behind Anderson, again, shoved his crotch up against Anderson's rear-end, and pretended to butt-fuck him.

"HEY!" The Champ scurried forward, to get away, but Rene had a hold of his trunks.

Sebastian laughed, "See zees! I am fucking your big <u>Chump</u>!!"

Dyer held on to the ropes and tried to pry Rene's hands off his trunks. The Ref smacked both of them on the shoulder and warned about continuing the action away from the ropes.

Rene backed up and stood center ring, his arms raised as if he was victorious.

Anderson came away from the ropes, and fidgeted with his trunks, trying to cover his red ass cheeks. For some reason, he was more embarrassed by them, than his exposed genitals.

The two men circled and Rene couldn't help but make cracks about the state of the Champ. "Why do you pretend? Your penis shows 'ow much you love losing to me!"

Dyer didn't like that. He came in quick for the lockup and in a flash went for another headlock. Rene was able to block it, and push away, but as he did, Dyer landed a loud, echoing forearm smash across Rene's muscular pecs. SHA-WHAP!

"OOF!" The big muscles in Rene's chest bounced and turned as red as Anderson's ass. He moved back, with his eyes shut.

WHAP! WHAP! The Champ was on him, delivering a left and right forearm across his chest. Before Rene could open his eyes, Dyer had him lifted up by the shoulder and crotch.

"NO! NO!" Sebastian begged. His eyes were open now.

Dyer waited one moment, enjoying the pleading of his conniving French Challenger.

WHAM! Rene was slammed, center ring. He bounced and rubbed is arched, agonized back, with his eyes twisted shut.

Dyer quickly had him up violently by the hair. He slung him into the corner, front-first, and pulled Rene's arms over the ropes. The Champ was now smiling. He slowly hooked his fingers up under each side of Rene's powder pink trunks and YANKED them up into his ass crack, higher than they ever should have been able to go.

Rene struggled, in silent agony. Dyer then took his big, thick hands and SPANKED the Frenchman's butt as hard as he could. SMACK! SMACK! SMACK! SMACK!

Rene groaned and writhed in the corner in a way that might lead someone watching to think he enjoyed it.

Dyer rubbed the French Man's butt, then grabbed it. "DAMN! That is one NICE ass!" He squeezed it, and leaned in with his chest against Rene's back, and his hard-on rubbing against Sebastian's exposed butt cheek. He said in Rene's ear, "It's pretty obvious that you love this kinda treatment, too, Jobber boy!"

"Mmm." Rene couldn't argue.

The Ref once again stepped forward to put an end to their good time, "Take it out of the corner!"

Dyer imitated The Frenchman, when he thought he had an easy win, just minutes before. His arms were up, and the audience hooted and hollered, loving the sight of the Champ, ass, dick, and balls out, swinging and bouncing. He milked the moment, but when he turned back around, he got a surprise. Rene had a drop kick waiting for him. BULLSEYE! It hit him square in the chest.

Dyer was hurled backwards, into the ropes, but rebounded with a clothesline.

BAM! Rene was hit square in the chest, just as he was getting up to his feet, and was back down on the canvas, seeing stars.

Dyer bent down, grabbed one of Sebastian's arms and twisted it, as he pulled Rene up to his knees. He swung himself around, behind the Frenchman, and had him in a tightly wrenched arm-bar. Sebastian was between Anderson's legs, his arm and butt sticking straight up, as his face rested on the canvas. Dyer torqued Sebastian's arm up, HARD, and used his crotch on his opponent's lower back for leverage. Rene yelled out and pounded the canvas with his free hand.

Dyer worked the arm bar with just one of his meaty mitts clamped on his Challenger's wrist. He flexed his other arm, letting the crowd know he was mere seconds away from victory. Rene struggled and tried to stand up, but Dyer slid forward and planted his feet wide. This caused the arm bar to be cranked forward and

Rene's face to be ground down into the canvas. The French man screamed out.

Anderson grabbed Sebastian's hair and pulled his head back. He crooked his own head forward and looked into the Challenger's eyes. With a smile, he said "Nice try, French fry!" Dyer thought he was pretty funny, and laughed out loud at his own joke.

Rene's expression went from pain to devious contemplation. His free hand snuck up in between Dyer's big, wide thighs.

The Champ's expression fell from victorious arrogance to fearful surprise. Whatever Rene Sebastian was doing between Dyer's legs caused him to drop his adversary's arm and jump up three feet. He held his bottom and Rene rose to his feet.

The Challenger laughed at the Champ, and The Champ responded by throwing a punch that hit Rene in the center of his chest, and clearly hurt. The crowd went silent. No one expected this sexual, friendly match to become a real fight. Rene's hands were up and he threw his own punch back toward the Champ's face, who dodged it. It just grazed the side of Anderson's face.

Dyer's eyes flashed red. Rene could do anything he wanted to Anderson's cock and balls, but for some reason whatever he did between The Champ's butt cheeks, and now this attempted punch, was too much.

Monsieur Sebastian had seen that look before, in his matches with The French Bull, Edouard Du Jardin, just after he had pulled one dirty trick too many. Subsequently, Du Jardin always flattened him.

Dyer put all his weight behind a right hook that struck Rene's jaw squarely. The Frenchman went down like a ton of bricks, and ended up flat on his back. KNOCK OUT!

With hands on his hips, The Champ surveyed his prey, before lowering himself onto one knee, next to his victim. He grabbed that big, French erection in the Challenger's trunks, as if it now belonged to him, and covered Rene Sebastian for the count.

BAM! BAM! BAM! "ONE! TWO! THREE!" echoed through the arena. "DING, DING", the bell sounded, calling out Dyer's victory.

Dyer stood up as the Ref raised his right hand. The ovation from the crowd was deafening. The Ref handed Dyer his belt. He was just about to exit the ring, but he handed his belt back to the Ref, and knelt back down. He lightly smacked the Frenchman's cheeks, reviving him, then pulled him up to his feet. Rene was dazed. Dyer retrieved their belts, and helped Mr. France out of the ring, up the aisle, and back to the locker room.

Rory was able to see this match alone in his room, but only because of his secret manipulations of the parental controls, allowing access to all restricted programming.

He was now 14, and Wrestling was his life. His set of friends consisted of all athletes, especially other wrestlers. All he thought about was turning 18, so he could join the All Worlds Pro Wrestling Federation.

2 ALL ABOUT CHRIS ENOS

JOHNSON WHITE vs. CHRIS ENOS

Rory became consumed with the tension surrounding the World Heavyweight Championship saga. Chris Enos campaigned relentlessly for a rematch with Dyer Anderson, but as U.S.A. Heavyweight Champ, he had his own title to defend.

Johnson White was previously undefeated, before Chris Enos beat him and took his belt. He was a big, buff, 6 foot 3 inch, 250-pound Black Man, with a thick neck and shaved head. Sometimes he was billed as "Mr. White", and sometimes as "Mr. Johnson", or even "The Johnson". The first was ironic, but the last two were apropos. He sported, what was considered to be, "the biggest bulge in the business". It was huge, and always protruded conspicuously in any gear he wore.

His loss to Chris Enos was very controversial. Mr. White was the better wrestler, but Chris Enos was far dirtier. As Johnson

White was a consummate professional, Chris Enos was a Sexual Satan, who would stop at NOTHING to win.

This seemed to be a theme that played out many times over in Pro Wrestling, and it resonated strongly with Rory's desires and fantasies.

Outside the ring, Enos tried to present himself as a good guy, and what would be called a "face" in the wrestling game. In the ring, he immediately got into his opponent's head and trunks, and gained control in both places. He was obviously a fan of his French counterpart, Rene Sebastian, who rose to fame two years before Mr. Enos.

Had Enos not been able to use his dirty tactics, Mr. White might have squashed him. Although Chris Enos was a good wrestler, he was not the technician Johnson was. Johnson was no stranger to dirty tactics; he just never lowered himself to utilize them.

He was also famous for being one of the few wrestlers, in recent times, who managed to keep his trunks on in every match. The public had never seen Johnson's Johnson. He was always able to thwart attempts to expose it. Because of this, rumors ran rampant that his extra large bulge was fake. It was taken for granted that he stuffed, and being the gentleman he was, he never substantiated nor denied. He just didn't talk about it.

Chris Enos's primary goal, in their now legendary match, was to strip the Champ of his trunks, then his belt. Johnson was forced to work overtime to defend his manhood from The Challenger's knees, elbows, feet, mouth, and especially his fingers.

Unfortunately for Johnson, these distractions ultimately worked, and at a crucial moment, Enos had him down, with a firm grip on his trunks. Had Mr. White kicked out of the pin, instead of extricating Chris Enos's hand from his trunks, his penis would have been exposed.

Johnson White's fans and supporters rallied for a special-rules rematch, where trunks, and all dirty tricks were off limits.

Chris Enos ducked all challenges from Johnson, even though he claimed HE was the superior technical wrestler. Nobody knew better than Enos, himself, that he didn't stand a chance against Johnson White in a purely scientific match.

Mr. White's close friend, All Worlds Heavyweight Champion, Dyer Anderson publicly supported Johnson. He offered Enos a title shot, but only AFTER he gave White a rematch, with dirty tactics banned.

Chris Enos used double-talk and diplomatic bullshit to decline the offer, while still trying to appear that he would be up for it. He used the excuse that there was a long line of other contenders, just like Anderson had stated about his own title.

So, to spite Enos, and add fuel to their fiery drama, Dyer Anderson announced that Johnson would be added to his list of Challengers, just after Mr. Canada, Tommy McGee.

DYER ANDERSON vs. TOMMY McGEE

Tommy McGee was the nicest man in, and out of the ring. He was another Strength Competitor turned wrestler, and was one of the many heralded as "The Strongest Wrestler In The

World". He was 6' 4 1/2" tall, 275lbs, and very handsome, with curly brown hair and hazel eyes. He was immensely muscular, but instead of the typical weightlifter body, he had a perfect bodybuilder physique. His shoulders were huge, wide boulders and his waist tapered down to a tight, shredded 8-pack. For a big man, he was incredibly flexible and light on his feet. What he lacked in killer instinct, he more than made up for with sheer athleticism.

His match up with Dyer Anderson was well anticipated. Dyer was a former power lifter, so many thought this would be a pure strength match.

Tommy started strong, out maneuvering Dyer, as he was much faster. McGee was able to pick up The Champ, in a crotch and shoulder lift, which was usually the set up for a slam. Instead, Tommy brought Dyer up to his chest, adjusted himself under the Champ, and pressed him overhead. Everyone in the arena was in shock, including The Champ, himself, who, with wide-eyed surprise, looked like a child on a roller coaster.

He obviously didn't get Dyer to submit, but when he slammed him down to the canvas from that height, the ring shook so violently it looked like the ring posts might topple. Dyer had never been slammed like that before. His face contorted, and after he bounced, he slowly sunk back down to the mat.

Tommy moved back to the corner, allowing Dyer to recover and get to his feet. This was normal for Tommy McGee. He couldn't stop being a gentleman, no matter what. Even the announcer commented on what a bad trait that was for a wrestler.

The way Dyer was lying, dazed, center ring, and the dopey

slowness of his crawl to the ropes, it appeared that Tommy McGee could have easily gotten the pin. The Ref even asked Dyer if he was ok to continue. He didn't say anything, just limply waved his hand at the Ref. When he finally got to his feet, turned around, and took one step away from the ropes, Tommy sprung to action. Dyer was slung across the ring, by his wrist, and as he rebounded off the ropes, McGee jumped up into the air, and clamped a flying head scissor on the champ. He rolled down to the mat. Dyer followed, and was flipped over onto his back. BAM! The Champ was seeing stars, wondering what just happened. McGee managed to maintain the scissors, and squeezed them with all his might.

Anderson struggled and clawed at Tommy's huge, bodybuilder thighs, but those giant slabs of muscle were flexed hard. It was like having two columns of granite choking the life out of him. Dyer's head went from red to purple, and looked like it might pop.

Tommy let up for one second, holding The Champ's head between his thighs. Dyer caught his breath, then Tommy leaned back, propped himself up on his arms and SQUEEZED, again. Anderson kicked and flailed. He tried to rock himself to his knees and force Tommy onto his back, but Tommy easily flipped Anderson back onto his side.

If this was any other Challenger, Dyer might have thought about resorting to dirty tricks, after all, Tommy's penis was bouncing just an inch from his face, in his red, spandex trunks. Whenever either one of them would move, it would rub against Dyer's chin. It took every bit of restraint for Anderson to keep his hands away from that vulnerable bulge. Instead, Dyer pushed his chin up, and in, and began grinding under Tommy's testicles. He tried to make it seem like he wasn't doing it on purpose. It didn't slow McGee down, though. If anything, he seemed to like it.

Anderson tried to bridge his torso up with his feet flat on the canvas. That didn't help. Tommy, again, pushed up onto his hands, and FLEXED his giant thighs, squeezing on Dyer's neck. Anderson dropped back down. This happened two more times, resulting in Dyer looking like a limp, wet rag. The Ref asked him again if he wanted to stop the match.

"Nnnn!" was all he could manage.

The Ref asked again.

"NNNOOO!"

Anderson worked several different moves before he was able to turn himself onto his hands and knees, and get McGee on his back. He finally got his feet under him, planted wide on the mat. Tommy's legs were straight up in the air, still flexed tight around Anderson's neck.

Tommy worked to flip him back down, but Anderson held on.

The Champ then began an assault on Tommy's washboard. He sunk several hard fists into Tommy's abs. The scissors didn't let up, but Dyer had Tommy's shoulders down, and held onto his legs for leverage.

The Ref decided that Anderson had a legitimate pin, so he dropped down to slap the mat.

McGee was able to kick out on the first count, but as he did, he broke his scissors and flung Dyer Anderson back onto his ass. Tommy kicked right up to his feet.

Anderson crawled over to the ropes, and held on, taking a few moments to massage his neck and move his head around.

The Challenger was on his toes, ready to circle as soon as The Champ got to his feet. Dyer shook his head and thought about how much he liked Tommy McGee, but couldn't wait until he could gain control over him, and humiliate him, center ring.

The Ref put his hand on The Champ's shoulder and asked, again, if he was ok to continue. When Dyer grunted, "Yeah!" and gave him a dirty look, The Ref told him to resume wrestling, or be counted out.

Dyer stood up, and made a half step away from the ropes. Tommy was on him, and muscled him over into a side headlock. BAM! Dyer slammed a fist into his hard, ripped, slab of abs.

"OOOF!" Tommy felt it, but it didn't stop him from cranking the headlock tighter.

BAM! BAM! It took two more hard fists before Tommy loosened up his headlock, and a fourth one before he released. BAM!

Anderson didn't waste a second. He grabbed the big, buff Canadian by the wrist and whipped him into the ropes, which were just two feet away. WHAM! He hit Tommy with a clothesline that rattled the big man, and almost sent him backwards over the top rope.

Dyer grabbed McGee's wrist, again, and propelled him across the ring, but this time, Tommy flew off the ropes with a cross body block. Dyer caught him, mid-air, thinking he could parlay it into a slam. Tommy was just too big, and Dyer stumbled backwards, then landed flat on his back, with McGee on top of him.

The Ref dropped down, but Dyer easily kicked out before the first count.

Once again, instead of capitalizing on his advantageous position, Tommy stood up and gave the Champ a chance to recover.

Dyer was grateful, but not as honorable. As he rose, feigning exhaustion, he was able to lunge forward and slam another hard fist into the Challenger's abs. WHAM!

Tommy hunched forward and held his midsection. Anderson pushed him against the ropes, grabbed his neck, and bent him back, over the ropes.

SMAAACK! He gave McGee such a big chop to the pecs the whole ring shook. Tommy's big, bodybuilder-sized chest bounced.

SMACK! SMACK! Dyer gave him two more. Tommy's mountainous pectorals were now completely red. He writhed on the ropes, his eyes shut and teeth grinding.

Dyer took McGee's wrist once more, and slung him across the ring. The quicker, bigger man again went for a cross body block, as he rebounded. This time Dyer was ready for that move. He caught him in midair, but instead of trying to hold him up, he twisted and power-slammed Mr. Canada. They both landed hard - McGee's back into the canvas with Anderson on top of him.

The Champ hooked the Challenger's leg, and the Ref dropped down for the count. "ONE! TWO!..."

Tommy was dazed and seeing stars, but he managed to kick out just before the third slap of the mat.

Anderson quickly got to his feet and pulled Tommy McGee up by his curly hair. He scooped him, and SLAMMED him, again. The Challenger bounced and grimaced, but didn't move much after that. One knee went up, but he stayed on his back. The Champ covered him and hooked a leg, but, once again, McGee kicked out!

Dyer kneeled next to the big man, and PUNCHED the canvas. He was desperate, wondering what could put this big, muscle man out.

He straddled Mr. Canada and began POUNDING his 8-pack. The Muscle Boy bounced with every punch, and attempted to grab Dyer's wrists, but couldn't. The Champ was unrelenting.

"Nnnn, ggghh" Tommy made an incoherent attempt to submit, but neither the ref nor Anderson understood.

Anderson reached back and hooked both of Tommy's huge granite legs. He leaned forward, his crotch in McGee's face, and had Tommy in a huge muscle roll-up.

Tommy didn't kick or struggle and the Ref pounded the canvas, "ONE! TWO! THREE!", then called for the bell "DING! DING!"

The match was over.

The Champ dropped his defeated opponent's legs and sat on top of him for a few moments, as the failed Challenger covered his face with his hands.

The Ref pulled Dyer's right arm up, and The Champ rose to his feet.

The audience was going crazy. Anderson was more thankful than cocky. There were a few moments, in the first part of the match, when he thought the muscle man at his feet would take his title. He leaned down and extended his hand. Tommy grabbed it, and allowed the Champ to help him up. He congratulated him on a tough match. Tommy congratulated him on the win.

McGee slowly padded back to his corner. The Ref handed Dyer his belt and he held it up, to the cheers of his fans.

DYER ANDERSON regroups.

The Champ was getting worried. His recent title challenges were close matches, and this one, with Tommy McGee, made him especially anxious. He had never been dominated so completely by any wrestler who was using purely technical wrestling moves. He doubted his strength and wrestling skill, and feared they might be no match for Tommy McGee, or future challengers.

It was one thing to lose control to Chris Enos or Rene Sebastian once they starting pulling him around by his penis or testicles. That was every man's weakness, but Dyer had always been one of the strongest, best wrestlers in the Federation. If he wasn't either of those things, anymore, could he hold on to the belt?

Chris Enos never gave Johnson White a rematch, so Anderson officially booked a title match with his old friend. Enos went crazy, and cried "foul!" When interviewers pointed out that all he had to do was give Mr. White a rematch, he worked himself up into a lather, and threatened to hit them. He pointed out that Johnson White was not a current belt holder, but no one else seemed to care.

So, the belt was on the line, again, but Anderson had scheduled it several months in the future. He wanted to hone his skills before facing a man who was just as good a wrestler and just as strong, if not stronger.

Duane Birdsong, Rory's first boyfriend.

Rory's whole life was directed toward his future Pro Wrestling career. He and Todd James were incredibly strict with their training regimen.

Rory ended up going to a different high school, but they still met every week for workouts, and became very close friends. When Rory was 16, and Todd almost 18, Rory came to realize that he was in love with Todd. Unfortunately, Todd was straight, and had a girlfriend. Rory kept his feelings to himself, and Todd had no idea Rory was even attracted to men until a senior on the football team asked him out.

Todd should have known. Many girls were interested in Rory, but he never went out with any of them. His indifference toward them was irresistible.

One day at school, Duane Birdsong walked up to Rory in the hall, and introduced himself. He was a senior, and linebacker on the football team. As a standout player, he had already been offered scholarships from good colleges.

They knew the same group of guys, but had never officially met. Duane was a big, handsome, 6'5" tall, 250 pounds guy, with the proverbial jaw "chiseled from granite". Even though he was only 18, he was already all man.

They stood in the hallway, and chatted for a bit, then Duane asked Rory to go to the beach. He also told Rory he would take him to lunch at a place he really liked, overlooking the ocean.

Rory thought that was great, and as inexperienced as he was with boys, he had no clue that Duane had just asked him out on a date.

When they took off their t-shirts, on the beach, and changed into their rash guards, Rory was in awe. Duane had apparently started lifting weights before he learned how to walk. Rory caught Duane checking out his body, too, and when Duane realized it, he just smiled, no embarrassment. Rory blushed and looked down, feeling like he had done something wrong.

While they were surfing, Duane made sure he stayed near Rory and watched out for him. Back on the sand at the end of the day, Rory dropped his board, pulled off his rash guard, and sat on his board, facing the ocean. Duane did the same, but sat next to Rory, on Rory's board.

Rory was uncomfortable, but in a good way. He liked Duane. In fact, he really liked Duane, but had no idea what Duane's inclinations were. "Thanks for inviting me today. I'm having a great time!" Rory kept his eyes focused on a spot way out near the horizon.

Then, Duane did something that made Rory feel stupid. He moved closer, and put his arm around him. "I'm having a great time, too! Thanks for coming with me." Duane also looked far out to sea, but with a big, happy grin on his face.

Rory couldn't believe he hadn't known this was a date, and that Duane liked him. Suddenly, all the signs and indications were crystal clear. Chills ran through him.

They talked for a long time, shared a lot of laughs, and Duane admitted that he had wanted to ask Rory out for a while. Rory didn't know how to respond to that, so they sat silently for a few minutes.

Duane shifted his position, and turned his head to Rory.

Rory turned toward Duane to see what he was looking at. He was looking directly into Rory's eyes, with that big smile still on his face. Rory's mouth went dry and his palms were clammy.

Duane looked into Rory's eyes for another 10 seconds. His smile went away, he closed his eyes, and pressed his mouth against Rory's. Rory kept his eyes open as Duane gave him a very nice kiss.

Rory liked the feeling of it, but didn't do too much in return. Duane opened his eyes, his lips still touching Rory's, "Sorry. Is this ok with you?"

Rory blushed, and said, in a low, breathy voice, "Yes."

Duane closed his eyes, kissed him again, and this time Rory kissed back.

Rory felt this kiss throughout his entire body. He put his hand on Duane's shoulder. His other hand felt Duane's back. His heart was beating faster and he had an overwhelming urge to touch every, single part of Duane's body.

Rory pulled away, and looked down. It felt very wrong, to him, to be out in public as sexually aroused as he was. The erection, which had swollen in his wet trunks, made him feel exposed and completely vulnerable.

At first, Duane was self conscious, but when he saw the dopey smile on Rory's face, he beamed, and squeezed Rory, pulling him closer.

They dated a couple of weeks, then Duane asked Rory to be his boyfriend. After two months, Duane told Rory he loved him. Rory was more excited than he thought he would be, but didn't say it back.

They went together the rest of the school year. In June, Duane graduated and in August he was scheduled to leave for college. They spent the summer together, surfing mostly, and often would end up wrestling on the beach.

Although Rory was a better wrestler, he couldn't always beat Duane, because Duane was 5 inches taller and 70 pounds heavier. It wasn't easy moving around that much muscle. But, it was fun for both of them, and always led to them making out in the sand. Todd and his girlfriend tagged along a few times. Rory thought it was funny how Todd looked embarrassed but his girlfriend was amused. Todd and Duane became good friends. Rory was happy.

He had never been with a man before, but Duane had. There was a group of guys from different high school teams, and most of them were straight and dated girls. One of the guys had a swimming pool, and they would have gatherings there. The way Duane described them, they sounded like young athlete orgies. There were a few guys from the football team, some from the swim team, and even a couple from the wrestling team, that Rory knew very well. He was shocked, but not surprised.

Rory was interested, but didn't push it. That was perfect because Duane said he was done with all that, now that he had Rory, and didn't like talking about it, too much. He didn't want to share Rory with anyone.

Duane found out about Rory's Wrestling Fetish without Rory ever saying a word. Their wrestling matches on the beach would be continued in Duane's bedroom. Rory would become extremely aroused. In fact, their first wrestling match led to their physical relationship becoming more passionate.

Up to that point, Duane would initiate with a kiss. Kissing would lead to fondling, then disrobing each other, and all sorts over very nice, pleasurable activities.

Once wrestling was introduced in the bedroom, all bets were off.

Their last day together, Duane took Rory to the beach and to lunch, just like their first date. He looked across the table at his young, blond, blue-eyed boyfriend.

Rory smiled back, until he saw the sadness in Duane's eyes. "What's wrong?"

Duane forced himself to smile, but it wasn't real, "Rory, I'm thinking maybe we should break up."

"Oh, ok." Rory was shocked. He appeared rather stoic, but he was as sad as he had ever been in his life. Anyone watching might think he didn't care too much about the whole thing, until he looked up and asked, "Why?"

Duane's head was down. "Well, since I'm going away to college... and you have two more years left... I guess it's just the smart thing to do."

Rory frowned and looked up at Duane, "Ok, I guess. If that's what you want to do."

Duane was a bit surprised by Rory's reaction, "It's not what I WANT to do, but I mean..."

Rory was now more confused, "If you don't want to, then why? ... I don't understand. Did I do something?"

"No!" Duane shook his head. "I love you, Rory. I think you're amazing, and I wish you loved me back, but... I, just, uh..."

Rory thought about it for a second. He knew his feelings weren't quite as deep as Duane's, but he did love him. "I do love you."

Duane sat straight up. "What? You do?"

Rory nodded his head. He wondered if there was a way these kinds of interactions normally went.

Duane was completely perplexed. "Why haven't you ever told me?"

Rory shrugged. "I don't know. ... I'm sorry. I guess I didn't really know, for sure... I don't know why."

Duane laughed out loud. "I don't know whether to be happy or sad, right now."

"Don't be sad! I'm sorry, Duane. I just never did this before."

Duane didn't know what to think of that, but he also knew they were on different pages. He reached across the table with an open hand. Rory placed his in Duane's, and Duane closed his fingers around Rory's and squeezed. "Ok, how about if we don't call it a 'break up'? We just sort of..." He was smiling, but sad. "I'll be back for Winter Break, and I really want to see you."

Was he stupid not to feel as deeply about the relationship as Duane? "Yes! For sure!" He squeezed Duane's hand back. "And, we can chat all the time!"

Duane stood up. "Let's go."

When they got to Duane's car, Duane put his arms around Rory and looked him in the eye. "I'm gonna miss you so much!"

Rory put his arms around Duane and kissed him, with his eyes open, "Duane, I'm gonna miss you, SO MUCH, too!" He didn't want Duane to go.

Duane smiled. They kissed, then kissed some more.

3 PURE PRO WRESTLING FEDERATION

After Rory's breakup with Duane, his life became very interesting. He began thinking about relationships.

Both Duane and Todd were now off at College. Rory had other friends, but none as close as Todd or Duane. He wondered if he should actively search for another boyfriend. Is that what people did when they got older? Would he be expected to have a significant other from this point on?

After several days of intense thought, he decided to throw himself completely into training. Instead of searching for a replacement for his best friend and boyfriend, he focused on finding good training partners.

One day after wrestling practice, he had an idea that cemented his destiny. He knew he would try out for All Worlds Pro Wrestling in two years. In order to stand out from the thousands of men, worldwide, who also had the same dreams, he decided to form his own local federation. He called it Pure Pro. That night, he configured his own viewing channel, and assembled all the right media outlets.

He approached the guys he thought would be interested, and was able to put together ten: three from his high-school wrestling team, two from the local wrestling gym where he worked out, four from the football team, and one from the swim team. Through these guys, Rory was able to find others who wanted to film, edit, and help him market his channel. He approached the owner of the wrestling gym for space, and they were off and running.

The first matches were very rough, but also kind of hot. It was a bit chaotic, and not at all what pure pro wrestling would be, but it was the most fun Rory ever had. Basically, it was high school boys horsing around, mimicking what they saw in videos.

Just thinking about it turned him on, so he wore two pairs of trunks, hoping to hold in his excitement. Even though it wasn't his ideal, it still fed into his fetish, and he was too shy to have an exposed erection in front of his friends.

Once the view count on their video channel exceeded their expectations, they started buying hot pro gear, and Rory put together matches that really made sense. He was the most dedicated wrestler in the bunch, and after two months he emerged as the Champion of the Federation.

NEW OBSESSION.

One night, while he was searching for hot new wrestling matches, a new man entered his life.

Tim Blakely had just won the All Kingdom Heavyweight Championship. "All Kingdom" is what the collective countries of

England, Scotland, Wales, Northern Ireland, and Ireland had become known as under the All Worlds Pro Title umbrella.

Blakely was 6 feet, 5 inches tall, and 300 pounds of muscle, with white skin, and freckles on his cheeks, arms, legs and shoulders. His fiery red hair made him look like a fierce, Celtic warrior.

The first time Rory saw him, standing in his corner at the beginning of a match, he found himself in pain. Mr. Blakely was such an amazing specimen of masculinity and muscle, it made Rory's entire body ache.

For a solid week, Rory searched for anything he could find about Tim Blakely. He watched Tim's videos over and over, sometimes until six in the morning. Then, on the seventh day, he turned off his computer, and stretched out on his bed. He realized that he had put more into this nonexistent relationship than he ever did with Duane. He felt stupid, and vowed to think of something he could do for Duane that would make him happy.

He tried as hard as he could to stop thinking about Tim Blakely, a man in England he would never meet.

A month later, Tim Blakely wrestled for, and won, the European Heavy Weight Championship, defeating the German Champ, Markus "Der Wolf" Wright. Rory watched the match between these two European muscle freaks, became sexually over-stimulated, pleasured himself, and then closed the book on Tim Blakely, for good.

The Anderson/Enos Saga

Dyer Anderson and Chris Enos were on similar paths with their titles. Both were expected to give Johnson White a shot, and both were taking matches with non-threatening opponents, trying to sharpen their skills.

Dyer was doing great, winning each match easily, sometimes against bigger guys, although all were rookies.

Enos was also doing well, but had a few close calls. Each new generation provided bigger, stronger men, who started younger and younger, and were able to avail themselves of the newest and most successful training techniques. But, for some reason, dirty tactics were not taught in training facilities. If they were, Chris Enos would be the number one professor.

In all his close calls, Mr. Enos was able to use his opponent's private parts against them. He never lost any of these matches, but had more than a few 2-count, near pins, where as Dyer Anderson had none. The closest he got to losing was a handful of 1-counts, with quick kick-outs.

Rory loved every one of Chris Enos's matches. He admired how Enos could act out all the dark, sadistic urges that Rory kept hidden deep inside him. His two biggest fantasies were to face Enos in a private match, and for them to become a tag team.

DYER ANDERSON vs. JOHNSON WHITE

Max Gunn, a spokesman for the Federation, announced at a press conference that Dyer Anderson could not officially offer a title match to a contender who was not holding a belt of a direct lower level.

Chris Enos made a lot of noise on the issue, saying that the Federation was finally showing some sanity. Dyer Anderson immediately announced that he would indeed put his belt on the line against Johnson White, no matter what the Federation said, and that if White won, he would gladly hand it over to Mr. Johnson. The Federation felt they had no choice but to sanction the match, and scheduled a time and place.

Enos threatened to "intercede". Anderson thought that was hilarious and encouraged him to "intercede" as much as he liked, and added that had Chris Enos offered Johnson a title shot, there would be no issue. He even offered the scheduled night at the arena for Enos to face Johnson, in case Enos changed his mind.

Mr. Enos ignored the offer and simply repeated his claims that Dyer Anderson was ducking him. At this point, Anderson took a page out of Mr. Enos's book and ignored him all together.

The Media Coverage became very different. Johnson also chose to completely ignore Chris Enos. Uncharacteristically, Dyer publically discussed his apprehensions about facing his friend in battle. Chris Enos's interviews consisted of ranting, raving, and throwing tantrums.

A couple of times, Anderson and Johnson gave interviews together. They spoke openly about each other's strengths and their own weaknesses and advantages. The biggest difference between them, was that Johnson had an aversion to nudity and dirty tricks. Anderson, not only, had no aversion, he liked them, and even reveled in them. But, for this match, he promised that he would not use any dirty moves or grabs, and stick to pure wrestling.

ANNOUNCER: "IN THIS CORNER, THE FORMER ALL-AMERICAN CHAMP, HAILING FROM DETROIT MICHIGAN, IN THE WHITE TRUNKS, 6 FEET 3 INCHES TALL, WEIGHING IN AT 250 POUNDS, MR. JOHNSON WHITE!!"

White didn't give a lot, in terms of fanfare. He nodded to the camera, and continued stretching out his muscles.

ANNOUNCER: "AND, THE CURRENT ALL WORLDS HEAVY WEIGHT PRO CHAMPION, FROM ATLANTA, GEORGIA, IN THE ROYAL BLUE TRUNKS, 6 FEET EVEN, 265 POUNDS, DYER ANDERSON!!"

After introductions, the two men met center ring. As the Ref gave them the once-over, they laughed, chatted and even used each other's shoulders to steady themselves when the Ref checked their boots. When the Ref sent them back to their corners, Anderson gave Johnson a pat on his butt for good luck.

The Ref called for the bell. The two competitors met center ring, gave each other a hearty handshake, and began circling.

From the beginning, it was back and forth, each scoring excellent technical moves, with the other countering. The balance of power tilted both ways. Two times after excellent combos, they stopped to congratulate each other for good wrestling.

Chris Enos emerged from the locker room and made his way down to the announcer's table. He was met with boos and cheers, equally. The two men carrying on the color commentary were both happy to see him and they moved apart to give him room to sit between them. They asked him who he hoped would win. He said it didn't matter because he could easily beat either man, and the All Worlds Title would be his, very soon. When one announcer pointed out that he already lost to Dyer Anderson, Chris sneered and said, "I think you are mistaken." The Announcers were dumbfounded.

Back in the ring, Dyer and Johnson were so evenly matched the back-and-forth went on for a solid ten minutes, until Anderson did something which surprised the entire arena. As Mr. White was rebounding off the ropes, he jumped up and successfully trapped Johnson with a flying head scissors.

THA-WHOMP! Johnson White flipped over and hit the canvas hard. Mr. Anderson's big, meaty thighs held on to White's head throughout the flip and hard landing.

The announcers went crazy. "That was an INCREDIBLE jump! He got HEIGHT for a man his size!"

The other announcer pointed out, "Tommy McGee hit him with that same, exact move in their last match!!"

Anderson pulled up on Johnson's head, making sure the hold was tight, and inescapable. Johnson kicked and tried to twist them both over, but he couldn't get enough leverage. Dyer was too broad a man, and his big arms, spread out, kept them right where they were.

Dyer smiled and rubbed his friend's stomach, who was now on his back, with his head locked an inch from Anderson's crotch. Dyer was proud to have obtained the first upper hand of the match. He thought about dishing out some big, heavy punches to White's vulnerable gut, but something stopped him.

Johnson arched up onto his tiptoes, trying to wrench himself out. Anderson just rubbed his stomach, again, and kept his big, beefy, muscular thighs flexed tight. Johnson tried again, though, and finally seemed to gain enough leverage to weaken the hold. BAM! Anderson pounded White's gut with a big hammer fist.

"OOOF!" Johnson flopped back down on the canvas, his sweaty muscles bouncing. His fingers dug into Dyer's thighs, who leaned back, and propped himself up with his arms, increasing the torque and pressure on Johnson's neck.

Mr. White kicked the canvas, furiously and yelled out. He arched up, again. Dyer was tempted to pull on Mr. White's huge bulge. There it was, again, just an arm's length away. A couple times his hand absent-mindedly made its way to the front of Johnson's trunks, but he pulled it back, remembering his promise. Johnson kept bridging up, and his big bulge bobbled around inside his trunks. It truly was the biggest package in wrestling, and it kept jiggling and bouncing.

Anderson looked away, and pounded his friend's gut, again. BAM! He had to get his head back in the game and stop focusing on his opponent's giant bulge. He yelled out, "ASK HIM, REF! HE WANTS TO GIVE UP!"

"HELL NO!" Johnson bellowed, before the Ref could ask.

Dyer held on, flexing his big quads, then leaned back, and brought his legs straight up, causing Johnson to have to come into a very awkward hunched over seated position. Anderson then swung his legs back down, crashing them, and Johnson White, back down to the canvas, with an earth-quaking THUD! Again, Johnson's wet and shiny muscles bounced and Anderson's muscley, beefy body jiggled.

Johnson's eyes rolled back in his head, and Anderson went for it, again. He swung those big, hairy thighs up, then back down to the canvas. BOOM! This time, he rolled himself up on top of Johnson as his legs came down. His knees were now pinning down Johnson's arms.

The Ref dropped down for the count. Johnson tried to kick his legs up to hook Anderson's arms, but Anderson batted them away.

Johnson wriggled his hands and grabbed Anderson's knees. Just as the Ref counted "TWO!", he lifted Anderson off of him and got his shoulder up. Anderson climbed to the side, and Johnson rolled the other direction.

Anderson was on his feet, but Johnson lingered at the ropes, on his knees, massaging his thick neck. Anderson crossed the ring in a split second. He pulled Johnson up by his still aching neck, and clothes lined him right there on the ropes. Johnson was now bent backward over the ropes, groaning. Anderson grabbed his wrist and sent him flying across the ring, into the opposite ropes. As he rebounded, Dyer dropped to one knee and had a big right fist waiting for Johnson's abs. WHAM! Johnson doubled over and dropped to his knees, holding his gut.

Dyer got to his feet, and went for it one more time. He shot his opponent into the ropes.

As Johnson rebounded, he dropped to one knee at the same time as Anderson, and threw a punch up to where The Champ's stomach had just been. Anderson did the exact same thing. Instead of hitting each other in the gut, they both landed a bull's-eye punch to the other's faces.

The Crowd went bananas. They had never seen anything like it.

The Challenger AND The Champ were almost knocked out, at the same time. They wobbled on their knees, grabbed each other, and slumped forward, chest-to-chest. Both heads sunk down to rest on the other's shoulder.

The Ref had to ask the pair if they were good to go on, and held up their arms to see if they had control of their motor skills.

Dyer put his hands on Johnson's shoulders and pushed up to his feet. Just as he did, Johnson wrapped his arms around Anderson's waist and stood up, throwing the Champ over his shoulder.

"WHOA!"

Johnson White had the All Worlds Champ on his shoulder, kicking and holding on for dear life. Johnson played it up, and even flexed for the camera. He then walked to the corner, turned around, ran diagonally, just past center ring, then dropped down to one knee, driving the Champ's stomach into his shoulder, and let go. The Champ rolled off and landed flat on his back with a huge THUD! He held his gut, the wind completely knocked out of him.

Johnson stood up and shook out the cobwebs. He took one step back, then two steps forward, jumped up in the air, and BAM! He landed a big leg drop across the Champs midsection. Anderson's head and feet flew up, and he let out a big "OOOF!" The Challenger covered him, hooked a leg, and yelled, "REF! GIVE

HIM THE THREE COUNT!!!"

The Ref dropped down, "ONE! TWO!" Kick out!

Dyer raised his shoulder, even with Johnson on top of him, then sunk back down to the canvas, holding his gut.

White stood up, dragging the Champ up with him, by his hair. He held a handful of that hair, and leveled a huge fist into Dyer's belly. BAM!

Dyer's jaw went slack, and he was, again, holding his gut. Johnson didn't give him a second to recover. He propelled the Champ into the ropes, and as he came off, drove a knee into his midsection. Dyer flipped over, onto his back, and hit the canvas. WHAM!

Johnson dropped to one knee, next to the fallen Champ, grabbed his wrists, pulled his arms up away from his stomach, and buried another big knee there. BAM! Spit flew out of Anderson's mouth. Johnson threw himself across Anderson for another cover, as he hooked his leg.

The Ref dropped down, again, "ONE! TWO!" Kick out!

The Champ was able to raise his shoulder, again.

Mr. White was becoming very frustrated. He yelled at the Ref as he slapped his hands together, quickly, "ONE! TWO! THREE!"

The Ref waved his hands at Johnson. "There's nothing wrong with the way I do my count!"

The Challenger gritted his teeth and slammed his fist straight down into Dyer's exposed belly. WHAMP! Spit flew out, again, and The Champ's body convulsed up, like the letter "V".

White got back to his feet, pulling Anderson up by his hair, again. He positioned himself behind Anderson and wrapped his arms around, in a reverse bear hug. His hands clamped together, indenting into the middle of the Champ's beefy belly.

"Annghh!" Anderson grunted and grabbed Johnson's wrists, trying to pull his hands apart. White SQUEEEZED his big arms, tightening the bear hug. The Champ struggled for air, and every few seconds Johnson would SHAKE him, and make him look like a big rag doll.

Anderson desperately tugged on White's wrists, and tried to pull his fingers apart. Johnson's arms were like steel, and nothing could weaken them.

Dyer planted his feet firmly under himself and started moving them both toward the ropes. Johnson leaned back and lifted Anderson off his feet and walked them *away* from the ropes. As soon as Dyer's feet were back on the canvas, he leaned forward and bucked Johnson's feet off the ground. He immediately walked them back to the ropes, hoping for a break. When Johnson's feet hit the ground, he did the same thing, and they were back to center.

They were covered in sweat, and Dyer's face was beet red. The struggle between the two bulls was taking its toll, on both. Johnson tried to keep Anderson off his feet, but he couldn't hold him up forever. Anderson got his feet firmly on solid ground, once more, and walked them into the corner, backward. Johnson's back was up against the ring post and Anderson held on to the ropes to keep them there. Johnson kept his bear hug clamped on, and tried to lift Anderson, but he held on to the ropes TIGHTLY.

The Ref smacked Anderson's chest and called for the break.

Johnson unlocked his arms and withdrew his bear hug. Dyer took a step forward, but then lunged backward with a big elbow to Johnson's jaw. WHAM!

"OOOOOH!" The crowd reacted, and   Johnson was caught off guard, thinking his friend would honor a clean break. His eyes rolled back in his head. Anderson took another step forward then spun around with a big fist to White's abs. BAM!

"AAUUGHH!" Johnson bounced in the corner, and held on to the ropes. His eyes crunched closed, and his mouth fell open, groaning.

The Ref warned Anderson, again, "OUT OF THE CORNER!"

Anderson took two steps forward and looked down at Mr. White's huge package. It was a very inviting. He thought about it for half a second, then put his hands on Johnson's shoulders and rammed his gut with a big knee. WHAM! Johnson's big, buff body undulated.

Dyer grabbed his old friend's wrist, whipped him across the ring, and Johnson's back slammed into the opposite corner post. Everything shook again. Johnson was numb, and all but knocked out. Anderson sauntered over, and put his hands on Johnson's shoulders again.

White put his hands on his friend's chest, and shook his head, "NO, man…"

Anderson bit his lower lip, and let out short breath. BAM! His knee rammed Johnson's stomach, again. The Ref smacked his shoulder blade and warned him to keep the action out of the corners. Anderson stepped back, and Johnson sunk to his knees.

Dyer grabbed White's chin to pull him up to his feet, but he couldn't stand. He also couldn't catch his breath. He held his gut with one hand, and leaned his face into Anderson to keep himself up. Anderson pushed him back, leaned down and WHAM! He slammed a big, mean uppercut into Johnson's gut.

Johnson gasped and fell forward, his face against Anderson's stomach. Anderson was getting pretty cocky. He propped Johnson up with one hand, then patted his own big, beefy tummy and yelled out, "DON'T MESS WITH DYER ANDERSON! 100 PERCENT CAST IRON!!!" He pounded a hammer fist into, as if it was a drum.

Anderson rubbed Johnson's head, then pushed it between his big, beefy thighs, and squeezed. He bent down, clamped his arms around Johnson's middle, and brought him up, in an upside down bear hug. He shook him, just as Johnson had shaken him a few minutes earlier. Johnson's legs kicked, and flopped. He wasn't doing well.

Anderson yelled out, "ASK HIM, REF!"

Johnson yelled, "NO!" and twisted his head side to side furiously.

Anderson gave him the rag doll treatment again, then SLAMMED him down.

Johnson's upper back crashed into the canvas first. He bounced, then his legs caused a second crash, and he was laid out, spread eagle.

The Champ knew he was victorious, and he raised his right hand as he sunk down to cover his friend.

The Ref was already down, "ONE! TWO!" but somehow Johnson got his shoulder up.

No one was more shocked than Anderson. He jumped to his feet, and tried to pull Johnson up by his chin. It was a no-go. Johnson could only get to his knees. He held on to Anderson's thighs to keep himself up. Anderson gave his friend a playful smack on his cheek, then leaned down and let loose another furious upper cut to his gut. WHAM!

"Ungg.. ahh." Johnson gasped, and drooled, his face still pressed against Anderson's stomach. Anderson smiled. He found the cameraman, and pounded his own gut again for the crowd. Johnson's face bounced as he did. He pushed Johnson down to the mat. The poor guy looked almost unconscious, on his back; his arms limp at his sides. Anderson jumped up, extended his leg out and brought it down HARD across Johnson's midsection. BAM!

Mr. White doubled up and spit flew.

Again, Anderson covered White, and again he was able to lift his shoulder just before the three-count. Anderson knelt next to the Challenger, his hands up, clawing at the air. He was frustrated, but also proud of his friend's amazing resilience.

The Champ stood up, and tried to pull Johnson to his feet, once more. This time he delivered the uppercut to Johnson's midsection instantaneously, thinking he wouldn't be able to get off his knees. BAP!

Unfortunately, Johnson had started to get to his feet, and it wasn't his midsection that Anderson punched, hard. His fist actually collided with Johnson's enormous bulge, dead on.

Mr. White's mouth dropped open, and he sucked in a huge gulp of air. His eyes went white, his knees buckled, and he fell on his side.

Dyer Anderson was shocked. He stood motionless with a big-eyed stare. He never meant to touch Johnson's privates, but there he was, in agony at The Champ's feet, cupping his enormous jewels.

Anderson looked at The Ref, then dropped down and covered his friend.

The Ref dropped as well, and pounded the mat, "ONE! TWO! THREE!" He signaled for the bell, "DING! DING!"

The match was over.

Johnson didn't move.

Anderson knelt by his friend, who he just defeated, unintentionally. He held Johnson's shoulder, and asked him, "Are you ok, man?"

Johnson groaned, still holding his genitals.

The Ref grabbed Anderson's right wrist and raised his arm. Anderson remained kneeling. The entire crowd was on their feet, cheering and hollering.

Finally, Johnson let out a big, long breath, and sat up.

Dyer helped him to his feet, and there was another blast of applause.

Johnson was walking very awkwardly.

Anderson helped him to the ropes, then sat on the middle one, creating a gap, which White climbed through. He helped him down from the apron, then put his arm around him, and headed for the locker room.

The Announcer intercepted them. Anderson profusely apologized to Johnson, on air, claiming the low blow was purely an accident. Johnson accepted his apology and said he knew it wasn't on purpose. He didn't say much more than that. His breathing was labored, and he was still in pain.

Anderson offered a rematch whenever Johnson was up for it. He even offered Mr. White a free shot to his own balls, at the beginning of the match. Johnson waved it away as a ridiculous idea.

At this point, Chris Enos stormed over. He decried Anderson's offer to Johnson, yelling the he was next in line for a title shot. He added, smugly, that he would also be taking Anderson up on the offer of a free shot to his balls.

Anderson stepped in front of Johnson, and affected an aggressive stance. He pointed at Enos, who was on the other side of the Announcer, and said that he would NEVER honor a match with Enos until he gave Johnson a shot at his Mr. America title. The Interviewer took up for Johnson, agreeing that he was long overdue for a rematch with Enos.

Enos screamed and yelled and the scene disintegrated into a melee. Security guards intervened and escorted Enos out of the arena. Anderson led Johnson back to the locker room.

Rory was so engrossed in the situation, he replayed the match over and over, especially the low blow. He couldn't wait to see Johnson take on Enos, and Enos to face Anderson. Even though Enos was now his favorite, he thought about all the exciting "punishment" the other two men could dole out.

DYER ANDERSON vs. CHRIS ENOS

Dyer Anderson stuck to his guns, insisting he would *never* give Chris Enos a title shot until he put his belt on the line against Johnson White. He was able to stand firm, until the Federation stepped in. Demand for the match had become overwhelming, and Dyer had exhausted his list of challengers, so Mr. Anderson was forced to face Chris Enos in another title match.

Anderson gave very few interviews leading up to the match. He referred to it as a "cake walk" and that he would finally shut that "cocky little bitch" up for good.

Enos was, indeed, beyond cocky, and called himself "The All Worlds Champ". He was as insulting as usual, and treated other people as poor unfortunates he felt sorry for. He became almost God-like in his self-assessments.

Johnson White was approached for comment. Instead of crying foul, as Chris Enos had done when White was offered a Title Shot, he was magnanimous and showed exemplary sportsmanship. He said it wasn't fair, but that he thought he would be given another shot at The American Championship once Enos lost to Anderson. Johnson even declined a rematch with Anderson, saying that he wanted to face him as the American Champ in their next title match.

ANNOUNCER: "THIS IS A TITLE MATCH FOR THE ALL WORLDS

PRO WRESTLING HEAVYWEIGHT CHAMPIONSHIP BELT!"

"IN THIS CORNER, THE CHALLENGER, IN WHITE TRUNKS, 6'2" TALL AND 230 POUNDS, THE A.W.P.W. AMERICAN CHAMPION, CHRIS ENOS!!!!"

Chris Enos stood center ring, wearing his American Championship Belt, hands straight in the air. He basked in the mix of cheers and boos, as if it was unanimous admiration. He struck his signature pose, and teased the crowd with the slow rub down of his perfectly muscled body. Anyone watching him would think he had just won the match of his life.

His shiny, shaggy, bleached-blond hair was a little longer, falling down to his shoulders, and his white trunks were smaller and tighter than usual. They had already ridden up, and were exposing the bottoms of his pumped up, all-muscle, butt cheeks.

He walked back to his corner. An attendant took off his belt and handed it back to him. He held it up for the audience to see.

ANNOUNCER: "AND IN THIS CORNER... IN THE ROYAL BLUE TRUNKS, AT 6 FEET, 265 POUNDS, THE A.W.P.W. WORLD HEAVYWEIGHT CHAMPION, DYER ANDERSON!!!"

The World Champ walked to center, and turned to all four sides of the ring, letting every corner of the arena get a good look at him.

He took his belt off, held it up, and reveled in the adulation. Unlike Enos, he received almost all-positive reaction from the crowd.

The Ref held out his hand, and Anderson handed him the belt. He raised it above his head, and walked it over to another attendant at ringside.

The Ref called Enos to meet them, center ring, so he could give them their instructions.

Enos had the strangest expression of serenity. It unnerved Anderson for a moment, but he brushed it off with a scoff. He knew that in five minutes the match would be over and the belt would be back around his waist.

The Ref turned to Enos, to give him his pre-match inspection. He patted his butt, and very lightly poked the tight bulge in the front of his trunks.

Enos took the Ref's hand and pressed it against his bulge. "You can feel it as much as you like. I have nothing to hide."

The Ref felt deeper, and was satisfied.

Chris raised his arms and said to Dyer, "You want to feel? I'm completely open. You can even look inside my trunks, if you want." His tone was creepily sincere, and oddly devoid of any irony.

Anderson looked down his nose at Enos, "No, I'm good. I trust the Ref."

Enos shrugged, "Suit yourself."

The Ref inspected his white wrist cuffs, and white boots, then turned to Anderson. He patted The Champs big, beefy butt, and lightly poked the front of his trunks, too.

Enos moved in close and gave Dyer's bulge a hard poke.

"OW!" Anderson jumped back. "What the fuck are you

doing?!"

"Oh, sorry. I forgot how much more sensitive yours is." Enos said, with that same strange sincerity.

Anderson raised his fist, ready to punch Chris Enos in the face. "Yeah?! Try that again!"

Enos put his hands up, "Sorry. I didn't mean to hurt you!"

The Ref got between them and blocked Dyer's fist with his open hand. "Hey! Save it for the match!"

Enos pushed his chest against the Ref's back and sandwiched him between himself and Anderson.

The Ref's hands rested on Anderson's chest as Enos's bump put him off balance.

Enos smiled, "I just want a good, clean match!"

"Yeah, I'll bet you do!" Anderson wanted just one clear shot at him.

"ALL RIGHT GUYS!" He pushed Anderson with his hands, and tried to push Enos with his back, but neither man was going anywhere.

Enos's face went blank, "I completely understand."

"ALL RIGHT, STOP! Or, I'm going to disqualify you both!" The Ref had had it.

"BUT, HE'S THE ONE..." Anderson was spitting mad.

"Who cares?!"

Anderson eased up, and moved back a couple of inches.

Enos did the same.

The Ref turned around. "YOU! Go to your corner!"

Enos had his hands up. "OK. I'm going."

The Ref turned back to Anderson, "And, YOU, to your corner…NOW!"

Anderson backed up, slowly.

Enos did the same, with a contented half smile on his face. "Good match, buddy."

Anderson sneered, and turned around. He wondered what Enos was up to. Why was he behaving so strangely?

The Champ worked himself up. He ran in place, flexed every muscle in his body, and shook them all out.

Enos stood, calmly.

The Ref called for the opening bell, "DING! DING!"

Anderson came out like a warrior, hands up, circling, ready for anything.

Enos skipped out casually, then circled as if he was up against a jobber.

Anderson came in hard for the lock up. He reared back, then slammed right in to a collar and elbow. Enos met him, with equal force. They struggled for a bit. Enos whispered something. Anderson broke it, and pushed the Challenger away from him.

"What the...?" The Champ had a strange look on his face. He was in disbelief.

Enos stood there, slowly rubbing down the muscles of his chest and abs, then his arms and thighs.

Dyer Anderson was visibly aroused. Chris Enos noticed.

Anderson walked away, and shook his head, trying to psyche himself up. He turned and began circling, again.

Enos didn't bother circling. He just headed straight for Anderson, and forced the lock up. They struggled for a bit, but Anderson pulled him down into a side headlock.

"Unngg." One of Enos's hands felt it's way all over Dyer Anderson's thick thigh. The other slowly reached around and rubbed his beefy belly, in a seemingly affectionate manner.

This had a double effect on Mr. Anderson. It confused him, and made the bulge in his trunks a bit bigger. He shook his head again, and cranked the headlock higher and tighter, in an attempt to stop the distractions.

"Uhnngh." Enos's hands flailed out, then resumed their rubbing and fondling of The Champ's beef and muscle.

Anderson HIP TOSSED Enos over onto his back, and kept a tight hold on the headlock, cranking it harder.

This is one of the situations Enos was looking forward to - being on his back, behind The Champ. He wrapped one arm around Anderson's burly thigh, and held it in place. His other hand slinked under Dyer's big butt and very lightly squeezed his balls. He fondled, and pulled very nicely, not causing any pain, just playing with them.

Anderson closed his eyes for one second.

Enos could feel Anderson's arousal, and he pushed up on it. Then, when he sensed Dyer relaxing for one split second, he reached up, grabbed his hair, threw his legs up, and caught Anderson in a head scissor. The Champ's headlock was broken, and Enos still had his arm around Dyer's big thigh.

The Champ's bulge had become a full erection, and completely vulnerable to the Challenger.

Anderson kicked, and writhed, but Enos's big, smooth, granite thighs were locked down tight around his neck.

Enos continued rubbing, nicely, and playing with The Champ's hard-on. Anderson moaned and his kicking stopped. He tried to pull Enos's hands away, but didn't have much power to do so. He obviously liked what was happening to him.

Enos moved his head down, right over the boner tenting Anderson's trunks. He put his lips gingerly around the head of the erection, then FLEXED his legs around Anderson's neck.

Anderson's moan turned into a grunt. He kicked his legs, again, and clawed at Enos's sculpted thighs.

Enos relaxed his thighs, and looked up to the Ref, "Ask him!"

The Ref was a feeling a bit uncomfortable, but he squatted down, and asked Anderson how he was doing. He grunted a definite, "NO!"

"OH, YEAH!?" Enos opened his hand, and SMACKED Anderson's balls.

"AAANNGG!" Anderson kicked, and bucked.

"Ask him, again." Enos was convinced this would do it.

"HELL NOOO!" Anderson didn't wait for the Ref to ask.

Enos slapped Anderson's balls again, and again. Every time he did, Anderson's whole body convulsed, he grunted, and his boner bounced, in his royal blue trunks.

Enos rubbed Anderson's belly, and licked the inside of his thigh.

"Mmm." Anderson was being forced to swing between pain and pleasure, and at this moment, he didn't seem to mind either, or both. He finally brought his legs together, trapping Enos's hand.

Even though Enos's hand was trapped, it was still moving around doing something that caused Anderson to buck his hips.

Anderson opened his legs and twisted around onto his knees. This brought Enos's legs, which were still wrapped around The Champ's head, straight up into the air. Enos was on his back, and The Champ straddled him, his own bulge hovering over Enos's face.

Anderson propped himself up with his two big arms, and intentionally GROUND his bulge into Enos's face.

Enos retaliated by FLEXING his shiny, sculpted muscle thighs.

"CLGHHKKK!" Anderson gagged, and tried to PULL the Challenger's legs apart, unsuccessfully.

Enos FLEXED his quads, again.

Anderson struck back with a BIG, HUGE PUNCH straight down into Enos's abs.

"UGLLGGHHH!" Enos's body undulated.

BAM! Anderson drilled another one into Enos's washboard stomach, and made his body undulate again. Enos's legs finally came apart.

"Unnnhhh." Enos was winded. One leg was bent, the other limp, straight out on the canvas.

Anderson positioned himself so that his bulge was covering Enos's mouth. He looked up at the Ref and yelled, "HEY! Why aren't you counting?!"

Enos had been pinned under him for a while, but the Ref wasn't about to start counting until either contestant had a controlled pin. He dropped down, and pounded the mat, "ONE! TWO!"

Enos twisted to one side, got his shoulder up, and Anderson's bulge off his face.

BAM! Anderson hammered another fist into Enos's gut, causing his legs to kick out.

"UHNNN.." Enos was in pain.

Anderson stood up, pulling Enos up to his feet, by his pretty, messed up, blond hair. He looked Enos in the face, and gave him a hard, open-handed chop to his six-pack.

"GLLLGGKKK!" Enos's eyes rolled back in his head.

The Champ pulled his arm back. WHAM! He SLAMMED

another punch into Enos's sweaty, ripped abs, as he let go of Enos's hair.

The Challenger collapsed down onto his hands and knees in front of The Champ. He held his stomach, and worked to get his breath back.

Anderson stuck out two fingers on his right hand, and angled them down, as if he was holding a gun. He pointed them at Enos and yelled, "THAT IS WHAT HAPPENS TO ANYONE WHO FACES ME!"

One of Enos's hands reached out, and rested on Anderson's thick leg. He was still gasping for breath.

Anderson grabbed a handful of that pretty blond hair, again, and directed Enos's face up, so he could make eye contact. "Ya ain't never gonna beat me, boy! Ya just can't do it!" He yelled out to the crowd, again, and he flexed his other big arm. "CHAMP FOR LIFE!!!" He looked back down at the Blond Pretty Boy and almost felt sorry for him. "You'll always be my bitch. Always." The sight of Chris Enos at his feet, groveling, made his excitement swell, and throb.

Enos looked up at him with doe eyes, and sighed, "Always." His other hand was now resting on Anderson's other big thigh, just an inch from Anderson's erection. He leaned forward and rested his head right where those two meaty thighs met. He lightly, and slowly rubbed his head against Anderson.

The Champ kept a handful of Enos's hair. He was ready to begin his next assault on Enos, but took a minute to enjoy the submissive conduct from his bitter rival.

Enos looked up, and maintained eye contact, as he put his mouth directly over Anderson's bulge, and his tongue delicately stroked.

Anderson would never admit it, out loud, but he had thought about this moment thousands of times, in daydreams. "Ah."

WHOMP! The next thing he knew, he was flat on his big ass!

Enos had wrapped his arms around Anderson's knees, pulled up on them, and lunged forward. Once The Champ was toppled, Enos threw his substantial legs over his shoulders.

Anderson was rolled up in a pin.

Enos dug his feet in, and worked to keep the leverage so Anderson couldn't kick out.

The Ref dropped down, "ONE! TWO! THR….!"

Anderson kicked out just before the third slap of the mat. The crowd was on its feet. Many thought the impossible had happened, and that they had just witnessed the upset of the decade.

Anderson, himself, was shocked. He rolled to the ropes. Enos followed, and slammed a BIG KNEE into the side of The Champ's head, as he got to knees. WHAM!

Anderson held on to the middle rope. He slumped across it, dazed. Enos swung one of his legs up and around the back of Anderson's neck, and pulled up on the middle rope, choking Anderson.

The Champ flailed his arms and gagged.

The Ref smacked Enos's back, "OFF THE ROPES!"

Enos climbed off of The Champ, took one step back. BAM! He hit Anderson with another knee, causing him to tumble out of the ring.

Enos raised his arms, and screamed out, "CHRIS ENOS! THE WORLD'S NEW HEAVY-WEIGHT CHAMP!"

The audience erupted in a strange mixture of sounds. There were cheers and boos, but also a lot of loud discussion. People yelled out things like, "DO IT, AGAIN! SUCK HIS DICK!", "STRIP THE CHAMP!", and, "WRESTLE NAKED!" They loved Enos's sexual attacks.

Anderson climbed onto the ring apron, kneeling, about to crawl back in, when Enos sauntered over, and slammed another knee into Anderson's face. The Champ flew off, and landed on the concrete, on his back.

The Ref warned Enos to stay back. He did, raising his arms, as if he had just won this Championship match.

The Ref began counting Anderson out. He climbed back up on to the apron, and put his hand up, telling the Ref, "KEEP HIM AWAY FROM ME!"

The Ref managed to block Enos long enough so that Anderson was standing on the apron, with his head and shoulders through the ropes. Enos sidestepped the Ref and slammed The Champ across his shoulders with a big elbow, WHAM!

"UNGGH!" Anderson dropped to his knees, holding on to the

middle rope, his head and shoulders sticking into the ring.

Enos straddled The Champ's head and scissored it, flexing his perfectly muscled thighs,

"UNNGGG" Anderson tried to pull his head back, but he was trapped.

The Ref slapped Enos's shoulder, "OFF THE ROPES!"

Enos jumped up, and came down hard, his feet crashing into the canvas with a THUD! Anderson screamed out, bouncing on the middle rope. Enos released the scissor, and sauntered away.

Anderson collapsed sideways onto his back, on the apron, then rolled himself under the ropes, just inside the ring.

Enos sauntered back, and pushed his boot down into Anderson's balls, while Anderson screamed and held on to the bottom rope.

The Ref grabbed Enos's arm, and PUSHED him back. "ENOUGH OF THAT! OFF THE ROPES!"

Enos stepped back a few feet, and yelled out, "THE CHAMP IS DONE! LOOK AT HIM!"

Anderson held his balls, and pulled himself up to his knees.

Enos turned back toward him, ready for another attack.

Anderson's hands went up, "NO! KEEP HIM AWAY FROM ME!" He almost took on a begging tone, "STOP! STOP! NO!"

Enos was in heaven. Having The Champ at his mercy, and begging, was almost too much for him. He stalked The Champ, backing him up into the corner. Enos walked right up into the corner, his boot between Anderson's legs. He leaned in, the front of his trunks pushing against Anderson's turned face.

Enos ran his fingers through The Champ's hair. He grabbed a handful, and jabbed a quick punch into the side of Anderson's face.

"AANNGG." Anderson tried pushing him back.

The Ref, once again, warned, "OUT OF THE CORNER!"

Enos stepped back, then forward, again, and gave Anderson another JAB to the temple.

The Champ was not doing well. He yelled out, holding the side of his face. He managed to pull himself up and sit on the middle turnbuckle before Enos was back with a big knee to his gut. He grunted, and slumped, his grip on the ropes the only thing holding him up.

The Ref pushed Enos back, and asked Anderson if he was ok to continue. He nodded his head, vigorously. His anger was brewing. He couldn't take much more of Chris Enos's humiliating treatment. He clenched his fists, and when the Ref moved out of the way, he CHARGED out of the corner, spearing Enos, who was completely surprised. They crashed to the canvas, Anderson on top of the winded Challenger.

Anderson shook his fists and worked himself up. He sat back on his knees, between Enos's legs, and started pounding on The Challenger's abs, "ASK HIM, REF!"

Enos tried to crawl backwards, but Anderson crawled with him.

The Challenger tried to roll on his side, away from Anderson, but Anderson grabbed his leg. They struggled, neither one of them at 100% strength.

Enos ended up on his stomach, with Anderson lying on his legs. Anderson crawled up on top of him, wrestled his big, beefy arms up under Enos's big, ripped arms, and trapped him in a full nelson. Enos's handsome face was being smashed into the canvas. The Champ twisted himself to the side, into a sitting position, off of Enos. He carried Enos along with him, and swung him around. Enos was now sitting in front of The Champ, the Full Nelson still being applied with a vengeance. The Challenger's chin was forced down into his chest. Anderson brought his big tree trunk legs around Enos's shredded midsection, crossed them at the ankles, and SQUEEZED.

Enos gurgled. His arms waved, trapped above his head, and his feet kicked the canvas.

"ASK HIM!" Anderson ordered, with a big smile.

Chris Enos shook his blond hair. At no point would he submit in this match. He would rather die, first.

Mr. Anderson rocked up and down, as he flexed his huge thighs and tried to bring his elbows together. The bulky muscles in his shoulders and neck swelled up to an extreme.

As much as Anderson was determined to win the match at that exact moment, with that exact hold, Enos was just as determined that he would not. Anderson looked like a giant kid abusing a rocking horse. He kept bouncing and squeezing with a big, child-like grin on his face.

Even though he was having a great deal of fun, at his opponent's expense, Anderson would never get Enos to forfeit. He sensed it, and released his nelson and scissors. Enos fell sideways onto the mat, and writhed, as he rubbed his neck and midsection.

The Champ stood up, pulling the weakened Challenger up to his feet, using a handful of that tousled blond hair. WHAM! He SMASHED a HARD PUNCH into Enos's brick wall of abs.

"OOOOHH UNNHH!" Enos could barely stand. He doubled over, his hands holding his stomach.

Anderson used Enos's hair, again, to pull him upright. He grabbed Enos's crotch and clamped on to Enos's shoulder with his other hand. Enos was scooped up, and unceremoniously slammed down.

Enos groaned at The Champ's feet, and turned onto his side, his entire midsection, front and back, in agony.

Anderson again pulled his battered foe up by his hair, scooped him up, but this time brought him down over his knee, in a back breaker. He pushed Enos's chin down with one hand. "So, you like playing with my dick? How do you like it when I do it?" He softly rubbed Enos's bulge, mimicking the way it was done to him, earlier.

Enos sprang to life. He kicked wildly, and desperately swatted Dyer's hand away. In that frantic moment, Enos's kicks built up momentum, and he flipped himself off of Anderson's knee, and landed flat on his face.

Anderson shook his head, and took a second to process what

had just happened. Enos was lying on his stomach, under him, his hands now burrowed into his groin area. His tight, white trunks had ridden up and were now exposing much of his perfectly molded butt cheeks. Dyer wanted to rip the trunks off and feel the smooth naked rear end of this fallen Blond God. Instead, he SPANKED, HARD, and enjoyed seeing the Muscle Boy's body jerk.

Anderson flipped Enos over, hooked a leg, and dropped his chest down across Enos's.

The Ref dropped down, and slapped the mat, "ONE! TWO!"

Enos called on every ounce of strength he had left, and kicked out just enough to get his shoulder up.

Equal amounts of admiration and frustration filled Anderson. He had to win this match, but he couldn't help but feel a bit aroused by the toughness of the Pretty Boy.

They both took a moment to rest, Anderson still on top of Enos, both hands planted on the canvas, one hand next to his opponent's shoulder, the other between his legs.

Anderson remembered what happened a few moments ago. He looked down at the front of Enos's extra-tight, white trunks, ran his fingers along it, then clamped down on the bulge.

Enos, again, snapped into some kind of frantic state. He ripped Anderson's hand away, swung wildly, hitting Anderson in the side of the head, then tried to squirm away to the ropes.

Anderson shook out the cobwebs, and lunged forward, He grabbed Enos by the hair, got to his knees and swung a fist of his own into the side of Enos's head.

Enos collapsed onto his stomach, and held his head. "Unhh!"

Anderson flipped Enos over, then straddled his head, his knees on either side, his butt resting on Enos's upper chest. He pulled Enos's head up by the blond hair, then squeezed his legs together. "Uh…" he let out a quiet moan when the Challenger's face touched his erection.

The Champ rolled onto his back, causing Enos to roll over, too.

The Challenger was now face down in Anderson's crotch, with his stomach on the canvas and his shoulders up against the back of Anderson's big thighs. The Champ's thick legs were wrapped tightly around his neck.

Anderson SQUEEZED and pushed Enos's face down.

Enos groaned, "UNNNHH." He was smothered by Anderson's bulge. He moved his head up, and pushed his chin against The Champ's balls, so he could breath. He tried to PULL his head out, but Anderson just FLEXED his bulky thighs harder. Enos slapped and clawed at those big slabs of beef.

Anderson propped himself up on one elbow, and played with Enos's hair, then pushed Enos's head down, again smothering the Challenger with his swollen bulge.

Enos ran his hands along The Champ's muscley, beefy thighs, and his head moved slowly and deliberately, upward.

"Nnnn.." Anderson moaned, and his hips jerked upward.

Enos's head then turned a bit to the side, and made small up and down motions.

"Oh, man!" Anderson tried to prop himself up on his hands. He closed his eyes for a moment, and settled back down.

One of Enos's hands rubbed Anderson's belly, and made a slow pushing motion from the top down to his crotch, as his head kept slowly churning around.

Anderson tried to flex his thighs together, but he could only flex his butt, and push his hips forward. Enos grabbed his erection, and pulled upward on it, very slowly.

Anderson intended to flex his scissor, again, but his legs came apart. He tried to push Enos's head away from his private parts. "Unnhhh. Stop!..." He looked up to the Ref for help, "Make him stop!"

The Ref shrugged. He poked Enos in the back. "Uh... continue wrestling!"

Enos looked up, and GRABBED Anderson's belly with two clawing hands.

"AAAAHHHGGGG!!!" Anderson's mouth dropped open. He grabbed Enos's wrists but couldn't pry them off of his belly. He fell onto his back, and threw his legs up, in another scissor attempt. The Challenger blocked them with his elbows.

Enos continued to claw Anderson's stomach with one hand. He hooked his other hand under one of The Champ's legs, and pulled it up over his shoulder. He wrapped his legs around Anderson's free leg, and pushed himself forward as far as he could, which brought The Champ's leg up pretty high.

"AAGHHUNNNGGG!!" Anderson was now tied up in a unique and painful pin.

The Ref dropped down for the count. "ONE! TWO!"

This pin might have worked on a smaller, weaker opponent, but Anderson was a strong bull. He THRUST his leg, that was over Enos's shoulder, down. It slid off of Enos's shoulder, and crashed to the canvas.

Anderson's shoulder came up, and the pin was broken. He propped himself up on his elbows.

Enos still had one of Anderson's legs grape-vined, and he pulled the other one over his shoulder, again. He wrapped his hands around the ankle of that leg, and PUSHED it away from the other.

Anderson was now the victim of a wide banana split.

"OOOHHH!!! AHHNNGGG!" Anderson moaned, gasped, and rubbed the inside of his thighs. "No! No! No! Stop! Stop! Stop!"

Enos had his shoulder braced against The Champ's big thigh, so he was able to hold that ankle with one hand. He brought his free hand above the front of Anderson's trunks, and let him see it. Anderson tried to grab it, but the hand was too quick. It clamped down on the big man's balls, and mercilessly yanked and shook.

"AAAGGHHHHH!!" Anderson yelled out, and threw his head back. He was as helpless as he had ever been, in any match he had ever wrestled.

Enos closed his eyes. The pleasure of the moment consumed him. "Ask him, Ref! Ask him how he's gonna get out of this one!"

The Ref knelt down next to Anderson. "You ok?"

Anderson nodded.

"You sure? You ok to go on?" The Ref couldn't tell if Anderson was extremely unhappy, or happy to be in extreme pain.

Anderson nodded, again. "YES! YES!" He maintained a very prominent erection throughout.

Enos PUSHED The Champ's legs apart, even further.

Anderson's mouth was open, but he didn't make a sound. He was beyond pain. His head and shoulders sank down to the mat.

The Ref warned him. "That's a pin."

The Champ didn't move.

The Ref lowered himself to the canvas, "ONE!"

Anderson got his shoulder up, right quick.

He grabbed at Enos's hand. "STOP!" He couldn't budge it away from his aching balls. He grappled with his own erection for a moment, trying to adjust it into a more comfortable position.

Enos twisted himself to the side, a shoulder now resting on Anderson's chest. This forced the Champ's shoulders back down onto the canvas.

The Ref counted, but only got to "ONE!", before Anderson had his shoulder back up.

Enos did that two more times, and two more times

Anderson was back up on the first count, though he was starting to fade. The pain was too much. He snagged a handful of Enos's blond locks, and pulled his head into his chest. He wrapped his other arm around Enos's neck, and SQUEEZED.

Enos YANKED on Anderson's balls, again.

"AAGHHH!" Anderson was forced to release Enos's neck. He rested back on one elbow, and whimpered.

"Give it UP! Just submit now! EVERYONE can see I'm the new Champ! And, you're my little bitch boy!" Enos PUSHED Anderson's legs apart, again.

Anderson yelled out, through gritted teeth, "UUUHNNNNNGGGGGG!!!" He leaned forward and latched on to Enos's hair, again, pulling his head up. He rammed his elbow into it. BAM!

"OOHHH!" Enos released his grip on Anderson's ankle, and balls, and grabbed his own head, still with legs wrapped around one of The Champ's.

Anderson propped himself up with one hand, and rubbed his balls with the other. His head was spinning, and one big leg was still draped over Enos's shoulder.

Enos shook his head and opened his eyes real wide. He turned and looked at Anderson, who was still in great pain. He grabbed Anderson's wrist, and pulled it away from his crotch as he SMACKED Anderson's balls with his other hand.

"ANNGGHHH!" Anderson's torso fell backward and he held on to his balls with both hands.

Enos grabbed Anderson's ankle and pushed his legs apart, again.

"Nnnnnggghh." Anderson moaned, held his breath, and began panting.

Enos rolled backwards, across the Champ's chest.

Anderson's legs went up in the air, in a wide "V", and his shoulder went down to the canvas.

The Ref dropped down, counted to "ONE!" and Anderson pushed off the canvas, and thrust his hip. His legs went down and his shoulders came up. Enos tried it two more times, and two more times the same thing happened. Anderson ended up in a sitting position with his big, thick, muscular legs being spread wide by the Blond Challenger.

Enos tried it one more time, but gave Anderson a big smack to his balls, first.

"UNNNGH!" Anderson pushed out again, but the Ref made it to the second count this time.

Anderson grabbed Enos's hair, again, but Enos YANKED on The Champ's balls, quickly. Anderson released and fell back, only to have the Ref start counting, again. Anderson pushed himself back up.

Enos started playing with The Champ's hard-on. "You having as good a time as I am?"

Anderson held on to Enos's arm. "Stop! Come on! Stop it!"

Enos smiled at Anderson, then leaned down, and BIT the tip of Anderson's erection.

Anderson's eyes rolled around in his head. "UNNGGG!!!"

"ASK HIM!" Enos shouted at The Ref.

"You ok, Champ?" The Ref held Anderson's head up, so he could look him in the eye.

Anderson just made a noise. "Unnnngg."

Enos quickly rolled The Champ back again, in the wide "V", leg-split pin. Only, this time, he PULLED down on The Champ's hard-on for extra leverage.

The Ref dropped down, "ONE! TWO! THREE!"

Enos was stunned. He kept Anderson in the hold as the Ref called for the bell.

"DING! DING!"

"WHOAAAAA!" A stunned roar rose up from the crowd. No one, except Enos, ever thought he would win.

The Ref pulled on Enos's wrist. "Come on! The match is over!"

Chris Enos closed his mouth, and forced himself back into the moment. He popped up to his feet and threw his hands in the air, like he had done dozens of times before, only this time he actually won.

The Ref held up The new Champ's right hand, and called for the belt.

Anderson sat up, blinking. "No! What happened? That wasn't..."

The ring attendant handed the belt to the Ref and the Ref

handed it to Enos. Another attendant entered the ring with Enos's American Championship belt.

Anderson got to his knees, and motioned to the Ref. "No! That wasn't a three count!"

The Ref came over, and leaned down. "Sorry, man. Yes, it was."

Anderson shook his head. "No!... That couldn't…"

Enos looked at the World Belt in awe. A smile crept across his face, and he said to the attendant. "Put it on me!"

He did so.

Enos was handed his American belt. He held it high in the air, to his usual mix of CHEERS and BOOS, and flexed for the crowd.

Anderson walked over to his corner, and grabbed the top rope. He lowered his head and let out a big, long breath. He was humiliated, and would rather have died than to lose to Chris Enos.

The new Champ stood center ring, and basked in the partial glory he was receiving. A lot of Anderson's fans were yelling out insults and the "BOOS" were unending. Enos climbed out of the ring, and slowly made his way up the aisle, with one belt around his waist and the other over his shoulder. He acted as though every single person in that arena was flooding him with love. Thousands of fans leaned over the barricades, some trying to touch him, most screaming obscenities. It didn't matter. He thanked everyone as he passed. In his own eyes, he was much more than just a Champ. He was a Golden God.

4 THE AMERICAN CHAMPION

Enos refused to give back The American Championship belt, until the Federation warned him that he would have to defend that belt against Johnson White, immediately. They went on to state that if he lost that belt, his All Worlds Title would be in question. He relinquished The American belt.

A tournament was held. It was the first one since Dyer Anderson ascended to All Worlds Champion four years prior. The competition was the hardest the country had ever seen. Along with many of the best well-known wrestlers, several new men had earned a spot in the Tournament.

After several amazingly tough matches, Johnson White regained the Title. His old friend, Dyer Anderson was ringside for each one. White also shot himself up to the top of the list of contenders for Enos's new World belt.

The new World Champion was up to his old tricks, though. He dodged all the top contenders and filled the first half of his year with cakewalks.

Dyer Anderson demanded a rematch almost immediately. The Federation made several announcements that this would definitely happen. Their matches were some of the most anticipated, viewed, and publicized in the history of the sport.

Enos declared Dyer Anderson a "loser", and told anyone who interviewed him that the "old man" didn't deserve another match with him. He wasn't in his league, and he was "washed up". He said it would be unfair to wrestlers who truly deserved it, to grant him another title shot. This line of reasoning backfired because Johnson White's name would come up, and Enos wanted to face him, even less.

The African Champ, Modu Habe, from the Ivory Coast, called Enos out, in an interview. He was a beautiful, black muscle giant, 6' 7" tall and 325 pounds. Enos didn't even respond, and no one blamed him. Habe came to America, and showed up at Enos's matches.

 Suddenly, Enos was surrounded by huge security guards, when he appeared in public. He was forced to announce that Modu's name was now on his list of contenders, but down toward the bottom.

Markus Wright, the blond-haired, blue-eyed German Champ also wanted his shot. He was the thickest man in wrestling, at 6', 280lbs. He told Enos, via interviews, that after he beat him and took his title, he wanted them to form a tag team. Markus was strong, and won his matches with sheer, brute strength. They would be the "two most dangerous blonds" in wrestling.

He wasn't fast, and many commentators rated Enos as a better wrestler, so Enos naturally placed him higher on the list. Early in his career, Wright wrestled as "Markus Wolf". He was quickly dubbed with the ridiculous moniker of "Big Bad Wolf". The "Wolf" part stuck, and he was often referred to as, simply, "Der Wolf".

Rene Sebastian also threw his hat back in the ring. He already fought Dyer Anderson and lost, so he should have been placed at the bottom of the list, but demand for an Enos/Sebastian match was high. Plus, Enos, himself, was eager to face the Frenchman in the ring, happily stating that he didn't consider him in the same league.

Tim Blakely, Europe's undefeated Champion, was conspicuously uninterested in The World Championship. When asked, he said he was happy with his titles, but would beat Enos, if he were offered a match.

This reignited Rory's obsession for Mr. Blakely. It was almost too much for him, imagining the Redheaded giant manhandling the Blond muscle boy. He couldn't have this occur, and not be a part of it. The unbearable ache of desire forced Rory to take another break from Blakely.

Wrestling fans had long been discussing the fact that, as Enos was quick to sexually manipulate and dominate his opponents, he never reacted well to reciprocation in this area. Even interviewers asked The New Champ point-blank about his reactions when Anderson simply touched the front of his trunks. In rare Enos form, he simply ignored the question. This caused quite a buzz amongst fans. They ALL wanted to see how he would fair against Rene Sebastian, the second most sexually ruthless man currently wrestling.

MIKE WALL – RORY'S 2ND RELATIONSHIP

Even though Rory had decided not to pursue a new relationship, some of the guys at school approached him, and he was even invited to one of those all-boy pool parties. He wanted to go, but politely declined, out of respect for Duane. He never accepted any dates, until an exceptional senior walked right up and asked him out.

Rory was stunned. He said "Yes", because Mike Wall was a beautiful, built, blond, young man, with dark brown doe eyes. He was clean cut, and wore nice clothes, but seemed aloof and just a little bad. His haughty jock-walk reminded Rory of Chris Enos.

Mike was also a friend of Duane's from the Football team. Rory kept in contact with Duane, although they hadn't emailed or video chatted in a while. He thought about asking Duane before he accepted the date with Mike, but didn't want to upset him at college before he even knew if he was interested in Mike. He figured he would talk to Duane when he came home for his winter break, if he and Mike were still seeing each other.

Mike took Rory to a virtual sports experience, then a nice dinner. Rory thought it was funny. It seemed so old-fashioned, and something Duane would do. It turned out that not only was Mike not haughty or arrogant, he was actually a little shy. Rory found it endearing that one of the handsomest, best athletes in school was shy, and even a little dorky.

Mike was quick to laugh, and a few times, when Rory caught his eye, he smiled, blushed and looked away. Rory began to feel something he never had before, not even with Duane.

As Mike drove Rory home, he admitted he had never dated a guy before.

"Well, Duane was my first." Rory turned to face Mike. "Hey, I should have talked to you about this, before, but, uh, I think I need to talk to Duane."

"Oh!" Mike stole a quick glance, then shot his eyes back to the rode. "Are you guys still, together, or something?"

"No. But, I don't want this to be uncomfortable for him." Rory realized he was being presumptuous. "Oh, I mean, uh, if you want to go out, again."

Mike just took that for granted. "Well, yeah! I mean, if YOU want to."

Rory nodded. "For sure." He smiled when he realized they were both kind of dorky guys, who really only knew about the sports they played. He had to laugh at the awkward exchange they just had.

Rory felt guilty that he never showed Duane as much affection as Duane showed him.

He wanted to hold Mike's hand, but he held back. "So, I mean, I'm going to talk to Duane when he comes back for Winter break, next week. You're ok with that, right? BUT, don't… I mean, it's not… I don't know how to do stuff like this. I'm just thinking because you guys are friends. Does that make sense?"

"Yeah, it does. Do you think I should have talked to him before I asked you out?" Mike also didn't want to hurt Duane.

"I don't know. I'm not that experienced with this kinda stuff." Rory appreciated that Mike felt the same.

At a stoplight, Mike smiled at Rory and took his hand.

Rory loved the feeling, and ran his other hand along the top of Mike's. They sat in silence for the rest of the ride.

Duane saw Rory the second day he was back. Rory invited him to the beach, then to lunch. It was too cold to surf, so they took a long walk. Duane put his arm around Rory, and Rory leaned in to Duane. They talked about how much they missed each other, and all about what they were doing in School.

After an hour, Rory asked Duane to sit down next to him, facing the ocean. "Duane, there's something I need to talk to you, about. I think I probably should have when it happened, but... I didn't know how, exactly..."

Duane sat silent, not reacting to Rory's sudden change in mood.

"Duane, I really do love you. You're one of the greatest people in my life. If what I did was wrong, and you want me to stop..." Rory was glad he wasn't looking Duane in the eye. Suddenly he felt so guilty, like he was confessing to cheating. "A friend of yours asked me out, and we have been... kind of ... seeing each other."

"Oh, wow." Duane didn't seem very surprised. "Who is it?"

"Mike." Rory put his hand on Duane's knee.

"So, you guys like each other?" Duane's voice sounded very sad.

"Duane, if you don't like this, I'll stop seeing him..." Rory repositioned himself, so he could look Duane in the eye. "Duane, I'll even get back together with you, if that's what you want. I miss you."

Duane hugged Rory, hard. He rubbed his back, and let out a lot of emotion with each deep breath. "Rory. Don't feel bad. I kinda knew something like this would happen." He leaned Rory back, so they could look at each other. "It's ok." He still looked sad.

"But, Duane, it's true. I miss you, so much." Rory held Duane's hand with both of his.

"I miss you, too, Rory. Every day… But, I have something to tell you… I've kinda been seeing somebody, too." Duane tried to smile.

Rory needed a moment. That information hit him dead in the heart. "Oh… Wow. Why did I never think of that, before?" Rory could feel some water in his eyes. He put an arm around Duane. "I'm sorry. Did it feel like this for you, when I just told you about Mike?"

Duane nodded.

Rory pulled Duane into him, kissed his cheek and hugged him, hard. "I'm sorry. I'm so sorry!"

They hugged each other for a good, long while.

Duane rubbed Rory's back, and slowly ran his fingers through Rory's hair. "It's ok, Rory. I think our time-lines can't match up at this point." Duane slowly rocked Rory. "Go out with Mike. It's totally ok… Do you mind if I don't see him, this trip, though?"

Rory pulled back, again, to look Duane in the eyes. "No, that's ok. Whatever you need. I won't tell him… But, can I see you, again, before you leave?"

Duane nodded. They stood up.

Rory held Duane's hands. "I just want you to really understand, that I love you. I love you, a lot!"

Duane smiled, and pointed his big, thick finger at Rory's face, and touched his cheek, "And, I just want YOU to understand that I love you, too, A LOT!"

They kissed each other, lightly, lovingly, and for a long time, hugged, then took the long walk back down the beach.

Mike took Rory to dinner two days later. Rory told him all the good things Duane said, and that it was ok they dated. Mike not only understood, he felt for Duane, and offered to back away, if that would make Duane feel better. Rory assured him that it was not necessary, but the gesture was touching.

That night, Mike took Rory to his house. His family was gone for the weekend. He brought him up to his room, and they sat on the edge of the bed for a while, talking. Rory held Mike's hand. It was shaking.

Mike was very nervous. Something about Rory allowed him to be vulnerable, though. "Rory, um... You know I never dated a guy."

Rory moved closer to Mike, understanding what Mike was about to tell him.

"I've never done it, like this... I mean." Mike awkwardly put his arm around Rory's shoulder.

"Wait, what do you mean, 'like this'?... You HAVE done it?"

Rory was confused.

"Rory, I've messed around with guys… kinda, I mean, a friend of ours, had these, kinda parties…"

"Yeah, Duane told me." Rory really wanted to know about those parties.

"Well, it wasn't like this." Mike caressed Rory's hand, and shoulder.

"Oh! You mean, like… wait, what?" Rory thought it better if Mike actually said the words.

"I've never been with a guy I like… I mean, like you. A guy I really like." Mike shook his head. "You know what I mean."

Rory ran his fingers along Mike's cheek, and leaned in. He slowly, softly touched his lips to Mike's.

"Ah." Mike found that very nice.

Rory very lightly kissed him.

Mike seemed to be entering a world he thought might only exist in dreams. He was very tense, holding himself back, but every second was pleasure.

Rory kissed him, again, and ran his fingers through Mike's hair. He kissed him harder and held his cheeks, pulling him in closer.

Mike was breathing very slowly, and halted after each breath. He kissed Rory back, softly, slowly, and very carefully.

Rory kissed Mike's cheek, his ear and his neck.

"Oh, God." Mike's whole body seemed to be responding to the slightest touch, or kiss, from Rory.

Rory kissed along the collar line of Mike's shirt. He unbuttoned it, and slowly pulled it off.

Mike let him.

Then, Rory pulled off Mike's white tee shirt.

Mike let him.

He ripped off his own shirt, and kissed Mike's neck, down, toward his collarbone. He ran his tongue along Mike's tight, rounded, muscular chest. Rory had to stop for a moment to look at Mike's beautiful body. He had the torso of an elite athlete. One would think he did 1000 pushups a day. His pectorals were smooth, and his nipples were a perfect pink. Rory smiled, thinking how much of a man Mike was, but how his nipples were so innocent looking, and vulnerable.

Rory kissed them, and licked them. His tongue had to remember just how perfect that chest was. Mike's skin was so delicious Rory couldn't stop.

The attention he was giving Mike's body brought him to the brink. Mike held on to Rory's head, and as much as Rory worshipped his chest, Mike's hand seemed to feel the same about Rory's hair.

Rory's mouth found it's way down Mike's hard, carved stomach. He reached down, to undo Mike's pants, and an electric shiver ran through Mike's body. He grabbed Rory's hands.

Rory sat up.

Mike held on to Rory's hands, breathing hard. He took a big, gulping swallow, "No, uh…."

"What?"

Mike's face was red. He was embarrassed. "I already… um…"

Rory smiled, and pulled Mike's head forward. He rubbed his cheek to Mike's, and kissed him. "It's ok. Don't worry about it."

"Mmm." Mike made a sound somewhere in between a moan and a whimper.

"It happens." Rory leaned Mike down on the bed.

They kissed for a long time. Mike held Rory's head tight. Their tongues worked very well together, their lips, their hands, and their beautiful, tight, muscular skin against each other.

"Do you want to take a shower?" Rory whispered in Mike's ear.

"YES!" Mike pulled them both up into a sitting position, on to their feet and led Rory into the bathroom. He turned away to take off his pants, remembering that he already had an orgasm. "Oh, I'm so sorry about that."

Rory rubbed his back, and came around in front of him. He helped him off with his pants, and wet underwear. He took Mike's penis lightly in his hand. It was already erect, again.

"Ohh…" Mike's body jumped. He looked up at Rory, almost with an expression that asked for mercy. He was so outrageously sensitive to Rory's touch.

Rory took off his own pants, and underwear, revealing his erection.

He slowly brought his hips forward, and touched the head of Mike's penis with his own.

"Oh, man!" Mike was in bliss. Anything Rory did was almost too much for him to handle, in the best way possible.

Rory leaned forward and kissed Mike, again, as his hand lightly fondled Mike's testicles.

Mike had to move back. "Wait, wait! It's gonna, um… do it, again!"

The fact that Mike was red with embarrassment turned Rory on all the more. He thought it was so cute that this "man", who was a bit older, a bit stronger, and more muscular, was virtually putty in his hands.

"It's ok if it does." Rory brought Mike's hand to his own penis.

Mike took Rory's erection between his fingers and handled it like it was a priceless jewel. "But, I want it to last… " Mike slowly, lightly stroked it, and licked his lips. He nuzzled Rory's neck, and led Rory into the shower.

While Mike turned the shower on, and felt the water, Rory kissed his neck, and his hands felt along his body, erection, and balls.

Mike's convulsed, again, and he let out a short, grunting laugh. "Wait!" He pulled Rory's hand away, again.

Rory took Mike's face into his hands, and kissed him. "That

is so FUCKING CUTE!"

Mike tried not to smile, "It's NOT cute!" He pulled Rory into the shower, and kissed him under the water.

Mike took Rory's erection in his hand, again, this time, gripping it firmer.

"Unhh." Rory leaned his chest against Mike's, and his head fell back.

Mike stroked him, and licked Rory's neck.

Rory guided Mike's other hand to his testicles.

Mike began fondling, as he continued stroking Rory.

"Oh! Unnghh" Rory reached out, and started doing the same to Mike.

"Uhnng... Oh... Wait!" Mike moved back, again. His hands were up, and he had a big, dazed smile on his face. "Wait... just wait."

Mike's over-sensitivity was unbearably arousing. Rory kissed Mike deeply. Mike kissed back.

Rory's hands returned to Mike's extremely sensitive erection.

He loved it, but moved back, again, and smiled, "Wait! ... I have an idea." He turned Rory around, so the water hit Rory's chest, and he pressed his own chest against Rory's back.

Rory leaned in to him. "Oh, man."

Mike slowly pushed his erection up under Rory's butt

cheeks, through his legs.

"Uhngg." Rory brought his legs together.

"Uhnng" Mike leaned forward and kissed the back of Rory's neck. He soaped up his hands, and reached around to Rory's erection. The soap washed away, but he kept stroking Rory, fondling, and lightly pulling on his balls.

Rory's head dropped back, and he rubbed his cheek against Mike's. He flexed his ass, and undulated, feeling Mike's erection under his butt cheeks and through his legs.

"Oh, God, wait!" Mike couldn't stop it, this time. He kept going, and kept stroking Rory. "UNNGH!! UNGHH!"

Rory felt hot liquid hit his balls. "Oh!"

Mike came and slowly stopped undulating his own hips, but his hands kept working on Rory.

Rory rubbed his own stomach, and one of his hands pushed down on his pelvic bone, just above his hard-on. "Oh, God! OH, GOD! YEAH… KEEP IT GOING! KEEPT IT GOING!" Rory's helped Mike find the right spots around his balls, while his other hand pressed down on the pelvic bone. "UNGGH UNNGHHH!!" He came, squirting onto the tile wall of the shower.

Both of them kept working until Rory's head bowed, and he pulled Mike's arms around him, tight. Mike kissed his neck, and rubbed his face in Rory's wet hair.

They made out, hugged, and washed each other for the next hour. When they got out, they dried each other, and their mouths explored every inch of each other's beautiful, athletic bodies.

They returned to the bed, and fell into each other's arms, completely naked. Both immediately drifted off into heavenly sleep.

The Enos/Anderson Saga Continues.

Enos had compiled a long list of contenders he moved in front of Dyer Anderson, and other threatening wrestlers. His list consisted of Champions from round the world he thought he could beat relatively easily.

Victor Octavio was Mexico's beautifully built Champion. He was the Latin Lover type, and very handsome, at 6', 220lbs. Octavio was a great wrestler, and tough when he needed to be, but for some reason, he was no match for Enos. The World Champ seemed to control him from the first bell. The fight and fire he normally showed just wasn't there. Enos outmuscled him, and easily dominated him sexually.

Public Demand once again forced the Federation to step in. Enos was well loved, as the Champion people most wanted to see suffer. His match against Octavio was hot, and sexy, but the fans were almost unanimous in their desire to see him face Anderson, again. The Federation had to respond, and strike while the iron was so damn hot. Not only did they force Enos to sign a rematch with Anderson, but they also announced *another* rematch, 6 months after THAT match. So, the first rematch would take place in the beginning of summer, and the second rematch was scheduled for New Years Day!

Enos went public, trying to rally his supporters to campaign against the rematches. Unfortunately for him, even his fans wanted to see him wrestle Dyer Anderson. No one supported his efforts. The entire Wrestling community came together, and these two matches were the most anticipated events in sports history.

More Pure Pro Wrestling

Rory's tiny federation was growing. People were watching it from all over the world. Guys came from other cites to compete. Rory lost his title to a guy almost 50 pounds heavier. Mike Wall joined, as Rory's tag partner, and they became the Tag Team Champions.

Everything was a very amateurish and low level at the beginning, but their talents grew quickly, especially Rory's. They finally found a wrestling gym that would rent them their ring, at a reduced rate. Because of insurance and liability, they couldn't do all-out pro matches, and the manager had to be present at all times. They had to pull back on real moves and holds, and nudity was prohibited.

Some of the guys became very sexual in their matches, but Rory could never put those up on his channel, as half the guys were under 18. A few Porn sites contacted Rory and gave him a list of The Pure Pro boys they were interested in meeting with, the second they became legal. His name was on the top.

Pure Pro gave him a small taste of fame, and he loved every minute of it, but he longed for all-out, sexually charged, real-time Pro matches in the A.W.P.W.

Summer drew closer, and Mike graduated. He would be going off to college, soon. Rory didn't want to think about it. It just made him sad. It brought back memories of Duane leaving, so he reached out to him, just to make sure he was doing ok.

Some of the guys in Rory's Wrestling Fed wanted to get together to watch the Enos/Anderson rematch. He made up an excuse why he couldn't, but asked Mike to watch it with him... alone, in his room.

At first, Mike laughed when Rory proposed that they wear their pro gear while they watched the match, but he absolutely saw how hot it could be. He had come to learn the extent to which Pro Wrestling aroused Rory, and was more than happy to oblige.

CHRIS ENOS vs. DYER ANDERSON

Current All Worlds Champ vs. Ex All Worlds Champ.

The match was broadcast as a Virtual Event, which they enjoyed from the comfort of Rory's bed. They scanned themselves, in their pro gear, and were downloaded into the experience. Rory's excitement appeared, fully rigid, as they donned their gear.

Mike was excited as well. He kissed Rory, and fondled him through his trunks. Rory wrestled his hands away, and asked him to slow it down. He took Mike's hands, held on to them, tight, and moved closer, rubbing his arm and leg against Mike, as the match finally started.

Announcer: "WELCOME TO THE MOST ANTICIPATED

MATCH OF THE DECADE! THE BATTLE FOR THE ALL WORLDS PRO HEAVYWEIGHT BELT!"

Dyer Anderson was already in the ring, his head slightly lowered, his eyes narrowed. His fists were clenched, and he was ready to fight.

Announcer: "IN THIS CORNER, THE FORMER CHAMPION, IN THE ROYAL BLUE TRUNKS, STANDING 6 FEET TALL, AND WEIGHING 255 POUNDS, DYER ANDERSON!"

Anderson was still well loved. Rory couldn't hear one "boo" from the crowd. Even Enos's fans wanted to see Anderson, in this very match. He looked leaner, and his big muscles popped a bit more, but he was still a meaty, solid powerhouse.

Announcer: "AND, NOW! ENTERING THE RING, THE CURRENT HEAVYWEIGHT ALL WORLDS CHAMPION, IN THE WHITE TRUNKS, STANDING 6 FEET, 2 INCHES TALL, AND WEIGHING 230 POUNDS, I GIVE YOU, CHRIS ENOS!!!!"

Chris Enos entered the ring, wearing the belt, with his hands high in the, air, taking in the cheers from the crowd.

Rory couldn't help but admire the beauty of this Male Blond Bombshell. Enos was probably the most handsome wrestler in the Federation. Rory's hand felt Mike's thigh, and gave it a squeeze as he took in every inch of The current Champ. His body was without a single flaw, and through his Virtual Headset, Rory could see him as if he was two inches away.

Enos wore his belt as the Ref gave them instructions. Anderson glared at him.

Enos looked back with an understanding expression. "I'll

go easy on you, tonight. I know how humiliating our last match was... for you."

Anderson's whole body shook and quivered as he held himself back from decking Enos right at that moment. His jaw was flexed and he growled without even thinking about it, "Rrrrr..."

Enos kept trying to get under Anderson's skin, "You want to touch my belt one last time, before I win, again?"

Anderson's breathing became louder. Enos thought he was rattling Anderson, but he was saying all the wrong things. In their last match, he confused The Champ, now he was just pissing him off.

The Ref had them return to their corners, then called for the bell. "DING! DING!"

Enos casually turned around, and came out, slowly circling.

Anderson's fists were up, and he cut Enos off, stepping right in front of him. He threw a quick left jab that Enos easily sidestepped.

BAM! Anderson's right hook predicted Enos's bob, and nailed him right in the ear.

"OOHH!" Enos had no idea what hit him. His eyes bulged out, and he stepped back, his hands up, guarding his head.

Anderson kept coming, and threw a hard right, then a left, from his hip, straight up into Enos's abs, WHAM! WHAM!

"Unnngghhh" Enos held his stomach, backing up even further, until his back was to the ropes.

Every single person in the Arena was on their feet, including the Announcers. They were worked up into a fevered pitch, and it was only the first 20 seconds of the match.

Enos's face was vulnerable, and Anderson backhanded him straight across it. WHACKKK!

That rang Enos's bell. His head flew back and to the side, and he bounced backward against the ropes. As he rebounded forward, Anderson had two more gut punches that drove Enos down to his knees. BAM, BAM!

"PANDEMONIUM!" The Announcer screamed, "ANDERSON IS BACK!!! THIS IS WHAT ENOS WAS TRYING TO AVOID! WHEN IT COMES TO A FIST FIGHT, ANDERSON TRULY IS THE CHAMP!"

Anderson clawed a handful of Enos's soft, beautiful Blond hair, and raised his right hand in the air. The thunderous ovation from the audience was unbelievable.

Enos held his stomach, gasping and struggling to catch his breath, at the feet of the Ex Champ. He looked up to see Anderson reveling in the admiration from his fans. He couldn't lose this match. Growing, right in front of his face, was his greatest strength, and Anderson's biggest weakness. He made a fist and jabbed it.

"Uuuhh!" Anderson let go of The Champ's hair, held his penis and testicles, and leaned forward. Enos was between him and the ropes, which he grabbed on to.

Enos pushed him back, swatted his hand out of the way, and SMACKED the bulge again, as he pulled himself up to his feet.

Anderson hobbled to the side, and leaned on the ropes, both hands cradling his groin.

Enos shook his head. He couldn't believe such a tough, savvy competitor could be so stupid. How many times would he leave his weakest part open to such an easy attack?

Enos got behind Anderson, and grabbed his hair. He pulled him two feet to the corner, and SMASHED his head into the top turnbuckle.

"Unhh…" Anderson kept a hold of his crotch. His head hurt, but didn't affect him nearly as much as the pain in his cock and balls.

Enos bashed The Ex Champ's head against the turnbuckle, again.

"Unhh" Anderson shook his head, grabbed a handful of Enos's hair, and BASHED his head into the same turnbuckle.

"UNGHH!" Enos had a much harder time with that. His eyes rolled back in his head and he was seeing stars.

Anderson slammed another fist into The Champ's abs.

"OOF!" Enos doubled over.

Anderson brought his knee up, and into Enos's face, then let go of his hair.

Enos's flew back, landed on his backside, and slowly suffered on the canvas, all but knocked out.

Anderson needed a second to regroup, and made sure his family jewels were out of Enos's kicking or smacking range.

Enos held his head and sat up.

Anderson got behind him, cranked his knee, and slammed it into Enos's back.

Enos arched in pain, and yelled out. He held his back, in a very awkward position at Anderson's feet. Anderson leaned down, and pulled backward on Enos's chin, as he pushed his knee down and forward, hard into The Champ's back.

The current Champ tried to pry the Ex Champ's big, sweaty hands away from his face, with no success. He yelled out, and Anderson PULLED back harder.

Anderson glared at the Ref, who snapped back into reality and squatted down in front of Enos, "You ok? You want to give?"

"NO! NO! GET HIM OFF ME!" Enos screamed, as if Anderson was doing something against the rules.

The Ref clarified, "I can get him off you, if you submit. Are you sub...."

"NOOO! NO! JUST GET HIM OFF ME!" Enos grabbed The Ref's shirt, and shook him.

The Ref pulled back out of Enos's clutches.

Anderson slid his knee down Enos's back, really forcing it forward.

Enos stopped yelling. Hard grunts came out, as his breathing became staccato.

Anderson brought his other knee down slowly into The Champ's back, as he kept pulling back on Enos's chin.

The Champ flailed his arms and tried to stand up, only to have Anderson lean forward to bring him back down. Anderson then brought his face down next to Enos's ear, and said, "Whatcha gonna do in this position? You can't get at my fucking dick and pull any of your tricks! Just give it up. You can't wrestle! You were never a real Champ!" Dyer Anderson smiled. Those words blew off a lot of steam he had been holding in since he lost his belt. He kept his lips up against Enos's ear, and breathed hard.

Enos pushed up from the canvas, trying to stand, again, and Anderson moved his weight down and forward, to keep him on the ground. Enos grabbed Anderson's wrists, and pulled, adding to the downward momentum, as he rolled his hips back, and shot his legs up. He CAUGHT Anderson's head between his calves, and crossed his ankles.

The crowd roared, and the Announcer commented, "A GENIUS use of balance and flow. You can knock Enos all you want, but the man knows how to wrestle!"

Enos straightened out his legs, and flexed them as hard as he could.

Anderson grunted. Enos had him hunched forward. They were both trapped, and both in pain, struggling to outmuscle each other.

Enos's body displayed amazing flexibility. He was folded together, with his chin pushed against his thighs. He could hardly breath, and his entire upper body was in agony.

Anderson couldn't break The Champ's head scissor. He got one of his knees up, and planted his boot firmly on the canvas. He let go of Enos's chin, and brought his other knee up. As he got his other foot on the canvas, he clamped his hands on both sides of Enos's torso, and pulled himself up to a standing position. This allowed Enos's upper body to roll down.

Anderson wrapped his arms around Enos, who was now in his upside-down bear hug. Enos's legs were still scissored around Anderson's head, and they both continued to squeeze each other.

The Commentator excitedly noted, "This is an interesting position for both of them. A wrestler's first instinct in Anderson's position would be to pile drive his opponent, but if he does that, and Enos keeps that Head Scissor on him, he's in danger of having his neck broken as Enos hits the canvas. I'm thinking that is what Enos is betting on, so he's not about to let go!"

There they were, in a stalemate of sorts. Anderson SHOOK Enos, but it didn't have any real effect on him. Anderson realized he was just as vulnerable as Enos, because of where Enos's face was at that moment.

It was too late. Enos grabbed hold of Anderson's bulge, and TWISTED IT.

"AAGGHHHHH!" Anderson released the bear hug, and pushed Enos's hands out of the way. He lost his balance, and they went crashing forward, Enos on his back, Anderson on top of him.

Enos's kept his legs together, until they hit, which meant that Anderson's head smacked the canvas. Enos's legs fell apart, and Anderson rolled off of him.

Both wrestlers were down, and suffering.

Anderson was on his back, staring up into the lights. His big, beefy chest, and solid belly rising and falling with each deep breath.

Enos moaned, and turned to roll away. He looked over, and saw that Anderson wasn't any better off than he was. He rolled back, and climbed on top of him, their stomachs together, his head at Anderson's feet, and vice versa. He dug his knees down, around Anderson's head, pulled it up, and scissored it, again.

"Unhhh." Anderson grabbed Enos beautifully muscled and oiled legs, and worked to pry them apart.

Enos then began fiddling around with Anderson's bulge. He TWISTED it, again.

"AGGHHHHHHH!!" Anderson tried to buck Enos off of him, and roll onto his side, but Enos's hands, planted on the canvas stopped that.

Enos TWISTED Anderson's bulge again, and told the Ref, "ASK HIM!"

The Ref was confused, and was about to drop for the count, because Enos actually had Anderson pinned underneath him.

"AGGGHHHHHHH!!! NOOOOO!!" Anderson screamed up at the Ref, "YOU ASK HIM!" He burrowed his hand in under Enos and TWISTED his bulge, the same way.

Enos made a sound no one had ever heard before, "UUHNGGAACCCHKKK!" It was completely alien, and sent shudders through The Ref and Anderson. The Champ was off of Anderson, and over at the ropes in a blur. He rolled out.

Anderson sat up, completely flummoxed by The Champ's behavior.

The Ref told Enos to get back in the ring, or he would count him out. Anderson stood up and joined him at the ropes. They looked down at Enos as if he was a unicorn, or something else completely unreal.

Enos yelled as he held his bulge, and pointed at Anderson, "HE FUCKING VOILATED ME! HE TOUCHED MY…". He looked down, and very carefully adjusted his trunks.

The Ref couldn't believe what Enos was saying. "He just did what you've been doing to him FOR YEARS!"

"BUT, I'M THE CHAMP!!! I'M THE CHAMP!!!" Enos screamed, his face turning red and spittle forming at the corners of his mouth.

The Ref responded by starting Enos's count out. "ONE!... TWO!"

Anderson put his hand up in front of The Ref. "NO! I don't want to win by count out! I'll let him back in the ring."

Anderson backed up, to the other side.

Enos climbed up onto the apron, and whispered heatedly to the Ref.

The Ref cocked his head, and backed away from Enos, "What?... NO! I don't understand what you're saying. Just get back in the ring, and start wrestling!"

Enos stood gripping the top rope. "Keep HIM away from me!!!"

Anderson opened his arms wide, showing Enos that he would stay back and allow the Temporary Champ a wide berth.

Enos pointed at The Ref, "KEEP HIM BACK!" His eyes locked on Anderson as he cautiously climbed into the ring. Once he was in, Anderson stepped forward with his fists up. Enos backed into the ropes, and yelled, "KEEP HIM AWAY FROM ME!"

The Ref wasn't interested in humoring Enos, "Start wrestling or I'll count you out!"

"You CAN'T count me out! I'M THE CHAMP!"

Watch me!" The Ref wasn't intimidated in the slightest.

Anderson came closer and threw his hands forward, feigning an attack.

Enos flinched.

Anderson scoffed at him. He couldn't help but feel extremely cocky. He knew, in his heart, that their last match was just a fluke. He pretended to back away, but when Enos eased up, and took a step away from the ropes, he sprang forward and nailed Enos right in the gut.

"Oooh AAAACCH!" Enos's hands went up, his eyes shut, and his mouth flew open. His knees gave out, and he sat on the middle rope.

Anderson kept coming. He slashed a vicious chop across Enos's tan, smooth, ripped chest.

"UNNHH-ANNHH!" Enos's red pecs bounced.

Anderson followed with a big, hard, backhanded bitch slap, and Enos fell sideways to the canvas.

Anderson stepped on Enos's throat, and pulled down on the

ropes.

Enos kicked his legs and punched at Anderson's calves.

The Ref pulled Anderson off of Enos, and gave him a warning. "OFF THE ROPES!"

Again, Enos rolled out of the ring. On his knees, he held on to the apron, and massaged his throat.

The Ref started counting him out. "ONE!... TWO!..."

Enos didn't even look up, but he held out an open hand, "Shut up! Give me a minute!"

Anderson walked over, leaned across top rope, bent down, snagged Enos by his Blond hair, and proceeded to pull him up onto the ring apron.

Enos screamed bloody murder. He held on to the middle rope and scrambled to get one knee under the bottom one. This caused Anderson to pull harder, and Enos screamed louder.

They found themselves in another situation where Anderson should have known better. He forgot whom he was dealing with, and should have backed away.

Enos reached through the ropes and engulfed The Ex Champ's big bulge in one hand. Anderson screamed out this time. He released Enos's hair, and held on to Enos's wrist.

The Champ brought his other hand into play, and now both were holding on to Anderson's private parts. Enos leaned back with his butt jutting out beyond the ring apron.

Anderson tried to pull him into the ring, but the sheer agony of his predicament left him a bit weak. He grabbed The Champ's Blond hair, again, but Enos yanked down on the now swollen penis. Anderson gagged and let go.

Enos had his center of gravity out over the edge of the ring, which caused him to fall backward. He held on to Anderson's erection and testicles as long as he could, but they couldn't support his weight. They were stretched to the utmost, before slipping out of his fingers. Enos fell onto the concrete floor.

Anderson howled like a wounded bull and fell backward, the opposite direction. Both wrestlers were on their backs, and both rolled into the fetal position.

Enos got to his knees, and threw his arms up onto the apron.

The Ref began counting him out. "ONE!..."

There was no time to recover. He swung one leg up and climbed onto the apron, then rolled under the bottom rope, by the time The Ref counted to "SEVEN!" His Challenger was still incapacitated, but had crawled to the corner, and was now in a sitting position. They both took a moment to recover.

Enos got to his feet, took a big, deep breath, then hobbled toward Anderson, who held up his hand. The Current Champ sneered down at the big Ex Champ and swiped that hand away. He pulled Anderson up to his feet, using a handful of his hair, and pushed him back into the ring post, HARD!

Anderson was in bad shape.

Enos leaned in and powered a low hook into Anderson's belly. It jiggled as Anderson groaned and slumped down. The Champ pressed himself into the struggling Challenger and pulled DOWN on his penis and balls again. Anderson sucked in hard, and held it.

The Ref slapped Enos's back, "OUT OF THE CORNER!"

Enos put his hands up and took two steps back. He had to smile when he saw that his opponent was still erect. The hard-on pushed to the side, as Anderson held it and rubbed. Enos stepped forward, again, and wrestled Anderson's hands out of the way, while he pulled and twisted Anderson's boner.

The Ex Champ threw his head back, and held on. It was hard to tell whether he was having an extremely good time, or an extremely excruciating one. Enos held on, and clawed Anderson's tough, big belly, at the same time.

The Ref grabbed Enos's arm, "OUT OF THE CORNER!"

Enos backed away, again, and Anderson was moaning, "OH...OHH..." He tried to readjust his trunks, but nothing helped.

The Champ came right back, with another grab and twist of Anderson's hard-on, and a simultaneous claw to one of his big pecs of beef.

Anderson held Enos's wrist, looked him in the eye, and begged, "Come on, man!"

The Ref yelled, again, "OUT OF THE CORNER!"

Enos whispered to Anderson, "Give it, Dy-boy. I own you, now." He smiled, and licked his lips.

Anderson was grimacing, but forced himself to smile back, which was a bit unsettling for Enos. Anderson ran a hand down Enos's side, across his stomach, and GRABBED The Champ's bulge.

Enos's face took on the strangest expression of fear, mixed with resignation. He pulled at Anderson's wrist, but couldn't pry it away. He punched Anderson's arm, and chest, "LET GO!"

Anderson grabbed Enos's shoulder, with his free hand, and changed places so Enos's back was against the ring post. He kept squeezing The Champ's bulge.

"REF! GET HIM OFF ME! OUT OF THE CORNER!!! HE'S...HE'S!!!" Enos was in a highly manic state. He PULLED on Anderson's erection, but that just made him moan. Nothing he did made Anderson ease up on his dick.

The Ref bumped Anderson's shoulder with the butt of his palm, "OUT OF THE CORNER."

Anderson let go, and backed away to center ring, and held his own crotch.

Enos glowered at him and the Ref, as if they had committed an unthinkable crime.

Mr. Anderson took a breather, adjusted himself, and began circling. Enos kept away, but didn't circle. Anderson approached, and Enos leaned out through the ropes, as he screamed to the Ref, "KEEP HIM AWAY FROM ME!"

"WRESTLE! OR, I START COUNTING!" The Ref, as much as anyone else, wanted to know what Enos was up to.

Anderson grabbed the back of Enos's trunks, and pulled. Enos struggled with him, and the top of Enos's butt was exposed. Enos held on to the ropes, so Anderson hit him in the lower back with a big elbow. BAM!

Enos yelled out, arching his back, still leaning out between the ropes with his amazing ass cheeks on display.

The Ref pulled Anderson back, "AWAY FROM THE ROPES." He approached Enos, "You ok to continue?"

"KEEP HIM AWAY FROM ME!" Enos kept a hand up, as if that would stop an oncoming wrestler.

"I'm telling you! Keep wrestling, or I'm gonna count you out!"

Anderson came up behind Enos, again, grabbed him around the waist, and PULLED him out from the ropes. He threw The Champ up, and back in a German Suplex. WHAM! Enos's upper back hit the canvas hard. His butt and legs were up in the air, and Anderson bridged, holding on to him for the pin.

The Ref dropped down and counted, "ONE! TWO!" before Enos kicked out.

Anderson let go.

Enos twisted and landed to the left, on his stomach. Anderson rolled on top of him, his chest on Enos's back, and wrapped his arm around Enos's neck. He cranked a headlock, really leveraging Enos's chin up. Anderson pulled so hard he brought The Champ's chest off the canvas, and painfully arched him backward. Enos had to push up on the canvas with his hands to alleviate some of the pressure. Anderson brought his knees up, and put his feet flat on the canvas. He was now sitting on The Champ's butt, and looked like he might be going for a camel clutch.

The Ref asked Enos if he was ok.

Enos waved him away, and got his knees up under him.

Anderson stood up, bringing The Champ up with him. He realized the vulnerability of this position, with a man like Enos, and punched him in the side of the head, before letting go.

Enos held his head, dropped back down to his knees, and rested his forehead on the canvas.

Anderson got behind him, and clamped onto two big handfuls of Enos's blond hair, and brought The Champ up to his feet in one quick motion.

Enos was speechless.

Anderson picked The Champ up, like a husband carrying is bride over the threshold, and brought him down hard over his knee in a back breaker. BAM!

The wind was knocked out of Enos, and he went limp. Anderson secured him in place by clamping an iron claw on The Champ's neck. Enos didn't move much, but he moaned.

Anderson ran his fingers along Enos's shredded ab muscles, tracing the cuts. "I gotta see what the hell is going on here." His hand made it's way down to Enos's trunks, and brushed along the restricted bulge.

Enos came back to life and tried to pull Anderson's claw off his neck.

Anderson fondled Enos's bulge, and gave it a light squeeze.

Enos kicked up a leg. Anderson punched it, and Enos groaned.

"What's your deal *Champ*? You can dish it out, but can't take it?" Anderson squeezed, again.

Enos started bucking and kicking, and Anderson had to work to keep him on his leg.

"BAM!" Anderson's fist sank deep, hard, and fast into The Champ's vulnerable six-pack.

"Unnnnhh" Enos held his stomach, immobilized for a moment.

Anderson squeezed The Champ's bulge, and again, he kicked like a bronco, then twisted and flailed like a caught fish. Enos's legs kicked out, away from Anderson, and his back slid off The Challenger's knee. Now, Enos was sitting in front of Anderson.

He took a breather, while Anderson pushed his knee into Enos's spine, and PULLED back on his neck.

Enos was suffering, but couldn't do much about it.

"ASK HIM!" Anderson demanded.

"You ok, there, Champ?" The Ref said, with a definite tone of disdain.

Enos ignored The Ref, and tried to get to his feet.

Anderson pulled him back down. BAM! The Champ landed hard on his ass. He pushed his knee harder into Enos's back.

"Unhh" Enos was worn out, but he tried to get to his feet, again, and again Anderson brought him back down.

Enos didn't move for a little while, so The Ref grabbed his

arm, lifted it up, and asked him if he was ok.

Enos pulled his arm away from The Ref, and tried to stand, once more. The same thing happened. Anderson PULLED him back down, and Enos's butt SLAMMED into the canvas, again. Instead of reapplying the hold, Anderson used the downward momentum to roll Enos back, pin his shoulders to the mat, and hook his leg.

The Ref was down, in a shot, pounding the mat, "ONE!... TWO!... THREE!"

Three whole seconds of silence passed, then the Arena erupted.

Anderson stoop up, and threw his hands up to The Ref, "Wait, what?"

The Ref signaled for the bell, "DING! DING!"

Enos sat up, and shook his head.

The Ref raised Anderson's hand, and called for the belt.

Enos sat on his ass, still in pain, shaking his blond hair. "WHAT THE HELL DO YOU THINK YOU'RE DOING! YOU FUCKERS CHEATED! THAT WASN'T A REGULATION THREE-COUNT!"

The Ref ignored Enos, took the belt from the attendant and handed it to The new Champ.

Anderson was still shocked at the quick win. He held the belt, and stared at it. Finally, a smile appeared as he realized he won back his title. He thrust the belt up in the air, and the cheers from the crowd surged.

Enos stood up and grabbed the Ref's shirt. "WHAT THE HELL?" He pounded his palms together in a blur, BAM! BAM! BAM! "YOU FUCKING CHEATED! THAT WAS NO FUCKING THREE COUNT!!!"

The Ref pointed at Enos, "Get OUT of my face! That was a perfect three count. You LOST!"

Enos stomped around, "YOU FUCKERS CHEATED!!!"

Enos tried to pull the belt away from Anderson, who struggled with him for a second, then punched him in the face.

Enos fell backwards, landing on his ass, again. He was dazed for a moment, then had an all-out, cry-baby tantrum. He rolled on the canvas, pounded it, kicked it, and screamed.

Anderson laughed.

He ran to all four corners, climbed up on the ropes, with his arms raised, and showed the fans who the REAL Champ was.

AFTERMATH

Enos was devastated. He followed Anderson to the locker room, and demanded the belt back. The Champ was ready to punch him in the face, again, but the locker room was full of wrestlers who got between them. Enos didn't have many friends in the Federation, so a couple of the wrestlers were rougher than they should have been, and Enos took a couple shots to the face, and body.

Anderson was escorted to a private locker room, with the belt.

In interviews, Anderson said that their previous match was a fluke. He welcomed their next rematch, as a chance to show the world that Enos was nothing but his plaything.

He admitted that Enos had his strengths, but couldn't match up in actual wrestling or fighting ability. Anderson also took every opportunity to point out that he, himself, had taken years of genital abuse from Enos, but Enos couldn't take one, light squeeze. He loved talking about that, and laughing at Enos's expense.

Enos, on the other hand, cried foul. He claimed The Ref and Anderson were in cahoots, and that the Ref counted him out *twice* as fast as normal. He rallied for a rematch right away.

In a move that stunned the entire wrestling world, he also filed a harassment complaint against Anderson and the Ref "who allowed it". The nature of the harassment was described as "sexual and inappropriate". When asked specifics, he would become outraged, "You saw the match! You saw Anderson blatantly attack my private area!"

Interviewers usually laughed, thinking Enos was having fun with them. Whenever they would point out that Enos was the worst abuser of genitals in all of Wrestling, Enos would argue back, "But THEY derive sexual pleasure from touching me! I'm just wrestling, doing my job, and trying to win the match!"

Anderson loved this new stunt of Enos's. At an interview, he held up the official Harassment Complaint papers, and admitted that he derived pleasure, sexual or otherwise, from every aspect of wrestling. He warned Enos that their rematch would a glorified cockfight.

Of course, The Federation didn't do anything about Enos's Harassment charges, but they loved all the publicity Enos was generating for them. The rematch was originally scheduled for the summer, but they talked about moving it up 3 months.

5 RORY TURNS 18

Rory only had a month with Mike, before he went off to college. They spent every day together, and when Mike was gone, they kept in contact almost daily. Rory realized that Mike had become more than just a boyfriend. He was now his best friend.

Rory was sad, but he had his hands full with school, the wrestling team, his tiny pro wrestling company, and his future in Pro Wrestling. He started compiling and developing footage that would look good on a submission reel to a Pro Federation. He also worked on his image, stage presence, and appearance. He was now 6 feet tall, and wanted to pack on more muscle. His goal was to be a ripped 225 pounds by the tine he was 18, but he was currently under 200.

One month before Rory turned 18, he began seriously editing the submission video. It included his competitive wrestling matches, mock TV promos for upcoming matches, and him talking directly into the camera, explaining why he should be hired as a wrestler. One week before his birthday, he sent it to the All Worlds Pro recruiting office in Las Vegas, and held his breath. He drove himself crazy checking every device and venue he gave them to contact, hourly.

SECTOR PRO WRESTLING FEDERATION

Rory *knew* he would be contacted on his 18th birthday. When nothing happened, he was crushed. He thought about it and realized it might take a little more time for them to get back to him. When a week went by, he decided he would go to the training facility, uninvited, and audition for them. There wouldn't be any possible way they would turn him down.

He re-sent his videos, pics, and biography to the Federation recruiter as a "Media Kit", then made plans for a one-way trip to Las Vegas. After carefully constructing a budget, he decided to leave In exactly four weeks to find a place to live.

He also started a strict regimen of bodybuilding. His goal was to gain ten more pounds of muscle before his audition. Nothing else mattered. He only saw his friends when they had wrestling matches for Pure Pro, or when he was working out. His family was concerned. They wanted him to go to college, but his mind was made up. He would wrestle, or die trying.

His anger stared to build. He couldn't believe the A.W.P.W. hadn't snapped him up, already. If they didn't want him, he figured a smaller federation would. He began research to find one, and other video wrestling businesses. Maybe he could combine his little federation with a bigger one and keep growing. He contacted several, and had some interesting interactions. A Fetish Sex Wrestling company offered him a job, and the porn companies told him they were still interested. He knew he wouldn't dive right into that, but thought it might be worth a meeting, at least.

Two small Federation recruiters agreed to meet with him. His plans changed. In four days he would leave for Palm Springs to meet the owner of Sector Pro. It was a small American Federation, which spring-boarded a few stars into the ranks of the AWPW.

DYER ANDERSON vs. CHRIS ENOS – Rematch.

All Worlds Pro Champ vs. Ex All Worlds Pro Champ.

The Anderson/Enos rematch had been moved up, and was happening that weekend. Rory decided to chill out, forget about all his anxieties having to do with wrestling, and just enjoy the match.

Mike came home from college, and they were excited to watch it, alone… together.

The Federation hadn't had so much interest in the drama between two particular wrestlers in a long time.

Anderson gained a little weight leading up to the match. He was meatier and his belly was a bit bigger. In fact he was bigger all over, including his face. He was a big, beefy, meaty musclebear of a man.

Enos, on the other hand, was still a ripped Greek God. He was also bigger, but it was 120% muscle. The man was genetically gifted, to the extreme.

Enos only gave one interview before the match, and the Federation had to force him. He was calmer than he had ever been, and didn't whine, or spout off about Anderson's "injustices". He just talked about winning the championship, and doing it with the least amount of "muss and fuss". That left his interviewer scratching his head. When asked to elaborate, he looked directly into he camera, and said, calmly, "I AM the Champ. Look at me. I was meant to be the Champ. I am a prototype of what a Champion should be. Can you argue with that?" The interviewer couldn't.

Anderson was as jovial as he ever had been. He gave only two interviews, and in both, he referred to the way Enos defeated him as a "fluke". He established that he was a better wrestler and fighter than Enos, and was tougher and stronger. When asked about the times Enos was able to sexually and genitally dominate him in the ring, Anderson laughed, and reminded the interviewer that Enos couldn't take any genital manipulation, at all.

This led to quite a bit of speculation about Enos and his ability to dish it out, but not take it. Fan forums erupted, wondering about his reaction to having his private parts touched. The Fans were desperate to see how Anderson would capitalize on this in the rematch, or if he'd have to.

Ring Announcer: "IN THIS CORNER, IN HIS PURE WHITE TRUNKS, 6 FEET, 2 INCHES TALL, WEIGHING IN TONIGHT AT 235 POUNDS, THE FORMER ALL WORLDS PRO CHAMPION, CHRIS ENOS!!!"

Mr. Enos stood in his corner, and stared straight ahead. He didn't showboat, in his normal fashion, even though the entire Arena was screaming for him.

The ringside Announcer was already worked up, "This match is like Christmas to this crowd! I have NEVER seen such an anticipated match in my entire announcing career! Fans of both fighters could watch them tear into each other EVERY DAY! Even the people who used to hate Enos have grown to love him!"

Ring Announcer: "AND, IN THIS CORNER, JUST ENTERING THE RING, IN HIS ROYAL BLUE TRUNKS, 6 FEET EVEN, 285 POUNDS, THE ALL WORLDS PRO CHAMPION, DYER ANDERSON!!"

The Arena exploded, like never before. Fans stood on their seats, and their screams didn't die down for a full seven minutes.

Anderson looked across the ring, and Enos met his gaze. It was an entirely different behavior than The Champ had ever seen from his adversary. He turned away.

The Ref called them to center. Enos arrived first, and the Ref patted him down. Enos didn't look away from Anderson, who stared at him as aggressively as he could. This didn't change Enos, at all. He scanned Anderson up, and down, then slowly and deliberately adjusted the bulge in his trunks.

Anderson smiled, "You sure you want to call attention to your dick? Remember what happened, last time?"

The Ref gave Anderson his inspection.

"Yeah." Enos licked his lips, with an expression that made Anderson think he might kiss him, if the Ref wasn't between them.

Anderson laughed, out loud. The thing he admired most about Enos was that he never stopped competing. He always had a psychological strategy. If Anderson were forced to, he would have to admit that it usually worked, to a degree. At the moment, he was confused, and his aggression toward Enos was a bit diffused.

The Ref directed them back to their corners, to wait for the bell.

Enos extended his hand to Anderson, "Good luck, man." He sounded sincere, very sincere.

The Champ's first instinct was to either smack his foe's hand away, or grab it, and pull him in to a crushing hold. Instead, he took Enos's hand, and they shook. Enos released, and walked back to his corner. Anderson watched him for a moment, then did the same.

The Ref signaled for the bell. "DING! DING!"

Anderson came out like a big bull, circling with his dukes up.

Enos had his hands up, and circled enough to keep himself in a position facing The Champ.

Anderson cut Enos off, and lunged forward for a lock up. Enos made an impressive martial arts dodge. He stepped to the side, deflected Anderson's hands, and landed a backhand punch to The Champ's ribs.

"Unfh!!" Anderson felt that.

Enos capitalized by swinging a roundhouse kick to Anderson's abs. BAPP!

"UNGGH!" Anderson doubled over, and held his gut.

Enos got in front of The Champ, pulled his head between his ripped thighs, and SQUEEZED.

Anderson groaned, and slapped at Enos's rock hard, flexed quads.

Enos leaned over, his chest against Anderson's back, and

wrapped his arms around him. He rubbed and fondled Anderson's belly, then leaned back, and tried to hoist The Champ up. That was not successful. Anderson spread his legs, and dropped his butt down. He was just too heavy, and knew how to utilize his center of gravity.

Enos grabbed fistfuls of Anderson's belly fat, and when The Champ screamed out, he tried to lift him, again. This time, he got Anderson's feet off the ground, but only about four inches, before he had to put him back down.

Anderson grabbed Enos's wrists, and stood up. Enos held on, and was now upside down, with a bear hug on The Champ. He quickly locked a head scissor on Anderson. He was very uneasy, as was The Champ, but Anderson had the advantage, if only just barely.

Anderson hobbled to a ring post, turned around, and thrust himself backward.

Enos's back slammed into it. He lost his scissor hold, and his legs hung over the top ropes. He also lost his bearhug. He pressed up from the canvas, trying to push up off the ropes. He wasn't able to before Anderson spun around, and laid a big, hard punch into his straining, ripped abs. WHAM!

"UNGAAHHH." Enos went limp, his arms hanging down to the canvas.

Anderson rubbed Enos's bulge, "Ah, there it is! Whatta ya gonna do now, Pretty Boy?!"

He was surprised when Enos didn't react. He just moaned, and tried to push up to dislodge his legs.

The Champ pushed down on Enos's knees, and pulled his feet from under, so his legs were locked around the top rope.

The Ref smacked Anderson, "OFF THE ROPES!"

Anderson planted a foot between Enos's legs and boosted himself up, with his right arm held high. The crowd cheered, while Enos yelled out, holding The Champ's boot, which was smashing his nuts.

"ONE!... TWO!..." The Ref started to count Anderson out.

Anderson hopped down off of Enos, who was silently suffering, cupping his balls.

The Ref helped Enos off the ropes. It was awkward, and Enos rolled over into the fetal position.

Anderson kept his right arm held high, as his fans started chanting, "ANDER-SON! ANDER-SON!"

Enos rolled out under the bottom rope, and limped around the ring, over to his corner. He climbed up onto the ring apron, and stood just outside the ropes.

The Ref walked over and asked him if he was ok to continue. Enos nodded, and The Ref didn't bug him about getting in, right away.

Anderson came over, all smiles, "Hey, buddy. How you doin'?"

Enos looked up at him, and nodded.

It was an unusually tender moment that left the Ref a bit puzzled. "Ok, get back in the ring, or I'll have to count you out."

Enos climbed back into the ring, and Anderson backed away to let him.

Anderson galloped around, circling hard. Enos kept facing him, slow and intentional. Anderson charged into another lock up, and again, Enos dodged to the side, and pasted another hard punch into Anderson ribs. BAM!

"Unghh!" Anderson held his rib.

Enos followed with another fast roundhouse to The Champ's gut. WHAMP!

"UNNGHH!" Anderson doubled over, holding his gut.

Enos followed with a kick in the opposite direction, which nailed The Champ right in his big, cushy butt. WHAMP!

Anderson was propelled forward a few feet. He stood up and held his butt.

Enos planted his hands on The Champ's back and pushed him forward until his chest was up against the top ropes. He pulled Anderson's trunks HARD up into his ass crack, and his big, muscley, chubby butt was exposed. Enos rubbed. It.

"Wow, soft!" SMACK! SMACK! Enos spanked The Champ!

Anderson held on to the ropes, and yelled out, his ass cheeks now red.

"OFF THE ROPES!" The Ref pushed Enos back.

Enos broke clean.

Anderson turned around quickly, and tried to adjust his

trunks back over his exposed butt. Enos was right back in front of him, though, and he hit The Champ with two rapid-fire forearm slashes across his broad, power lifter's chest. SMACK! SMACK!

"UHHAHH!" Anderson arched backward over ropes, his chest, and the whole ring, bouncing with each slash.

Enos grabbed at The Champs hairy, cuddly belly, and CLAWED IT.

The Ref intervened, again. "OFF THE ROPES!"

Enos let go, and stepped back.

Anderson rubbed his belly, and put his hand up. "Back off." He was more than a little overwhelmed.

Enos was right back on him. This time, before he resumed his assault, he smiled, and patted Anderson's chest. "This is gonna happen. You knew it would." Enos wrapped his fingers around The Champ's bulge, and PULLED him forward off the ropes.

Anderson held on to Enos's wrist, and had to follow.

Enos kept a hold of The Champ's privates, and laid a big, hard punch into that tough, hard belly. WHAM!

"Aaghh." Anderson was now hard in Enos's hand, but he felt that punch. He held his belly, and put his hand up, guarding against another punch. "No more."

"No more? Ok." Enos seemed to agree with him.

Anderson dropped his hand, and worked on trying to free his genitals from Enos's grip.

WHAM! Enos sunk another hard punch right directly into The Champ's navel.

"UNGHH." This time, Anderson slumped forward a bit. He held his hand up, again. "No more!!"

Enos slowly yanked on Anderson's hard-on and balls.

"Unghh!" Anderson's hip came forward, and he was forced to dance on his tiptoes for a moment. He kept working on Enos's wrist.

WHAM! Enos's punch found its mark just as Anderson let his hand drop, again.

Anderson dropped to his knees, as Enos lost his grip. The Champ slumped forward, resting his head against his Challenger's crotch.

Enos took a slow breath in, then out. This was very pleasurable to him. He ran his fingers through Anderson's hair, then pulled him back up to his feet, and lifted him up, one hand on The Champ's shoulder, the other gripping his crotch.

Enos walked The Champ to center ring, raised him high, then SLAMMED him down.

"UNGHH, AGGGHH!" Anderson arched his back.

Enos dropped down to his knee, slamming a fist into Anderson's raised gut, as he did.

"OOOFFHHH." Anderson fell back down to the canvas, holding his gut.

Enos covered his man, and the Ref dropped down for the

count, "ONE!... TWO!..."

Anderson kicked out, and managed to throw Enos up over him.

Enos went up into the air, and landed on all fours.

Anderson slumped back down on the canvas, needing a breather.

Enos was relentless. He tried for another pin, right away. He swung his legs around, getting a knee on either side of Anderson's head, and squeezed. He sat back, his balls smothering The Champ.

The Ref counted, again, "ONE!... TWO!..."

Anderson lifted Enos up, by his knees, as if he was bench-pressing him, and threw him to the side.

Enos landed and rolled back to his prey. He wrapped his legs around one of Anderson's, grabbed The Champ's other ankle, and rolled him up into a banana split, holding his beefy legs up in the air in a wide "V". This was the hold that helped Enos claim his one, and only, defeat of Anderson. He held on to The Champ's legs, as he leaned his back against Anderson's chest, and had his shoulders pinned down.

The Ref counted to "TWO!" before Anderson undulated his hips to get his big legs down, thus teetering him up into a sitting position. He pulled back Enos's chin, and wrapped one of his big, beefy arms around The Challenger's neck, and worked it into a sleeper.

Enos lost his grip on Anderson's ankle. He wildly tried pulling on The Champ's hands and fingers to release himself from the sleeper. He groped around for Anderson's hard-on and PULLED on it!

"UHNGGG...AHH" Anderson moaned, and his body convulsed, but he cranked the sleeper as hard as Enos cranked his boner.

Enos pushed his elbow down into Anderson's balls, and LEANED in HARD.

"AGHH!... NO... STOP!" Anderson was forced to release the sleeper, and push Enos's elbow away from his crotch.

Enos secured Anderson's ankle, and again forced his legs apart into an unbearable banana split. He rolled back, and pinned The Champ, one more time. As the Ref dropped down for the count, Enos pulled DOWN on Anderson's hard-on. This was the little extra that helped him score the pin, the last time.

Anderson howled, and rammed his elbow into the top of Enos's head, as he thrust his hips, and cantilevered himself back up into a sitting position, just avoiding the third slap of the mat.

Enos rolled to the ropes, and rubbed the top of his head.

Anderson sat, center ring, his legs spread, massaging his aching groin.

Enos pulled himself up, and Anderson rolled to the ropes on the opposite side of the ring. Enos followed, and rammed a big elbow into the nape of The Champ's neck.

"Uhnnahh." The Champ slumped forward, and he held on to the ropes.

Enos pulled The Champ up, and leaned his chest against that big, wide bulky back. He ran his hands up Anderson's sides, and felt around his big, burly pecs, then he twisted Anderson's nipples as he said in a low, soothing voice, "God, you LOVE these matches with me, don't you?"

Anderson grunted. He couldn't get Enos's hands away from his nipples. He even tried to push Enos back with his elbows.

Enos slid one hand down Anderson's muscle belly and burrowed his fingertips down in through the waistband of his trunks. He fumbled around, and untied The Champ's trunks, then pulled them down, and lodged them up under The Champ's balls. Anderson's boner sprung to attention, and he tried to cover his erection with his hands. The Crowd on that side of the ring stood up. Rory got a close-up shot of it on his virtual TV, and he couldn't help but manipulate his own excited penis.

Anderson tried to pull his trunks back up just as Enos rammed his hips forward and pulled up on the middle rope, grinding it into The Champ's balls.

"EEEYYAAAHHH!!" Anderson pushed down on the rope.

The Ref pulled Enos's arm, but was unable to move it. "OK! That's enough! Off the ropes!"

Enos grinned, "Wait, one more second." He kept pulling up on the rope with one hand, and pushed his other hand into the pubic bone just above The Champ's erection, then slowly moved the heel of his hand down.

The Champ's erection, and balls, were now in a vice created by Enos's hand, and the middle rope of the ring. Anderson's mouth hung open, and his hands shook, as he held them out just in front of his throbbing manhood, immobilized by pain, and a fair amount of pleasure.

The Ref jabbed the back of Enos's shoulder. "COME ON! OFF THE ROPES!"

Enos whispered in The Champ's ear, "I'll continue this in a moment." He released his vice on The Champ's boner, and backed away.

The Champ rested against the ropes for a moment, and massaged around his hard-on, afraid to touch it.

The Ref got between them, and put a hand up to Enos, as he asked Anderson, "You ok?"

Anderson nodded his head, and turned around. He cautiously raised his trunks, and lightly pushed his erection back in. "Ahhgg!" It looked painful, like a man with a sunburn putting on a shirt. His erection pushed out on his trunks, leaving an inch gap between the waistband and his waist.

Enos smiled at his handiwork. He stepped forward, The Ref still between them, and put his hand on Anderson's chest, "You ok, *Champ?*"

The Champ was breathing hard, hands on his hips.

Enos pushed The Ref out of the way, and brought his knee up, into The Champ's balls.

The Champ doubled forward, "Unhahh." His hands rested on Enos's chest. "Stop..."

Burgeoning heel, **EB** (5'9" 175lbs) controls **VINNY O** (5'8" 207lbs) – Rookie vs Rookie.

World Champion
DYER ANDERSON
(6' 265-285lbs)
vs
American Champion
CHRIS ENOS
(6'2" 230lbs)

A 5-year struggle for the title between Dyer Anderson, the tough, brawling, Reigning Title-Holder, & Chris Enos, the sport's current Golden Pretty-boy & dirtiest wrestler in the business. He will stop at nothing to win the belt. Even though Anderson is the superior fighter, Enos knows how to manipulate and distract him with excruciating pleasure.

Top Contender **FREDERICK SOURIS** (5'2" 160lbs) has Parisian Champ **RENE SEBASTIAN** (5'10" 220lbs) on the ropes in a Championship Tournament match

Enos did it, again, slower, this time, pushing up, and grinding his knee into Anderson's testicles.

"Unnhhhaaahh." Anderson rested his face against Enos's chest, which bounced as he balanced himself, his knee still up. He placed his hands on Anderson's shoulders and dropped his knee.

"Ohhahhh." Anderson had to hold on to Enos to keep himself up. He started to massage his balls, but had to stop. It hurt too much.

Enos pushed The Champ into the ropes, again, and raised his knee, once more. This time, he slowly pushed his knee down, forcing Anderson's hard-on down. He loved the feeling of The Champ's hard erection and soft balls rubbing against his big, muscled thigh.

"Aahh… Wait! Please… Stop!" The Champ pushed against Enos's rippling chest, but didn't have enough strength to move him.

The Ref was getting sick of telling them, "OFF THE ROPES!"

Enos moved back, and Anderson sank to the canvas, holding his groin. His head lowered down causing his big butt to stick straight up in the air. This was too inviting for Enos. He sat on Anderson's back, facing backward, and PULLED The Champ's trunks up his crack. He began spanking him. SMACK! SMACK! SMACK!

Anderson's muscley, beefy butt jiggled. He grunted and convulsed with each spank.

Enos was in heaven. His hand snuck down between Anderson's butt cheeks, through his legs, and found Anderson's aching balls, again. He gave them a nice little squeeze.

"No!" Anderson tried to grab Enos's hand.

Enos's other hand helped out. It grabbed a hold of The Champ's balls, and PULLED them back through his legs.

Anderson yelled out.

Enos worked his hand around, got a hold of The Champ's boner, and pulled it back through his legs.

Anderson screamed out. One hand tried to wrestle Enos's away, as he needed the other hand to keep himself steady.

Enos really YANKED back on Anderson's erection, "ASK HIM!"

The Ref winced. Just seeing The Champ in this situation made him uncomfortable. "Um... You ok, Anderson?"

Anderson screamed out, "MAKE HIM STOP!!!"

"You wanna give it up?" The Ref was ready to call for the bell, but Anderson shook his head, violently.

He kept working Enos's hand, trying to break free. Finally, he lost his balance, and fell on his side. Enos fell with him, and ended up with his legs around Anderson's torso, that big, bountiful booty right in front of him. He locked his legs at the ankles and FLEXED a body scissor.

"Unhhh" Anderson almost welcomed this pain, over the genital torture.

The Announcer said he had never seen a match like this, before. Dyer Anderson was basically Chris Enos's jobber boy.

Never had a Champion been so easily worked and abused, as far as he could remember.

Enos PULLED up on Anderson's trunks, really wedging them as high as they could possibly go, as he FLEXED and un-flexed his big, buff thighs.

Anderson grunted each time, and got himself up into a sitting position.

This forced Enos onto his stomach. He pushed up from the canvas with his hands, and FLEXED the squeeze on Anderson's midsection again.

"Unhh." Anderson could feel it, but it wasn't nearly as bad as anything else he endured in that match. He held on to Enos's ankles, and LEANED back.

Enos couldn't hold the pushup position and he fell, his chest slamming down into the mat.

Anderson kept a tight hold on Enos's ankles, as he got up onto his feet. This bent Enos backwards, in a sort of Boston Crab, but Enos still had his scissors applied, squeezing as hard as he could. It didn't have much effect, though.

Anderson LEANED back more, and pulled Enos's ankles up even higher. "ASK HIM, REF!"

The Ref shook his head, and decided that Anderson had the slight advantage, at that moment. He bent down, and asked Enos, "You ok?"

"YES!" Enos said in a tone meant to convey that he thought the Ref was crazy.

Enos pushed back up on his hands, and tried to power Anderson down. No go. Anderson was too big, and his big, brawny legs were too strong. Then, Enos walked his hands forward, toward the ropes. This was much easier, as Anderson was leaning back, and pushing with his legs, which added to the momentum. Enos grabbed the bottom rope, and yelled up to The Ref, "Break it up!"

The Ref reluctantly warned Anderson, "Break it! Off the Ropes."

Anderson patted Enos's legs, which were still squeezing him. "Uh, me break it?"

The Ref smacked Enos's big, granite thigh. "Break it!"

Enos yelled back. "Keep him off me!"

"All right." The Ref smacked his thigh, again. "Break it!"

Enos did and brought his feet down to the canvas.

The Champ stepped away from Enos, adjusted his trunks, bent over, and massaged his balls.

Enos stood up, and pushed on his aching back for one second, then resumed his attack.

Anderson stood up as Enos approached, and was met with a loud forearm slash across his big chest. SMACK! It bounced and jiggled. He sucked air in through clenched teeth.

Enos took hold of his big wrist, and slingshot him into the corner. WHAM! Anderson's back hit hard, and the ring shook like an earthquake.

The Champ groaned, and needed the top rope to keep him steady.

Enos spotted the head of Anderson's erection peeking out the top of his trunks. He stepped forward and fired another slash across The Champ's wide, round pecs. They bounced, and jiggled, again. Enos grabbed the head of Anderson's boner, and pulled down on it. The Champ's trunks came down, completely exposing his erection, again.

The Ref called for Enos to take the action "OUT OF THE CORNER!"

So, Enos walked backward, and PULLED the erection.

Anderson followed. "AAAHH! AAAH!" The Champ held on to Enos's wrist with both hands, trying to alleviate some of the torque on his engorged member.

Enos then began a slow, methodical assault on Anderson's chubby muscle belly. One HARD punch was dealt, while he kept a firm grip on The Champ's erection, and YANKED!

"UNNGHAHH!"

It was hard to tell if the punch affected Anderson at all. The rough manipulation of his penis seemed to elicit the most reaction.

The Announcer continued commenting on the match as a "Sexual Squash". He added that The Champ didn't seem to be himself, at all.

At that point, Enos had delivered his third punch and yank, when Anderson groaned and fired back a gut punch of his own.

"UNGGHH!" Enos felt it. He took a deep breath in, and then YANKED down on Anderson's penis, again.

"OHHH"

Enos saw that he was getting nowhere by working on Anderson's stomach, so he put all his weight into PULLING The Champ's boner straight down.

"AAAHHH! AAAHHH!" Anderson fell to his knees, put his hands on Enos's arms and PUSHED. He stopped that right away, gasping from the pain.

Enos let go. Anderson cradled his crotch, and slumped forward. Enos brought his knee up and slammed Anderson right in the face.

"Ungghh." Anderson fell to the side.

Enos pushed Anderson's shoulder down to the mat, with his boot, covered him for the pin, and hooked one of Anderson's enormous thighs.

The Ref dropped down and slapped the mat, "ONE!... TWO!", and Anderson got his shoulder up before the third.

Enos sat up and took a hold of Anderson's exposed erection. Only this time, he was tender with it.

Anderson appreciated the opportunity to recuperate, until Enos grabbed a viscous claw full of his beefy midsection.

Anderson screamed out, and sat up, his chest against Enos's shoulder. "STOP! ST...STOP!" He furiously pulled on Enos's hand.

Enos RIPPED his hand back, and Anderson's belly snapped out

of his claw, jiggling. Again, Anderson screamed out.

Enos stood up and pulled Anderson to his feet, using his hair.

The Champ wasn't exactly steady on his feet, "WAIT! WAIT!"

Enos didn't hesitate for one second. He scooped Anderson up, and held him high with a grip on his crotch and on his shoulder.

Anderson kicked and shook his head, "NO!"

Enos's face developed an almost sympathetic smile, "Oh, sorry. This is gonna happen, Buddy."

BAM! The whole ring shook on impact. The Champ's big muscles shook, and his body fat shimmied. He pushed up to a sitting position, his lower back arched in extreme pain.

Enos dropped down, pushed Anderson's shoulders to the mat, and covered him for the pin.

Again, The Champ got his shoulder up before the three count.

Enos was up quickly, pulling Anderson to his feet, scooping him up, slamming him, and covering for the pin, and, again, Anderson got his shoulder up.

One more time, Enos slammed, covered and pinned The Champ, and one more time, he got a shoulder up. Enos could not believe Anderson's stamina.

He rubbed The Champ's belly, then GRABBED it, and stood up. Anderson's erection was still sticking out, so Enos grabbed that, too. "GET UP!" He tried to raise The Champ by pulling on these two parts of Anderson's body, like handles.

Anderson's pelvis rose up, as he tried to get to his feet, but that just made his pelvis bend back down toward the canvas. Enos's grip on the penis and belly fat wasn't strong enough to lift the 285-pound muscle bear, so Anderson fell back down onto the mat.

The pain from his erection and belly being clawed and stretched had him rolling on the canvas, cradling his suffering parts.

Enos placed his boot on Anderson's shoulder and pushed the fallen Champ onto his back. He stood between Anderson's thick thighs, and pressed the heel of his boot down into The Champ's balls.

Anderson held on to Enos's boot, "UNH UNG, " and tried to push it away.

Enos gave Anderson's balls a tap with the toe of his boot, and Anderson's whole body jerked, again causing his big muscles to shake and shimmy, "Ung!"

Enos bent down, picked up Anderson's ankles, and hooked them into his armpits. He pulled Anderson up higher, then worked to twist Anderson over into a Boston Crab. It wasn't easy with such a big man, and Anderson was actively trying to make it more difficult.

Enos lowered his weight down and heaved his body to the side. Anderson spread his arms and bucked his hips. Anderson's whole body was so thick with muscle, it was like trying to wrestle a hippopotamus or a polar bear. Turning The Champ over was such a hard task that Enos had to stop and rest, with Anderson's boots still hooked under his armpits. The Champ tried to kick his legs again, so Enos placed his boot on Anderson's balls and PUSHED DOWN.

Anderson howled and grabbed The Challenger's boot. Enos took that opportunity to go for the crab, again. He withdrew from Anderson's balls and threw that leg over The Champ and twisted.

Anderson was so distracted by pain that it worked, and he was flipped over onto his stomach.

Enos leaned back and sat on Anderson's lower back. The Champ was bent back further than anyone thought he could be. He screamed and pounded the mat.

"ASK HIM!" Enos's voice echoed.

The Ref didn't think Anderson was anywhere near giving up, but he knelt down near The Champ's face. "HEY! How you doin'?"

"UNHH!" Anderson planted hands firmly on the canvas and flexed his brontosaurus quads in an attempt to straighten his legs and flip Enos off of him.

Enos tottered forward and lost one of Anderson's legs. He now had a free hand, which immediately went where it always did: between Anderson's huge, hairy legs. His fingers found their mark and Anderson's whole body heaved.

The Champ bucked, and flailed. He tried to get his hands back there to stop the ransacking of his nether region, but was helpless to do anything to stop the onslaught.

Anderson tried to scissor Enos, but he couldn't bring his ankles together, since Enos had one trapped under his arm.

Enos's eyes glinted and he licked his lips. He moved his hand slowly, then used his fingers HARD, just behind The Champ's balls.

Anderson grunted, gasped and he screamed out, "GET HIM OFF ME!!!"

"You want to give up?" The Ref didn't think he would, but The Champ's tone conveyed a touch of panic.

Anderson clawed into the canvas and walked them forward a couple of feet, as he stretched out to reach the ropes.

Enos raised his hand a few inches, and then SLAPPED the area just behind The Champ's testicles.

Anderson's head sunk back down and he rested his face on the mat. His eyes rolled back in his head and a bit of drool trickled from the side of his mouth.

"TALK TO HIM!" Enos directed. "HE WANTS TO SUBMIT!"

The Ref hunkered back down, and lowered his face to The Champ's. "You ok to continue?"

The Champ nodded, "GET... HIM... OFF... OF... ME!!!"

"That means you give up?" The Ref couldn't do anything about Enos. His sadistically sexual hold hadn't broken any rules.

"CALL THE MATCH! HE WANTS TO GIVE UP!!!" Enos was feeling the effects of having to hold up the big brute's lower body.

"I have to hear "I give", first!" The Ref made a dismissive, backhanded gesture.

Enos smiled, "Well, get ready to hear it!" His hand moved slowly, then quickly, then slowly, then HARD, pushing down and trembling, just behind Anderson's nut sack.

The Champ yelled out, held his breath, and his mouth fell open.

Enos gently rocked, as he worked his hand back and forth, then in a slow circular motion.

Anderson clawed the air, and whipped from side to side, trying to get a hold of The Challenger.

Enos really concentrated and bit his lower lip. His elbow cranked, his hand pumping up and down.

"No! No!... No!" Anderson tapped the mat.

The Ref was surprised. "Are you tapping out?"

"NO!... GET HIM OFF ME!!!" Anderson almost sounded like he was crying. His voice wavered and cracked.

Enos became very calm. "Ask him if he wants to submit... and I'll stop."

Anderson tapped the canvas, again.

The Ref took a hold of The Champ's shoulder, "Are you submitting?"

"MAKE HIM STOP! MAKE HIM STOP!!!" Anderson was begging.

Enos leaned back, as far as he could, and his hand started pumping like a jackhammer.

"AHH! AHHH! Make him..." Anderson closed his eyes, tight. "HE'S!.... HE'S!.... STOP!"

The Ref's heart went out to The Champ. What a way to go. "Do you want to give up? Want me to stop the match?"

"Yesss..." Anderson's whole body trembled.

"Say the words!" Enos instructed The Champ.

"No...." Anderson was just about done.

"Say, 'I give up'." Enos smiled.

Anderson's body convulsed in rhythm. "I...gi....give...."

Enos watched The Ref, who shook his head and signaled for the bell.

"DING! DING!"

Enos dropped the big bull's legs, and stood up, stretching out his arms and back. His head was down. He leaned forward, and rested his hands on his knees. He wouldn't have been able to keep up that hold one second longer.

Anderson kept his eyes closed, not completely aware of what had just happened.

The Ref called for the belt, and tried to hand it to Enos, who just raised his arms up. The Ref realized he wanted the belt to be placed around his waist. He did so.

Enos stood above the old champ, and accepted the almost universal cheers.

Anderson crawled to his corner. He slumped against the ring post, too exhausted, and humiliated to face the crowd.

Enos walked over, and extended his hand down to Anderson,

who looked up at The new Champ, halfway between fury and admiration.

The Ex Champ finally shook his head and waved Enos away, so The Champ knelt down in front of Anderson, and congratulated him. Then, he stunned Anderson, and the entire arena, when he leaned forward and embraced him. They whispered to each other in that position for a while, then Enos helped Anderson up to his feet, and said, "I'm sorry. I just had to have this belt."

Enos patted Anderson on the shoulder and headed back to his corner. He exited the ring, to another blast of applause.

Anderson watched him, and as he stood there, everyone could now see the big wet spot on the front of his trunks.

Rory was in an excited state throughout the entire match. When Chris Enos's hand felt it's way around Dyer Anderson's butt cheeks, then snuck down between his legs, Rory's whole body ached. He grabbed Mike's erection and pulled on it, roughly. Mike gasped and had to bridge his hips up.

"Aah.. unh... wait!" Mike held his hands up.

Rory wanted to sexually torment Dyer Anderson, but Mike was there, so he acted as proxy and bore the brunt of Rory's frustration. Fortunately, it was almost entirely pleasurable.

Rory had to know what it was like, so he flipped Mike over and sat on his back, reverse cowboy style. He thrust his hand down, under Mike's butt cheek, just like Chris Enos had done, and rubbed the area behind Mike's testicles, hard.

At first, Mike struggled, then made noises similar to the troubled Champion.

"Wait... Stooo..." Mike begged Rory to stop, but flexed his perfect, white ass cheeks as he humped the bed.

Rory figured this is what Enos's hand was doing to Anderson. He worked Mike, then relaxed, then worked him harder, matching Enos's moves.

The moment Anderson finally submitted, and Enos scored the victory, Rory couldn't hold back. He pressed his balls into Mike's smooth, muscular butt and worked his own erection like Enos worked The Champ. He came almost immediately, but kept working himself intensely, for a whole minute after he was drained.

Unfortunately, he hadn't gotten Mike over the finish line. Rory slid off him and reclined on a pillow, watching the end-of-match drama. Mike sat up and grabbed Rory's arms.

"Wait!" Rory pulled Mike into him, and held on tight, "I just wanna see this!"

When Rory saw the wet spot on the front of Anderson's trunks, he was ready to go, again. He couldn't believe that The World Champion was brought to climax, AND stripped of his belt! That was too hot for him to process. He kissed Mike, deeply, as he grabbed a handful of his hair. Mike did the same, and pulled Rory down onto his back, then slid on top of him. He pressed his hard-on into Rory's and relaxed, then pressed harder. Rory took a hold of Mike's amazing butt, with both hands - that perfect butt.

Mike slid himself up Rory's body, massaging his balls and

erection into Rory's stomach. He brought himself up to his knees, and straddled Rory's face, as he shoved his balls against Rory's chin. He pulled up on Rory's head, so he could work his balls as hard as possible. He grunted, groaned, moaned, and held his breath. Slowly, he slid up until he was able to wedge Rory's chin up into the area behind his balls. "OH, GOD!"

Rory still had a hold of that beautiful ass, and he helped ram his own chin into the underside of Mike's balls. He loved the perverse feeling of having his chin used that way. His mouth opened and he caressed Mike's nuts with his tongue

Mike's head fell back and his breathing stopped for a moment. He had to keep a hold of Rory's hair to make sure he didn't fall over.

Rory moved his chin up and down, really digging it into Mike's most sensitive area. He brought his legs up, hooked them around the sides of Mike's torso, and easily brought Mike down, backward onto the bed. He was now in a sitting position, with Mike's legs around him. He pushed them back, rolling Mike up. Mike's knees were now just above his own face. Rory leaned his head down and licked the area behind Mike's balls, then bit it, very lightly.

"Oh, God!" Mike grabbed one of his own pecs, with one hand, and flexed it, then pulled on his erection, with the other.

Rory sucked Mike's balls, and pulled one into his mouth. His tongue ran all around it.

"Oh... no! Oh, God!" Mike gave his penis one stroke, and stopped. "Wait!..."

Rory took Mike's other testicle into his mouth, now bathing both with his tongue.

Mike's body shook, "Wai….!" He was right on the edge.

Rory pushed the heel of his palm up into the area behind Mike's balls.

"NO! WAIT…" Mike tried to hold on, but it was too late. His orgasm had already started erupting. He furiously pulled at his penis as Rory kept up his expert use of hand and mouth, like some kind of sexual terrorist.

Mike came all over his own face and hair. He closed his eyes, and kept going.

When he was done, he gave his penis one last, long squeeze from the base to the tip.

Rory let Mike's legs go, and brought them down. He sat next to Mike, and watched him. His eyes were still closed and he was breathing hard. The sight of the very masculine, muscular Mike, covered with his own sperm turned Rory on even more. He wiped Mike's face with the bed sheet.

When Mike opened his eyes, he saw Rory looking down on him with a big, juicy smile. He sat up, and saw that Rory was hard, again.

Rory pulled him up, and into the bathroom. He turned on the shower, guided Mike in, and positioned his face under the water. He wrapped his arms around Mike, and kissed him long, hard, and deep. Then, when he was done, he kissed him, again.

Rory reached for the soap, and ran it all over Mike's body. He turned Mike around, and let the water rinse that flawless butt clean, then he lowered himself to his knees, and kissed it. He bit it, licked it, then kissed it, again. He soaped it up, again, and ran his hands up and down the muscles of Mike's legs and back.

Then, it was Mike's turn. He lathered up Rory's hard, defined pecs, and stomach, then let the water wash all the suds away. His mouth, tongue, and teeth, explored every inch of that beautiful, muscular chest, then pulled on those soft, pink nipples. Rory moaned, and pushed his boner up under Mike's, and stroked them together.

Mike lowered himself down to his knees, and licked the tip of Rory's hard-on, back and forth, then around. Rory leaned against the tile wall. Mike took Rory, all the way into this mouth, and sucked.

"Oh!" Rory held on to Mike's head.

Mike did it one more time, all the way in, then slowly out, and this time he pulled down, lightly, on Rory's testicles.

"Oh, Mike!" Rory held his breath.

Mike stood up, and they kissed, again.

He looked Rory in the eyes, and whispered, "Will you, um….?"

Rory knew what he wanted. He smiled, and kissed

Mike, then turned off the water.

They stepped out, and dried each other off, stopping to kiss, lick, and fondle every muscular, tan, beautiful inch of each other.

Rory opened a drawer, and pulled out a condom. He held it up to Mike, and flashed a somewhat mischievous grin. Mike pulled Rory into him, and closed his eyes. He nuzzled Rory's neck, and squeezed him, tight.

Rory licked his ear, and asked, "You wanna put it on?"

Mike looked at him, a coy smile on his face. He took the rubber from Rory, opened it, and pulled it out. He reached down, gripped Rory's hard-on, with his fingertips, and placed the condom on the tip of Rory's penis. He rolled it down, slowly, and used his finger to push as much of the lubrication to the head of the condom.

They kissed, again.

Rory turned Mike around, and pushed his torso down. Mike held on to the tile counter. Rory rubbed Mike's magnificent gluteus maximus and spread the cheeks, then pushed the tip of his hard-on into Mike's butt.

"Unhh!" Mike's body tensed. "Go ahead!"

Rory slowly pushed in deeper.

"Oh...Unhh!" Mike's back arched, and his head bridged up. "Yeah! Yeah! Keep going!"

Rory pushed himself in, all the way.

"Ohhhh!"

Rory slowly pulled out, then back in.

"Harder!"

Rory closed his eyes and smiled. He pulled out, and slammed back in.

"Yeah! Faster!" Mike pushed his balls back.

Rory thrust his hips back and forth, hard and fast, their balls slamming together.

"OH, YEAH! OH, YEAH!" Mike kept his hand down, holding his balls in place. His other hand pulled on the tip of his own erection, and stroked it in small, hard movements. "Oh, no!... I'm gonna..." He had to let go of his erection, and grab the counter to keep from falling.

Rory went fast. "I'm almost..."

"Oh, my God!" Mike started. He wasn't even touching his penis, but his orgasm had already started.

Then, Rory's started. "Oh, yeah! I'm com...ing!" His humping became shorter, and he rammed harder, both of them in ecstasy every time their testicles collided.

Mike was done, and both hands were now gripping the counter. But, Rory kept going, and it felt good. Mike became light-headed.

Rory finished. He leaned forward, and held on to

Mike for a second. He took in two deep breaths, then helped Mike stand up straight.

Mike turned and put his arms around him, "I love you, Rory."

6 ONWARD & UPWARD

One day, after a hard workout at the gym, Rory was walking to his car, checking his fone. There was a video message from a number he didn't know, but he recognized the facial icon. His head cocked, and he played the message.

It was Max Gunn, the AWPW World Champ, from fifteen years earlier. "Hey Rory! I'm Max Gunn. I'm a recruiter for All Worlds Pro Wrestling. I'm going to be in your area next week, and I'd like to set up a meeting. Call me back, and let's get this confirmed." Max smiled into the camera. The message ended.

Rory stopped dead in his tracks. This was for real. Max Gunn, THE Max Gunn, wanted to meet with him. Rory shook his head and said out loud, "That was REALLY Max Gunn!"

Max Gunn was a rough, tough, mean, violent wrestler, blond, very handsome, and now balding. Rory was stunned by how polite he was, and how he smiled at the end of his message.

Rory ran to his car, jumped in, and locked it. He hit the "call back" icon. It rang twice, then Max Gunn answered, "Hello?"

Rory was shaking with anticipation, and had a stupid expression on his face. "Uh.. hi."

"Oh, hey! It's Rory Pedersen, right?" Max smiled, again.

Rory nodded, "Yeah, hi! Yeah! I'm Rory Pedersen. How's it going?" He shook his head. He couldn't believe he just asked Max Gunn, "How's it going?" as if he was just some guy calling to shoot the breeze.

"I'm good, thanks. I'll be in your area next week, and I want to see you. You're on my list of guys we are very interested in. How about..." Max scrolled on his fone, checking available dates. "How about Tuesday, 2pm? I'm staying at the Regency. We can meet in the lobby?"

"Uh, yeah! Yeah! Of course." Rory was now smiling, his heart racing.

"Excellent. I'll see you then!" Max was done with his business.

"Yeah! That's awesome... Um, do I need to bring anything? Do you need anything else from me?" Rory had a million questions for him, including personal ones, but he restrained himself.

"Nope. Just show up. I gotta go, so I'll see you then. Thanks, Rory!"

"Yeah! Thanks! Thank you very much!"

Max hung up.

Rory stared at his phone. He let out a war cry, "FUCK YEAH!!!", and laughed uncontrollably. "I'm on a list of guys they are interested in!!! FUCK YEAH!!!"

He called Mike, as he drove home. They both yelled and

screamed and cussed a lot. Then, he called Todd and Duane.

When he got home, he remembered that he scheduled a meeting with Sector Pro. He called and apologetically cancelled the appointment, telling them he would reschedule in two weeks. He felt stupid. He KNEW he would be getting into The A.W.P.W., and was mad, at himself, that he ever doubted it.

Rory was in the best shape of his young life, but he worked out doubly hard in the days leading up to his Tuesday meeting. He even oiled himself, daily, in his bathroom with the door locked, checking every inch, every angle. He thought he looked good, but like every man who works out, he worried about his "flaws". He wished his arms and legs were bigger. He had a six-pack, but wanted it more defined. He should have been exhausted by all the extra workouts, but his excitement for the upcoming meeting gave him an electric sort of energy.

When Tuesday finally came, he got ready very early, and left his house one whole hour before he needed to in order to be on time. He arrived at the hotel, and circled it for a while. A half-hour before his meeting, he parked, then walked around for fifteen minutes. He entered the lobby, and sat down for what seemed like another fifteen minutes. When he saw a clock it had only been two. He couldn't take it anymore. He went to the front desk and told them he was there to see Max Gunn. They called up to his room, and told Rory that Max would be down in a few minutes.

Rory sat down, again. He checked his fone every two seconds. The fifteen minutes it took Max to come down from his room seemed like an eternity. Rory spotted him immediately as he walked through the doors from the elevators. He stood up quickly, and even though he tried hard not to, his face broke out in a smile.

Max saw him, and walked over, also smiling. He extended his hand, "Hey Rory! It's good to meet you!"

Rory grabbed his hand and shook vigorously.

Max had a good, hard, firm grip. He was big man about fifty years-old, 6 feet 2 inches tall. When he wrestled he was billed as being 250 pounds. He seemed heavier and a bit beefier, but Rory thought he looked good.

Their handshake sent chills through Rory. His excitement was beginning to have a very physical manifestation. He tried to think of things that would calm it down, and hoped Max wouldn't notice.

They made a little small talk, then Max asked Rory if he would be ok with continuing the meeting in his hotel room. Rory thought nothing of it, and agreed.

Max's room was a suite, with a living room, and separate bedroom. Max led Rory to the living room area. Rory sat on the couch, and Max in the chair across from him.

"We always like to meet with the guys before flying them out. Even though everyone has to send in a video, people sometimes don't look as good, OR they send in old videos. But, Rory, I gotta tell you. You look great!"

Rory smiled like a dopey schoolboy. "Thank you! You look great, too, Mr. Gunn!"

Max chuckled. "Well, thank you. I appreciate that, but I already got the job. And, call me Max... Like I was saying, you look good, you photograph great, and your wrestling looks good on your video. We are interested in bringing you out for tryouts."

Rory nodded. "Sure, yeah! Absolutely!"

Max's hands went up, "Sorry, one more thing, and if you are uncomfortable with this, we totally understand, but I'm going to need you to take your shirt off."

Rory blushed. He felt strange all of a sudden. "Um... yeah, ok." Was this standard practice? His pants felt a lot tighter, and he squirmed his hips to the side hoping to readjust himself.

Max was concerned about Rory's hesitancy, "I totally understand if you are uncomfortable with this,   BUT, if you want to be a wrestler, you WOULD be appearing in front of crowds almost, or sometimes completely naked." He said this in a way that made Rory feel like he was losing interest.

"No! No! I'm not uncomfortable." He stood up, and grabbed the bottom of his tee shirt, pulling it down over the fly area of his pants. "Do you want to see it, now?"

Max nodded. "Sure."

Rory whipped his shirt off, and his whole body blushed.

Max made a face that Rory couldn't read. Did he notice the bulge?

Rory pulled his stomach in, flexed it, and tried to nonchalantly flex the rest of the muscles in his body, hoping to draw attention away from his pants. "Is this ok?"

Max nodded. "Oh, yeah! You look great." Can you turn around?

Rory did.

"Yeah, that's awesome. You can sit down, now."

Rory sat down, "Cool", with his shirt still in his hand.

Max smiled, realizing that Rory was just a naïve, well-mannered kid. "And, you can put your shirt back on."

Rory did.

Max went over all the particulars, what was expected of him, rules, etc. They wanted Rory to come out for tryouts in two weeks. Rory asked about training, and what he should know when he arrived.

Rory was beside himself. This is what he had been dreaming about, and it was coming true.

When Max was done, Rory became nervous, again. He looked down, with a big, goofy grin, and said, "Uh, I guess you hear this all the time, but I'm a big fan of yours!"

Max smiled. "Thanks. That's good to hear."

Rory looked up and Max was smiling right at him. He couldn't believe how friendly he was. It made him feel funny, in a very good way.

Max stood up, and Rory followed. "I'm sorry I have to cut this meeting short, but I have a flight out."

They said their 'goodbyes' and Rory left. As soon as the

elevator doors shut, he danced, jumped, yelled, and laughed, until they reopened. This was the first time he had met a real Pro Wrestler. On the ride home, he fantasized about what would have happened if Max had made a pass at him.

He was in euphoria for a week. He smiled every time he thought about Max's big, strong handshake. He watched all the videos he could find of Max wrestling, and it turned him on. Max Gunn was now on his list.

PURE PRO

Mike was home from college that weekend. When Rory came over, he threw him down on his bed, and attacked him. He kissed his mouth, his neck, his face, and his mouth, again. He ripped Rory's clothes off, and didn't let him up for hours.

Afterward, they lounged in each other's arms, and talked endlessly about Rory's future in wrestling. Mike admitted that he was envious, and wanted to go with Rory to see the training facilities.

They had a meeting with all the wrestlers from Rory's federation, Pure Pro Wrestling. Every single one howled and jumped around when they heard the good news. They all swarmed into a big huddle and gave Rory a huge group bear hug.

All the guys expressed their admiration and envy. Two pulled Rory aside to ask for help with their own submissions to the A.W.P.W.

Rory told them all that he wanted to have as many wrestling workouts as possible before he left for tryouts. He wanted to videotape them for the Pure Pro wrestling channel. That worked them up into another frenzy. Every wrestler had ideas, and shouted them out at the top of their lungs.

The focus was on preparing Rory for his tryouts. One of the guys had the idea of Rory versus the entire Federation. He loved it.

Rory started center ring. All the other wrestlers stood outside, in the corners, just like a tag match. There were 3 per corner. Rory spun around slowly, asking, "Who's gonna start."

One guy jumped in, and Rory quickly gained control. Then, another guy jumped in, and they double-teamed him. There was some back and forth, until Rory got one guy down, and gained control on the other. He did pretty well, until the third and forth guy jumped in, then Rory pretty much became a plaything. Mike jumped in to help, but he was soon over-powered, and it just disintegrated from that point and became a free-for-all. None of them could stop laughing, and it ended with the guys dog-piling Rory.

They did several other matches, and every wrestler let Rory practice holds and moves on them.

The very last workout, before Rory's tryout, ended with the guys picking him up, and carrying him around the ring.

A.W.P.W. TRYOUTS, LAS VEGAS, NEVADA

Max sent Rory his itinerary. They would meet in the first class lounge at the Las Vegas airport. Rory flew alone, and maintained a high level of excitement for the entire flight. When he walked off the plane, he could hear his own heart beating. There was a noticeable bounce in his normally athletic step, and he couldn't stop smiling. He wanted to appear cool and calm, rather than the giddy way he was feeling.

Max was sitting with three young men when Rory entered the first class lounge. He took a really deep, controlled breath, let it out slowly, and walked over, a big smile still pasted across his face, "Hey!"

Max stood up, returned the smile, and grabbed Rory's hand for one of his hearty, manly shakes, "Hey Rory! Ok, we're just waiting for one more." He turned to the three other guys, "This is Rory."

He pointed to the first guy, "This is Scott."

Scott was a clean-cut athletic white guy, about 20 years old. He stood up, put his hand out and smiled, "Hey Rory. Good to meet you."

Max pointed at the next guy, "This is Eb."

Eb had dyed black hair, olive skin, and wore all white, tight clothing, with two big black wrist cuffs. He definitely had some kind of look going, He was a thin, yet muscular, Hispanic guy, who Rory figured could have been anywhere from 18 to 25. He just nodded and said, "Hey."

Rory was still smiling, "Hey, Eb."

The last boy sat two seats away from Eb. Max pointed at him, "And, that is Jeffry".

Jeffry was smaller than the other guys, and had distinctly

Mediterranean features, with dark, natural hair. He was plucked and groomed within an inch of his life, and was wearing tight slacks with a flowery collared shirt that was unbuttoned almost all the way down. He was rather effeminate. Rory thought he heard Jeffry make a clicking sound, and his face was scrunched up into an expression of disapproval and annoyance.

Rory's smile faded. "Yeah, hi Jeffry."

"Mmm!" Jeffry made a sort of grunt, and looked away.

Rory caught Max rolling his eyes, but he smiled back at Rory right away. "We're just waiting for one more guy."

Rory sat down and made small talk with Eb, and Scott, who Eb kept calling "Scotty". Max checked something at the front desk and Jeffry ignored them.

A very handsome, muscular, young black man entered the lounge. Rory noticed him immediately. He seemed to recognize Rory, and he nodded and smiled. Max walked over, shook his hand and led him over to the other guys. Rory and Scott stood up.

"Hey, guys. This is Bravon." He took Bravon through the same introductions. Scott and Rory both shook his hand and smiled, and the other guys did what they did before.

Max rounded them all up, and led them out to baggage claim, then the car. Bravon hurried up to walk next to Rory. "Hey! I watch your videos. They're great."

Rory smiled, "You do? Wow, thanks!"

Bravon continued, "Yeah, in fact, I was going to contact you to ask if you wanted to do some together."

"Whoa, really?" Rory didn't know what to say... "Yeah, that would be really cool."

"This is crazy that we're here at the same time!" Bravon nodded, "But it makes sense. I mean, you're really good."

"Well, thanks. I really appreciate that." That giddy feeling returned, and Rory could feel himself blushing.

They continued talking all the way to and through baggage claim. Scott and Eb had kind of paired off and Jeffry was on his own.

When they emerged from baggage claim, a black limo was waiting for them at the curb. Max motioned them all to file toward the trunk where the driver stowed their luggage. In the limo Rory ended up sitting next to Bravon, and they kept talking. Their conversation was so natural it seemed like they'd been friends forever.

The limo drove down the World Famous Las Vegas strip, and all the guys craned their necks to stare out the windows, except Jeffry. He pretended to look at his phone while he peered at the sights out of the corner of his eye. On Sahara Avenue, they turned right and headed west to the Queensridge neighborhood.

They stopped in the driveway of a mansion, and waited for the gate to open. This time, even Jeffry pressed his face up against the window to see. As they filed out of the limo, every boy's mouth hung open, and their eyes almost popped out.

Max Gunn smiled. "Get your stuff and follow me."

A good-looking guy named Christopher met them at the door. He was slim, about thirty years old, and wore a tank top and gym shorts.

Max introduced them. "This is Christopher. He is your house manager." He pointed at the boys. "Let me just warn you right off the bat: if you give him any problems, at all, you're out!"

That sobered them right up, except for Jeffry, who let out a derisive sigh.

Christopher smiled, "Well, I don't..."

Max pointed at the boys, again. "No, I mean it! You are here to <u>work!</u> We have had problems with new trainees in the past, and if you are not professional, we have no time for you, whatsoever. Does everyone understand?"

They all nodded... except Jeffry.

Max went to the office downstairs, and Christopher showed them to their rooms. Eb and Scott had already decided to room together, so they took the first one. Bravon turned to Rory, "How about us rooming?"

Rory nodded, "Yeah, that would be cool."

Jeffry heard them, and rolled his eyes.

At the next room, Christopher smiled, and said, "Sorry, guys, but we are full up, so the three of you will have to share."

Rory and Bravon shrugged and said they were all right with that, but Jeffry rolled his eyes, sighed, and asked, "You don't have *any* other rooms?"

Christopher's smile melted away, and he looked Jeffry straight in the eye, "No. We don't." He waited for Jeffry to say something else. It was clear that he didn't have time for this kind of problem. Jeffry grunted and entered the room. Both Rory and Bravon thanked Christopher and followed Jeffry. Christopher excused himself and said he would meet them downstairs.

In the room, there were two queen beds. Jeffry put his things on the first bed, and proclaimed, "I'll take this one. You two can have *that* one."

Rory and Bravon looked at each other.

Bravon put his things down, and closed the door. He took a deep breath, and turned to Jeffry. "Listen, Jeff. We have to get one thing straight here."

Jeffry put his hands on his hips, "It's JeffRY!"

Bravon smiled, "Ok, JeffRY. We are all here for the same reason, and it's going to be a lot of hard work. So, if you are going to be in this room, WE are all going to agree to treat each other with respect."

Jeffry rolled his eyes and snorted.

Bravon continued, "WE are going to be polite, compassionate, and VERY considerate to each other!"

Jeffry snorted again, and looked at Rory, as if Bravon was insane. "Whatever!"

Rory nodded. "I agree with Bravon. If you can't get along with us, then you have serious behavioral issues, because we will both treat you with the same respect you treat us."

Jeffry didn't soften up, at all. He rolled his eyes, again, unzipped one of his bags, pulled out a toiletry case and exited the room.

Rory hauled his biggest bag over to their side of the room, "That was awesome. I thought you handled that really well."

"Well, thank you, and thanks for the backup, but I think he's gonna be a huge pain in the ass." Bravon took a bag over to the closet.

Rory sat on the bed. "Oh yeah, for sure."

Rory and Bravon took a few short minutes to get settled, then headed downstairs to find out what they should do next.

Christopher was in the kitchen with Scott, Eb, and Russell, the cook-slash-nutritionist for the trainees. The four new guys were very interested in talking to Russell. They all had questions for him.

Then, Jake arrived.

Rory's eyes became three sizes bigger. Bravon suddenly went completely silent, and Scott couldn't stop smiling. Eb was interested, too, but kept his cool. Jake was more commonly known as "Big Jake Colt", a Pro Champ from a few years back. He was in his forties now, and up until a couple of years ago, wrestled sporadically with his iconic Cowboy Gimmick. His hair was now salt and pepper, and he had put on some weight, but his hyper-masculine charisma was tangible as he walked into that kitchen. At 6 feet 3 inches tall, and 280 pounds, he was an imposing figure.

Rory had quite an internal physical reaction to Mr. Colt.

Christopher introduced Jake as their Head Trainer, and the man they would report to every morning at the training facility.

He instructed all the boys to go to the living room. Their orientation would begin immediately. He looked around, and asked where Jeffry was. Bravon said he was upstairs and would go get him. Jake made a comment that it was odd he wasn't already downstairs, eager to get started. The three other boys exchanged looks.

Bravon met them in the living room almost immediately. Jeffry did not.

Christopher sat down, and Jake began the orientation. He told them what time they had to be in bed, what time they would wake up, what time their meals were, and what time they would need to be in front of the house to catch the van to the training facility. He was very clear, and repeated each one.

Then, Jeffry appeared. His lips were pressed together, slightly raised at the corners. It looked like an annoyed frown, but was an attempt at a smile. He sunk into a vacant chair.

Jake stopped talking. "Who are you?"

"I'm Jeffry."

Jake pointed at him. "I'm not even going to ask you why you were late..."

Jeffry feigned surprise at the perceived attack, "I didn't know!"

Jake pointed at the other boys, "They didn't know, either, but they came down to find out what the next steps were. This is a HARD program. Your tryouts will demand more from you than you have to offer. If you are late, or we ever have to come find you, you're out!"

Jeffry's mouth was open. "Ah!" For some reason, he couldn't believe that he was being singled out.

Jake shook his head. He was amused that there was one in every bunch. "I'm gonna tell you right now. If I don't like your attitude, you're out!" He pointed at Christopher. "If he doesn't like your attitude, you're out!" He pointed back at Jeffry. "You got that?"

Jeffry finally softened a bit. "Yeah."

Jake pointed at the other guys, "You got that?"

They all nodded, "Yes!" "Absolutely!" "Of course!" "Oh, yeah!"

Jake smiled, and it wasn't comforting. It was a bit unnerving. "I am the nicest guy you will EVER meet, but I don't put up with bullshit. Not ever. Not even for one second. I don't have time for it."

No one said anything for a solid minute.

Jake smiled and continued briefing the boys on what was expected of them during the tryouts. He finished up, excused himself, and said he would see them at the training facility in the morning.

Christopher took over and told them to relax. They would have dinner soon, then they should just take it easy, wind down, and get ready for a good night's sleep.

The guys talked about working out before dinner. Christopher stood up and with a chuckle said, "Don't work out. Just relax. I've been here a while. Take my word for it. I've seen guys work out, give it 100%, and then hate life when tryouts start. Jake wasn't kidding when he said that they expect 150% from you. Rest today. Trust me. I've been through it, myself, and you guys will be smart to take advice from the trainers."

That quieted them down.

Christopher asked them if they were hungry. All of them followed him into the kitchen, except Jeffry, who went back up to his room.

The guys had a snack, and Christopher showed them around. There was a huge living room, in which they just had their meeting, a den, and an entertainment room with both Holographic and Virtual Televisions. Outside, there was a beautiful patio kitchen, with grill, sink, oven, three large low tables with couch seating, a long stone bar with a dozen stools, and a giant turquoise pool, with a hot tub at each end.

The four trainees became very excited, talking about taking a swim.

Christopher put a stop to that. "Sorry guys, no swimming tonight."

"What?!?" Scott sounded like a child denied a Christmas present.

"Sorry, not until after tryouts. You'll thank me." Christopher motioned them back into the house. "Dinner is at 7, when the trainees get back."

It was two hours until dinner. The guys settled into the

entertainment room, except for Jeffry. They talked about wrestling, wrestling, wrestling, and the other wrestlers who would be there for dinner. Rory was beside himself. He was sitting there with three like-minded individuals, and couldn't believe how fast they seemed to have bonded.

Just before 7, the first vanload of trainees arrived. The guys came out into the entryway to meet them. The trainees were sweaty, dirty, and beat, but they couldn't help but be amused by the exhilaration of Rory and his band of rookies.

Rory, Bravon, Eb, and Scott stood there smiling, eager to introduce themselves. A couple guys just sort of nodded at them, then headed upstairs. Rory was surprised that two of them were older, in their late thirties or early forties, and were huge mountains of muscle and beef.

One went straight into the kitchen, but smacked a hand or two as he walked by and said, "Hey Newbies!"

The other three stopped and talked to them. There was Landin, a handsome white guy in his early twenties, and Ricky, a handsome black guy he introduced as his boyfriend. Tagging behind them was Adam, a bubbly, ginger white boy. He was feminine, but very friendly.

Those three excused themselves just as another 6 trainees arrived. Two muscle boys immediately made a b-line over to the four new boys. Marky was an Italian/Irish mix, and his friend Vinny O was an Italian-American bodybuilder, both Jersey types around 5'9", cocky, and very out-going. They seemed genuinely excited to see the new guys, and talked about how they couldn't wait to get their hands on the newbie's. Everybody laughed.

A Japanese/American guy named Hide made his way over. He was as short as Vinny, but looked about 40 pounds of muscle bigger. He was a 35 year-old tiny muscle monster. Then, there was Martinez, a cute Mexican boy in his early 20's, and Reeves, and big, black bodybuilder in his late 20's.

Marky and Vinny started trash-talking Hide, and a playful skirmish broke out. Christopher poked his head out of the kitchen, "HEY!" Everybody stopped. "Dinner in five."

All the guys, who just arrived, headed upstairs to clean up as the two Man-Mountains, who arrived in the first load, were coming down. The bigger one, Clint, nodded to the four newbie's, "Hey guys! How's it going?" He was 40 years old, with short black hair, 6 feet 4 inches tall, and 310 pounds of power lifting muscle. His resting face was hard and tough, and made him look mean as hell, but he smiled easily and often. "I'm Clint, and this is Sterling."

They all shook hands. Sterling was 6 feet 2 inches tall, blond, a bit scruffy, and only 275 pounds. He was a little chunkier than Clint, but obviously had been lifting weights his whole life.

Clint hooked a thumb up, indicating upstairs, "What's with that other guy in your group?"

"Uhhh…" Rory, Bravon, Eb, and Scotty all looked at each other.

Sterling smirked. "Is he always such a little cunt?"

The four broke up in nervous laughter.

"We stuck our heads in to say 'Hi' and he blew us off."

Clint scowled.

"Yeah, we don't know. We just met him at the airport, and he hasn't been cool with any of us, either." Bravon shrugged.

"I'll have a talk with him after dinner. That attitude won't fly here." Clint's huge arms outstretched and he sort of corralled everyone toward the dining room.

At dinner the new guys met the remaining trainees. There was Sean, a tall, white, extremely handsome clean-cut model-type in his early 20's and Marcos, a Latin, suave, lothario sort of gentleman.

Everybody was friendly, except, of course, Jeffry. All the guys tried to talk to him. A couple times he seemed to make an effort, but he kept receding back into himself.

They spent a good two hours at the dinner table. As the time wore on everyone's personalities really started to show. A couple guys were over-bearing, one or two were more reserved, but all in all, they seemed to be a cohesive group. There was a palpable sense of camaraderie. Rory liked it, a lot.

After dinner, the twelve trainees calmed down. Most of them showered and went to bed. They had given the five newbie's a lot of advice, and the one thing they all agreed on was, "Get as much sleep as you can. You're gonna need it!"

Rory, Bravon, Eb, and Scott were the last at the table. They cleared their dishes, then retired to their rooms.

Jeffry was lying on his bed, reading a book. He ignored them when they came in. Bravon stripped out of his clothes right away, and stood bare-naked, as he pulled a fresh pair of boxers out of his bag to sleep in. Rory couldn't help but look at Bravon's perfect bubble butt. He wished he could touch it. He glanced sideways and noticed that Jeffry was also looking.

There was a knock at the door. Rory took a step toward it, as Bravon said, "Come in", and pulled up his boxers.

It was Clint, fresh from the shower, wearing only a towel. His chest and shoulders were huge. He had a belly, but it looked hard as a rock. "Can I come in for a second?"

Rory stepped aside, "Sure."

Jeffry looked annoyed, and held up his book, thinking he wasn't a part of this.

Clint sat down on the end of Jeffry's bed, and glared at him, daring him to say something about it. He didn't, but at least he put the book down in his lap.

Clint motioned the other guys to sit down. They did, on the edge of their bed, facing Clint.

"A couple things I wanted to tell you guys. First of all, Jeffry, is it? You gotta drop your attitude, and I mean, now!" Clint looked directly at him.

Jeffry scowled.

"Seriously. You're not gonna make it here like that. If you don't have my back, if you don't have their backs..." He pointed at Rory and Bravon, "then we won't have your back. And, you'll be all alone."

Jeffry wasn't totally convinced.

Clint sat up, his huge chest puffed out, "How much do you weigh?"

Jeffry cocked his head, still not amused, "152 pounds."

Clint laughed. "Yeah, I'm 310 pounds. We are going to be working together. If you don't have my trust, when I go to slam you, or I have to do a leg drop on you, how do you think that's gonna end up? Which one of us do you think is gonna get hurt?"

Jeffry started to see his point.

"So, can we start over?" Clint extended a hand to Jeffry.

Jeffry lightened up, "Ok", and shook the huge man's hand.

Clint pointed at Rory and Bravon, again. "You guys all better have each other's backs. You're a team now, whether you like it, or not. You guys will all make each other, or break each other."

Bravon nodded, "That's cool. I didn't think of it like that, before."

Rory liked Clint.

Clint got up. "Oh, yeah, and one other thing. Do yourself a favor: Don't jack off, suck each other off, or fuck each other, until after tryouts."

Rory giggled, then stopped himself, "Wait, what?"

Bravon had a huge dopey smile on his face, "For real?"

Even Jeffry perked up, with an almost shocked, inquisitive expression.

"Oh, yeah. It takes you off your game, puts you just a beat behind. Wait 'til you make it, and you're in training. You'll see. We've all done it." Clint smiled, pointed at them, "We're all cool?"

Jeffry nodded.

Rory nodded, "Yeah, absolutely!"

Bravon put his thumb up, "Thanks, Clint."

Clint let himself out. "See you guys tomorrow."

Bravon looked over at Jeffry, who went back to reading his book. "So, Jeffry, we're cool, too?"

Jeffry put his book down, again. "Yeah, we're ok."

Rory added, "Yeah, cause I'd really like us all to be friends. I'm more than happy to have your back anytime you need it."

Jeffry didn't smile, but seemed a little different. "Yeah, all right, that's cool."

He pushed his lips together, and made it look like a smile, but his eyes didn't follow along.

Bravon stood up. "Ok, cool."

Rory stood up, and stripped down to his yellow briefs. He pulled on a pair of gym shorts, and picked up his toiletry bag.

Bravon had his toothbrush and toothpaste in hand. They both left the room.

There was only one empty bathroom. Bravon stood aside to let Rory enter.

"I just gotta pee. I'm cool with that if you are." Rory walked in.

Bravon followed, "That's cool. I gotta pee, too."

Rory peed while Bravon starting brushing his teeth. He looked over at Rory, "Damn. I was gonna ask you to *help* me out, before we went to bed." He started brushing.

"What?" Rory finished peeing, shook his penis, pulled his briefs and shorts back up, and turned around. "*Help* you with what?"

Bravon smiled, with the toothbrush sticking out of his mouth, "You know."

Rory couldn't help but smile, too. "But... what? I thought you were straight."

"I am. But, I fool around with guys, when I have to. Who doesn't?" Bravon turned to the mirror and slowly gave attention to each tooth, individually.

"I'm, uh, into guys... only." Rory blushed, as he prepared his own toothbrush.

Bravon shrugged and looked at Rory in the mirror. "That's cool... Aren't you totally wired, though? I feel like there is no way I could go to sleep."

Rory nodded.

Bravon spit out, into the sink, "I'm wired, I'm horny, I wanna fight, and I am so fucking excited to get in that ring tomorrow."

Rory smiled. "I'm exactly the same. THIS is what I've wanted to do my whole life. I want to wrestle, and wrestle, and wrestle, right now!"

Bravon rinsed his mouth out. "And, how can YOU fucking stand it? Just having all these guys around me makes me want to... I don't fucking know what! Did you SEE the size of Clint?"

Rory shook his head, and pointed at Bravon, "Promise you will NEVER tell anyone what I am about to tell you?"

Bravon turned to him and nodded, "Hell yeah. What?"

Rory was almost shaking, "I just wanna... I mean... " He clenched his fists together, and his whole body flexed as he thrust his hips forward, "I wanna just, BAM! BAM! BAM!" He pounded one of his palms with a hammer fist, as he held his toothbrush in his mouth with gritted teeth.

Bravon was laughing. "You act like that's a secret! Even I feel like that, right now!"

Rory whispered, "In high school, I was invited to some pool parties that were all guys. I never went, but I think about it all the time, and NOW I'm in this house with all these HOT wrestlers and that's all I want to do - just wrestle them all over this fucking house!!!"

Bravon couldn't stop laughing, "What? Why didn't you ever go?"

Rory spit out, "I'll tell you sometime. It's a long story." He rinsed his mouth out and started flossing his teeth.

"Oh man, I forgot mine. Can I borrow some?"

Rory handed the dental floss canister to Bravon. "So, what are we gonna do tonight? How are we gonna get some sleep?"

They stood there in the mirror, flossing together, both of them laughing, as it struck them funny.

Bravon asked, "Some kind of relaxation breathing exercises?"

7 ALL WORLDS PRO WRESTLING TRAINING FACILITY

The facade of the All Worlds Pro Wrestling Training Facility was impressive enough, but when Rory stepped inside and saw what was waiting for him, he almost cried. Photos did not do it justice. The ceilings were over fifty feet high, and a football field could have fit inside. There were 7 rings, broadcast cameras, and an amazingly modern workout facility. Rory's knees started to shake.

Bravon put his arm around Rory's shoulder, "Can you believe this?"

Eb did the same to Scotty, and said, "I'm so fucking excited, I'm gonna fucking cum right now!" Scott picked him up and spun him around.

Even Jeffry managed a smile.

All the trainers and trainees were already working out, some in the rings.

Max gave them a quick tour as he led them to the locker room. Again, Rory's knees were shaking. It was shiny and new, and as clean as a whistle. His entire fantasy was perfect down to the tiniest detail.

Max assigned them lockers, then gave another one of his speeches. "There are NO maids in this facility. YOU are required to leave every inch of this place cleaner than when you found it. Is that understood?"

The guys nodded, happy to accept any terms just to be there.

"Get suited up. Meet me at the practice ring in five minutes!" Max left the locker room.

The guys changed quickly into gym shorts and tees, except Jeffry, who appeared to be sporting some kind of tight yoga ensemble. They were done and out in three minutes, and practically ran to the practice ring.

Max was there with Big Jake and two other men, one of whom made their mouths drop and their tongues hang out. Rory couldn't believe his eyes. Standing there, not more than six feet away was Dyer Anderson. Rory looked him up and down, three times. He was wearing a tight black t-shirt and gym shorts.

Max put his hand on the shoulder of the first man, "This is Bart Kolchek."

Once more the newbies were in awe. Rory hadn't noticed him because of Dyer Anderson, but Bart Kolchek was also known as Bart Colt, a former champ and tag team partner of Big Jake's. He was a very handsome dark-haired 40 year-old man, 6 feet 4 inches tall, and 254 pounds of smooth muscle. He wasn't cut, or ripped, but a strapping, beautiful man. He was a baby-face, but when he wrestled with Big Jake, he was as tough as they come.

Bart was one of Rory's favorite wrestlers, and he smiled at

Rory when Max introduced them. Rory smiled back, but had to look away. He felt that Bart would be able to see what he was really thinking.

Then Max pointed at Dyer Anderson, "And, I'm sure you guys know this loser."

Dyer shook his head, and smirked. "You son of a bitch."

It had only been a few weeks since he had lost his belt to Chris Enos, in that unusual match, with the climactic ending.

Anderson's legs looked even thicker than they did in virtual TV, and Rory had the strongest urge to hug this huge, beefy man.

Rory made a wish that he would be alone with Dyer at some point, so he could ask him about every detail of his matches with Chris Enos. During the introductions, he lingered on Rory, held his hand after the shake, and asked, "Wait, what's your name?"

"Rory... Uh, Rory Pedersen." Rory held on to that big, meaty paw and felt something. He had to adjust his gym shorts.

Dyer smiled and gave him a wink.

Jake started the tryouts with some warm ups, stretching, and cooperation exercises. He explained, "Even though you will eventually be competing against each other, *if* you are chosen, during tryouts I need you to work as a team. There will be no injuries or blood on my watch. Even when I have you spar, you will be looking out for each other's safety. Do I have everyone's agreement?" He went down the line and pointed at each of them, individually, making sure they all answered in the affirmative.

When he got to Jeffry, he asked again, "You agree to cooperate with me AND your fellow trainees?"

"Yes!" Jeffry didn't give him any attitude.

After the warm up, Jake got them all in the ring, and had each of them demonstrate all the basic Pro wrestling moves and holds: arm bars and arm drags, dropkicks, suplexes, headlocks, nelsons, etc. Since there were five of them, they went in a round robin style of rotation, being giver and receiver.

Rory, Bravon, and Scott knew all the moves and holds Jake threw at them. The ones Eb and Jeffry didn't know, they picked up on quickly. Rory was surprised at how good Jeffry was. He thought, because of his attitude he would not know what he was doing. He became frustrated a few times, but kept up.

Then Jake brought in some of the trainees they met the night before. Clint, Hide, and Sterling stepped in the ring. They were all wearing gym shorts, and tee shirts, like the newbie's.

Clint smiled, and winked at Jeffry, "Remember me, little guy?"

Jeffry blushed.

Jake smacked Clint's big shoulder, and gave the five newbie's a rather evil grin. "This is my favorite part of the tryout. See these guys? They're gonna work holds and moves on you, and we are gonna see how much you can take."

Clint, Hide, and Sterling rubbed their hands together in an effort to psyche out the newbie's. It worked, only partially. Jeffry was the only one who appeared worried. The other four guys smiled, and became even more excited.

Jake noticed this, and called out, "Jeffry!" He pointed to a spot on the canvas just in front of Clint. "Step up!"

Jeffry walked up in front of Clint, and looked up at him. Clint looked like a huge, adult man standing in front of a toddler.

"But... I would never face a guy this size." Jeffry was properly scared.

Jake pointed to Jeffry's four peers. "Oh yeah? These guys wanna face him. So, get ready."

Clint patted Jeffry's shoulder, then clamped on, grabbed his crotch, and hoisted him up. Jeffry kicked and held on to Clint's shoulder, for dear life.

Clint smiled, "You ready?"

Jeffry kicked more, "NO! NO!"

"Well, get ready, cause it's happening!" Clint lifted him high, then, WHAM slammed him down. He bounced, slid, and ended up at the feet of his four fellow trainees. They bent down to help him up.

"NO! DON'T TOUCH HIM!" Jake motioned them back. "We need to see how well you can hold up to what can happen to you in a real match."

Jeffry was on his back, rolling in pain.

Jake stood over him. "Get up! Stand up!"

Jeffry glared up at him, rolled over, crawled to the ropes, and slowly pulled himself up. He struggled to catch his breath, then turned and gave Jake and Clint another dirty look.

"GOOD JOB!" Jake was impressed. He thought Jeffry might cry, or something.

Clint walked over to Jeffry and lightly squeezed his shoulder. "You ok, Jeffry?"

Jeffry nodded.

Jake pointed at Jeffry. "That's what I want to see. Whatever happens to you: keep going! Good job."

Jake had Hide, Clint, and Sterling slam them, clothesline them, scissor them, drop legs and elbows on them, and anything else wrestlers might do to each other in a match. They all recovered fairly quickly. Jeffry stopped glaring at one point, and the other four stopped smiling at one point. They all just tried to hang on and survive.

Finally, Jake called an end to this portion of the tryouts, and gave the guys a break. "Lunch, guys. Then strip down to your best gear, and back here in 30."

The guys were beat. This was the hardest workout they ever had, and the day was only half over.

When they returned from the break, Jake was standing in the ring with three different trainees lined up against the opposite ropes. There was Vinny O, the Jersey Bodybuilder boy, his friend

Marky, and Adam, the redhead boy with freckles.

Vinny O's body was amazing. Every wrestler, in the facility, had a nice one, but Vinny's was as near to perfect as a human could achieve. He was 5'8", 200 pounds, completely clean-shaven, tan, and even his eyebrows and hair were perfectly groomed. He wore white mid-calf boots and tiny powder-blue posing trunks that just covered his package and part of his ass. His hard muscle butt cheeks peeked out the bottom.

Dyer Anderson was in the corner, just outside the ropes, leaning on them. He was in his Royal Blue trunks, matching boots and nothing else. Rory peered at him out of the corner of his eye. He had a funny feeling in his stomach. All this man-flesh standing around him was distracting enough, but to have the 280-pound ex champ so close made it impossible to focus.

The newbie's were also suited up, nervous, but proud. Bravon was the tallest, at 6 feet 2 inches. His 225 pound body was tight and muscular. He looked amazing in his shiny black trunks with silver crossed swords sewn on the crotch. Scott wore simple navy pro trunks. He was a total white boy, with extra white skin, and a lean jock body, at 5 feet 10 inches, 180 pounds. Then, Eb was a bit more in character. He had on long black sheer tights with random holes, small black trunks, black kneepads, shiny black boots that laced all the way up, and shiny wrist gauntlets to match. Eb also had an athletic body under all that glam. At 5 feet 9 inches and 175 pounds, he was similarly built to Scott, but his skin wasn't pale, it was sort of an almond shade, and glimmered with just a touch of body oil. Rory was impressed.

Jeffry's body also surprised Rory. At 5'7", 152lbs, he was the smallest guy there, but he was also the most ripped, with completely etched out abs. He even had pecs that looked big and tight on his frame, and wore tiny metallic purple wrestling trunks.

Then there was Rory, himself, who didn't notice the other guys checking him out. His 6', 200lb lean muscle body looked inviting in his small yellow trunks, boots and wrist bands to match. Dyer Anderson made no pretense and stared openly at him.

Jake went down the line, and gave them each the once-over. He and Dyer pointed out what they liked and didn't like about this new group, but over all, they weren't displeased.

He started the next part of the training session. "Remember when I said that last thing was my favorite part? Well, THIS part is my favorite, actually."

Marky, Adam, and Vinny laughed.

Jake called out, "Which one of you thinks you're the toughest guy in the group?"

None of them was dumb enough to claim that.

Jake nodded, a grin on his face. "Ok, then. Which one of you guys is *totally* straight?"

Bravon looked at Rory. Scott and Eb looked at each other and avoided eye contact with the others. Jeffry sneered at the question. Bravon shrugged, and his hand slowly came up.

"Nice!" Jake's hand made a quick jerk toward himself. "Come 'ere!"

Bravon cautiously walked over. Jake took Bravon by the shoulders and positioned him across from Adam, who was licking his lips and sizing Bravon up, below the waist.

Jake narrated to the guys trying out, "Ok, let's say you're in a match, and you get your opponent in a headlock." He snapped his fingers at Bravon. "Go ahead, get him in a headlock."

Bravon was tentative, but he loosely wrapped his arm around Adam's head, as Adam bent down for him.

Jake frowned. "Is that the way *you* apply a headlock?"

Adam smacked Bravon's stomach, "Come on, I can take it!"

Bravon looked at his fellow trainees, all of whom were just as anxious as he was. He then proceeded to crank the headlock as tight as he could. Adam gurgled and held on.

Jake smiled. "Then, your opponent decides to take matters into his own hands."

At that point, Adam showed all the trainees his right hand, then took it and wrapped his fingers around Bravon's ample bulge. Bravon gasped, and grabbed at Adam's wrist, while Adam's fingers squeezed.

Vinny O and Marky laughed.

Jake smiled. He loved it. "So, you're gonna let go of your headlock and give him the advantage?"

Adam let out an evil laugh, and began pulling and playing with Bravon, who was now grimacing.

Bravon looked at Jake, then down at Adam. He pulled himself back into the moment, wrapped his arm back around Adam's head, took a few quick steps, then hip tossed Adam over onto the canvas, flat on his back. As he did this, Adam's grip was RIPPED away, and Bravon was left in agony. He yelled out, and held his aching bulge.

This time Jake laughed, along with Marky, Vinny O, and Adam, who slowly rolled up to his feet. Bravon gave Jake a dirty look, then traded looks with his compatriots. Rory and Scott had big, compassionate eyes for him. Eb was intrigued and Jeffry looked like a hungry wolf, who was blissfully eager to be involved in the same predicament.

"Walk if off, man." Jake motioned Bravon to return to his place in line, against the ropes.

Adam traded congratulatory handshakes and smacks with Marky and Vinny O.

Bravon backed up next to Rory, keeping his eye on Jake and the guy who just humiliated him in front of his friends.

Rory grabbed Bravon's shoulder, "You ok?"

Bravon nodded and said in a low voice, "Yeah, yeah!" He wanted to just move on, silently.

Jake pointed at Rory. "You're next, Pretty Boy."

Rory gulped. Up until this moment, all he ever wanted to do was become a part of the wrestling world, and one of its biggest attractions was the opportunity to do what was just done to his friend, Bravon. But, at this moment, the last thing he wanted was for anyone, especially The Ex World Champion, who had made him sexually excited on so many occasions, to find out about this particular proclivity. He inhaled, taking as much time as he could to walk over to Big Jake Colt. His anxiety was palpable.

"What's wrong, Pretty Boy? If you're afraid to have your

eggs scrambled, then you won't be able to make it in this business." Jake's hand rested on Rory's shoulder.

Rory jolted upright. He suppressed a hurt expression. "I can take it!"

Jake had that evil grin, again, "Good!" He snapped his fingers.

Marky had already come up behind Rory. He trapped him in a full nelson, as Vinny O stepped forward and clamped a hard hand around his bulge.

"Aghh.. unnh." Rory knew it was coming, and internally scolded himself for not being ready.

Jake stepped back, "You're in a tag team match. If you're outwrestling your opponents, the first thing they're gonna do is go for the gold."

Bravon stepped forward, about to help Rory out.

Jake anticipated this, and stepped in front of him, with his hand up. "So, whatta ya gonna do. How are you gonna get out of it, if your partner can't get in to save you?"

Rory looked over at Bravon. He got his feet firmly on the ground, and pushed himself and Marky back into the ropes. Vinny O followed, at an arms length, his hand still holding on to Rory's now hard bulge.

Rory got one foot up, and was able to tap Vinny's bulge with it, causing him to release his grip.

"Oh...Unh!" Vinny was smiling. He obviously liked that. He massaged the tip of his bulge lightly with his fingertips.

Marky held on to the nelson, and whispered in Rory's ear. "Nope. You gotta work Vinny harder than that, if you wanna get away."

As Vinny stepped forward, Rory threw his legs up and caught him around the waist in a leg scissor.

Vinny's eyes closed. He rubbed Rory's muscular thighs and moaned. His hands slid up to the top, just to where Rory's trunks met his thighs, then both hands clamped on to Rory's completely erect bulge.

The three of them moaned and groaned, and tried to out-do each other.

Jake pointed at them. "Ok, now, that's some HOT action!"

Dyer climbed into the ring. "I'll say." He walked over to the three, to get a closer look.

Rory kept his eyes on Vinny, knowing that if he looked at Mr. Anderson, he would lose it.

Jake stepped forward and patted Vinny O on the shoulder. "Ok, break it up, guys."

Vinny O let go, and rubbed Rory's thighs. Rory let go, and planted his feet back on the ground. Marky released his nelson, and Rory leaned back against him for a second, trying to adjust his trunks. He had a very noticeable erection, and was blushing bright red. He kept his head down.

Vinny rubbed Rory's head, sporting his own erection, now. "You're a fucking hot fighter, man."

Jake could see that Rory was mortified about his boner, so

he pointed it out to everyone. "THAT will happen. And frankly it's what your fans want to see!"

Dyer put his arm around Rory's shoulder, and walked him a couple feet beyond Jake, Marky, and Vinny. He said, in a low voice, "You ok, man?"

"Uh, yeah!" Rory wasn't. He knew that his woody would never go away, now that Dyer Anderson's arm was on him - that big, beefy, mass of muscle.

To make matters worse, Anderson leaned his body into Rory. "That was really fucking hot! We can see that you love it, AND you got this whole turmoil thing going on!"

Rory let out another long, hard breath. He wanted to disappear. He understood that they liked his involuntary physical reaction, but he couldn't shake the feelings of embarrassment. He just wanted to get on with the tryouts, "Thank you, Mr. Anderson."

Mr. Anderson bumped him with his hip, "Call me Dyer."

Dyer removed his arm from Rory, who turned quickly to walk back to his place against the ropes. Dyer smacked his butt, and said, "Good going, kid!"

Rory kept his eyes on the canvas as he stepped back to his spot between Bravon and Eb.

Bravon grabbed the back of his neck, and laughed. "Wow man!"

Eb leaned into him, and whispered, "So fucking hot!"

Rory just grunted an unintelligible, "Thank you."

Eb was called up next. Unlike Bravon and Rory, he was ready. Marky stood in front of him and Vinny shifted back toward the opposite ropes. Eb focused on Marky, who was trying to lock up with him, but Eb got a hold of his fingers, in an attempt to keep his hands busy.

Vinny snuck back behind Eb and began pulling his tights down. When Eb's hands shot behind himself to stop it, Vinny pulled his arms back and up in a hammerlock.

Marky was now free to do whatever he wanted. He smiled and looked Eb directly in the eyes.

Eb shook his head, "No!"

Marky slid his hand inside Eb's tights, causing Eb's body to convulse. Marky slowly fished around before clamping down hard.

"No! Man... What the fuck?" Eb tried to kick, and pull his arms loose, but he was trapped between the two Muscley Jersey boys.

Scott leapt forward and shot a quick look to Jake, who simply stepped back and made a welcoming arm sweep toward the action. Scott rushed behind Marky, clamped his arms around him and pulled him back away from Eb.

Marky was completely taken by surprise. He gripped Scott's wrists, trying to pull them apart. Scott threw Mark up and over in a German Suplex.

Vinny was also surprised. Eb planted his feet down hard, and pushed them back into the corner.

Scott was up, facing Marky, who was slower to get to his feet.

Marky's smile was back, and Scott was ready to take him down, again.

Jake stepped forward, "Ok guys! Excellent!"

Scott moved in on Marky, still in fight-mode.

Jake clamped a hand on Scott's shoulder, "Ok, that's it, guys!"

Scott settled down.

Marky grabbed Scotty's right hand and pulled him in for a quick back pat, "Nice work, man!"

Vinny let go of Eb, and they both stepped out of the corner. He rubbed Eb's chest, "Nice!"

Scott turned to Eb, "You ok?"

Eb put his hand on Scott's shoulder and walked him back to their spot against the rope, "I'm good. Thanks Scotty."

Jake snapped his finger and pointed at Scott. "Wait! You're not done!"

"Uh oh." Scott smiled and shook his head nervously.

"Let's turn the action around." Jake pointed at Vinny O. "You! Keep Eb trapped in the corner." He pointed to the corner where Eb just had Vinny. "Make sure he can't get out and help his partner."

Eb walked over, and leaned against the ring post. Vinny pressed his back against him and rested his hands on the ropes.

Jake grabbed Scott by the shoulder and turned him,

"Marky. Bear hug him from the back!"

Marky stood behind him, and Scott got ready. Marky didn't touch Scott for a few seconds to build the tension.

Vinny O planted his feet down on the canvas, and clamped his fingers around the ropes, pressing Eb back into the corner.

Scott looked over and Marky made his move. He wrapped his arms around Scott, one hand clamped to his own wrist, the other clamped on Scott's balls. His arms squeezed Scott's waist at the same time his fingers squeezed Scott's nuts.

"Anghh!" Scott clawed at Marky's arms. His whole body jerked as he tried to pull Marky's hand away from his aching balls.

Marky lifted Scott up off his feet then brought him back down, his feet pounding the canvas with a THUD!

"AACHHH!" Scott's mouth hung open and his whole body convulsed.

Meanwhile, Eb stopped trying to power out of the corner, and decided to use some dirty tactics, himself. His arms wrapped around Vinny's waist. One hand had a handful of balls, and the fingers of the other hand pulled Vinny's erect penis in the opposite direction. Vinny's tiny poser trunks were being stretched, and he was now half exposed.

"Ooh! Unhhh!" Vinny had a huge smile on his face. He was in pain, but didn't hate it. "Oh... man... uhnn... stop!... Let go!" He told Eb to let go, but his own hands never left the ropes, and never attempted to physically stop the attack on his private parts.

Marky was still bear-hugging Scott, and manually working

his balls. Scott's usually white face was now apple-red. He grabbed Marky's forearms and held on tight. He spread his legs out in front of him, so his weight caused Marky to hunch over just a bit. Then Scott pushed his feet into the canvas. He was able to force them back against the ropes.

Jake stepped between the two couples of wrestling meat, "Ok, guys!"

Marky loosened his grip, but didn't let go. He whispered into Scott's ear, "Fucking, fucking, fucking hot!"

Scott gingerly pulled Mark's hands away from his throbbing balls. He took a step forward and lightly massaged them. "Oh, man!"

Vinny didn't let go of the ropes, so Eb didn't let go of his cock or balls.

Jake smacked Vinny in the chest, "Ok, enough already."

Vinny closed his eyes, let out a deep breath and let go of the ropes.

Eb released his grip on Vinny's penis and testicles. Vinny continued leaning against him, with his eyes closed. Eb's hands slid up Vinny's abs to his big, ripped pecs, and he moved Vinny forward, then stepped out of the corner. He walked over to Scott, and wrapped his arm around his shoulder, "How you doin', Scotty?"

Scott smiled gritted his teeth, and drew in some air, with a pained smile. "I'm doing great."

Vinny stepped forward, half of his very noticeable erection

still exposed. He messed up Scott and Eb's hair, and said, "Good job, guys! ... Can't wait for 'Part Two'", his erection bouncing whenever he moved.

Marky also congratulated the other tag team, then pointed at Vinny O's big boner. "He's back!" They both laughed, and Marky flicked it with his finger, as Vinny flinched. "Aah!"

Eb once again led Scott back to their spot, his arm still around his shoulder.

Jake congratulated them, "You guys are all doing pretty well! I'm impressed!" He pointed at Jeffry. "Let's see if you can keep it up!"

Jeffry smirked and sauntered right up to Jake. He threw his hands up, and jutted his pelvis out. "Bring it!"

Jake gave him a sideways glance. "Ok." He snapped at Adam, who was chomping at the bit.

As Adam made his way over to his victim, Jeffry turned to him, his arms still up, the front of his trunks totally vulnerable.

Adam ran his fingers down Jeffry's chest, abs, and slowly across his bulge. He felt around for a moment, then wrapped his fingers around the entire bulge and gave a quick PULL.

"Unh!" Jeffry's body flexed. "Is that all you got?"

Adam shifted his stance, and his arm trembled as he worked to get a tighter grip.

Jeffry moaned, "Mmmm. What is this? A massage?" His hands glided along Adam's pale chest, and his fingers gripped the sides of his pectoral muscles. He clawed them, HARD.

"AAAH!" Adam let out a quick snort.

Jeffry pushed them over to the ropes, Adam's back against them. They both worked their clawing, clamping fingers against each other.

Jake nodded. He was impressed, again.

Jeffry managed to push Adam so he was leaning back over the ropes. SAAA-MACK! Jeffry delivered a hard, fast forearm smash across Adam's now red chest.

Jake nodded to the other newbies. "Well, I guess we have a winner!" He snapped his fingers, "Ok, guys! Good work!"

Adam let go, and Jeffry gave Adam's pecs two quick taps with his hands before stepping back. He turned to face his peers, sporting a pair of tented trunks. Very cocky, now, he strolled back to his place next to Scott, who greeted him with a high five.

Adam, Marky, and Vinny O regrouped and made comments about the action to each other.

Dyer stepped in, next to Jake and smiled at the newbie's.

Jake was nodding, "Well! All of you can take some abuse, that's for sure." He pointed at Jeffry, "Some more than others. We had to make sure you can take it. We've had guys freeze up when their cock and balls come into play. As you all know: totally fair game. And, in case you didn't know, in your first few matches, that's what your opponents will go for. They're gonna test you, and try to throw you off your game. And, probably a lot harder than these three did." He gestured toward Marky, Vinny O, and Adam.

Jake put his hand on Dyer's shoulder, "And, sometimes, that's all they'll work on."

Dyer closed his eyes, shook his head and let out a deep breath.

"But!" Jake continued, "That's all we want to see of those kinds of tactics during your tryouts! We know you can take 'em, and anyone can do 'em. Now, we just want to know how good you can wrestle, and how good a show you can put on!"

The guys stared at him. No one said a word

"Is that understood?" Jake put his hand to his ear.

All the newbie's answered in the affirmative.

"Excellent!" Jake pointed at the three trainees. "Ok, thank these guys for helping out. You won't be working with them, again, until tomorrow."

Adam blew the newbie's a kiss, and climbed out of the ring.

Vinny O pointed at the newbie's, then at the semi he was still sporting in his trunks, and said, "Hot action, guys! Can't wait to get a hold of you for more." He and Marky laughed.

Marky gave a quick head pump to the guys, "Good job!" He grabbed the front of Vinny's trunks and gave it a yank. "Come on, man, let's go!"

"Anh!" Vinny smiled, gave them a head pump, and followed Marky out of the ring.

Jake rolled his eyes, "And, those are the guys you'll be

working with, if you make it through try outs." He clasped his hands together in front of him. "Next, you're gonna take a break, then back here for some round robin sparring. You can keep your pro gear on, or change back into your gym clothes – whichever is more comfortable for you." He clapped his hands twice. "Ok, back here in 15!"

The guys filed out of the ring.

Dyer and Jake conferred with each other, while looking at them, and pointing.

The newbie's all made their way to the locker room to pee. As they walked, Bravon nudged Jeffry with his elbow, "So, you got balls of steel, huh?"

Jeffry threw his head back, "You better fucking rec-o-nize!"

The guys all laughed, and talked about how weird that last part of the tryouts was, but how hot it was, as well.

Bravon and Rory finished up and made their way out to a table set up with snacks and water. They grabbed stuff and sat down.

Scott came out and sat next to Rory. "Hey! Was it weird getting, you know..."

Rory didn't know, exactly. "Whatta ya mean?"

Scott blushed and leaned in closer, "You know. Getting a boner in front of everyone."

Now, Rory blushed... again.

Scott became very animated. "Being in that ring was everything, but I was really nervous that I was going to pop one, too!" He maintained eye contact with Rory.

Rory looked away. "I know. It was..."

Bravon leaned in, "No! I'm sorry. I thought it was pretty hot. We couldn't look away." Bravon leaned in all the way, a hand on both of Rory's shoulders. "And, Dyer FUCKING Anderson! He was getting off on it!"

"Shut up!" Rory let out an anxious laugh.

"Oh yeah! I was watching him! He was really into it!" Bravon playfully shook Rory.

"Yeah!" Scott smacked Rory's arm. "He didn't come over and put his arm around any of us!" Scott lowered his voice. "How cool is it that we are here with guys like Dyer Anderson?!?"

Bravon nodded, "AND, Jake and Bart Colt, AND Max Gunn!"

This was about the hundredth time they talked about "how cool" it was to be meeting some of their favorite wrestling legends.

Scott laughed. "Yeah!"

Rory also nodded and stared off blankly. His dream was coming true, and it contained some of the men he had fantasized about for years.

Eb and Jeffry came over. Eb took the seat next to Scott and leaned into him. He looked over at Bravon and Rory. "You guys gonna change out of your Pro gear?"

"Nope!" Rory had a big, dopey grin on his face.

Bravon twisted his head from side to side. "Hell No!"

Eb was pleased, "Excellent!" He directed his thumb toward Jeffry, "He's not, either."

A sly smile slid across Bravon's face, "You're not?"

"Of course not!" Jeffry adjusted his tiny bikini trunks and his bulge jiggled as he pulled up on the side straps. "I've always wanted to wrestled here, and I'm gonna milk it for ALL it's worth. AND, I want more of what we just had!"

The guys laughed.

Bravon jutted his index finger at Jeffry. "Dude! You might have the toughest balls of any of us!"

Jeffry let out a cocky snort. "No question about it!"

Bravon liked this side of Jeffry's attitude.

The rest of the day was devoted to sparring. Jake warned them that there would be times in their careers when they would be forced to wrestle their friends, especially in the beginning. He then extended both of his arms to point at Eb and Scott. "Everyone, but these two, climb out onto the apron."

Scott shot Eb a concerned look, as the other guys climbed out, and leaned across the top rope in the corner.

Jake directed Eb and Scott to the center of the ring. "Ok.

This is a real match, with real stakes. Your job depends on you winning."

Scott was noticeably uneasy.

Jake could see. He raised his hand, and brought it down with a snap. "Ding! Ding! Start wrestling, guys!"

Eb put his hands up, ready to circle. Scott did the same, but his heart wasn't in it.

Eb grabbed Scott's hands, and looked directly into his eyes. "Come on! Let's just do this! It's ok! Get into it!"

Scott gave one quick snap of a nod. "Ok!" His hands went up, and they began to circle.

They came together in a hard, rough lock up. Eb went down to one knee, and tried to slide around behind Scott, but Scott was too quick. He pivoted, easily, and trapped Eb in a side headlock.

Eb had some moves, but Scott countered every one. He was much faster. Eb would escape a hold, but Scott would get him in another.

When Jake called an end to their sparring, Scott looked worried. Eb was all smiles, though. He hugged Scott, patted his back, and whispered something in his ear.

Jake kept it going. He paired Bravon and Jeffry. It was a comical match. Bravon basically toyed with the much smaller man. Jeffry became frustrated, and resorted to bopping Bravon in the balls.

Even though Jeffry tried to hide it, Jake saw. He yelled out a warning, and Bravon pushed Jeffry, HARD. He flew backwards and landed right on his ass.

Jake made Jeffry get up and start all over. Two minutes later, he was in a headlock, screaming. Once again, he took it to the dirty side, and yanked on Bravon's dick.

"Aaagh!!!" Bravon cradled his pained penis, and when he saw the smug look on Jeffry's face, he lost it. He scooped Jeffry up, and threw him six feet across the ring.

Jeffry landed on his back with a SPLAT, then skidded into the ropes. He slid out under the bottom rope, pounded on the ring apron and screamed at Jake, "THIS ISN'T FAIR!"

Jake shrugged. "Well, I told you NOT to work the cock area, anymore. I told you that! What do you think a guy's gonna do in a real match?"

Jeffry didn't answer.

Jake pointed at Bravon. "Pretty much what HE did, but in a match, he'd follow after you and continue beating the crap out of you!"

Jeffry glared up at him, and whined, "Well, what am I supposed to do? How am I supposed to wrestle a guy his size?"

Jake gave him an incredulous look. "Just the way you were doing it! You were taking it, and you weren't giving up! You think you're gonna dominate every match? HELL NO! Most of you are gonna have your asses handed to you your whole first year of wrestling! So, get used to it! I thought you liked getting worked!"

Jeffry was offended. The other guys kept quiet and traded

looks.

"Now get your attitude in gear and hang out in the corner." He pointed to where the other guys were standing, on the apron.

Next, Jake had Eb and Rory spar. It was similar to Eb's encounter with Scott, except one time when Jake was giving them a tip, Rory turned to look at him, and Eb took the advantage. He was behind Rory, and kicked the back of Rory's knee forward. His arm came up between Rory's legs, and he rolled him up backward for the pin.

Rory kicked out, right away, and it took him a while to regain control.

Eventually, all the guys matched up. Everyone was able to dominate Jeffry. Eb had a particularly good time with that, since he wasn't able to out-wrestle Scott, Rory, or Bravon. Jeffry didn't have much fun, though. He lost his temper a couple more times, and Jake had to tell him to get his attitude in check.

Bravon, Scott, and Rory, all had pretty even match ups, completely give and take. Rory had a harder time with Bravon, mainly because he kept worrying that he would get hard.

They were having the time of their lives, except Jeffry, and he was very relieved when Jake called an end to their day. He had them change, and clear out of the locker room before the trainees finished up. They were packed up in their van, to go home, with a warning to eat dinner, then get to bed. "Tomorrow will be a lot harder."

They were all tired, but chattered on and on about how

amazing the experience was, all the way home in the van, up the stairs to their rooms, and even into the bathrooms to take showers.

Each bathroom had a separate room for communal showers, enough for 6 guys at a time. Bravon, Rory, Eb, and Scott stripped down, and Jeffry went to one of the other bathrooms.

They all began their showers turned away from each other.

Bravon turned to face them. "Oh man! If we weren't told not to get off during tryouts, I'd have all three of you guys working my dick over!" He pulled on the head of his penis.

The guys laughed. Scott and Eb exchanged sideways glances. Rory tried not to touch his own penis. He was really worked up, and already sporting a semi.

Bravon soaped himself up and turned around liberally to talk, while the other guys strictly faced forward. Bravon walked over between Scott and Eb, and put his hands on their shoulders.

Scott looked at Bravon's hand, at Eb, then down.

"You guys are boyfriends, aren't you?" Bravon smiled, as if he was proud of himself.

Eb easily turned to him. "Yeah, we are. "

Scott nodded and said, "Yes", but didn't look up.

"Oh, man! How do you guys keep your hands off each other, while you're here?" Bravon earnestly wanted to know.

Scott blushed.

Eb let out a chuckle, and a deep breath of frustration, "Last night was one of the hardest nights of my life! Literally! I don't know what the hell we are going to do tonight! We might have to sleep in separate rooms. In that ring, I wanted to FUCKING...." Eb clenched his hands tight, and looked over at Scott, who was laughing, blushing, and shaking his head.

Bravon walked over, stood behind Rory, his penis almost touching Rory's butt. "I'm so fucking horny, I don't know how I'm gonna keep 'Prettyboy' off me tonight!" He gripped Rory's shoulders and growled.

Everyone laughed, again, but Rory didn't turn around. His excitement was almost fully realized. He tried to turn away.

Bravon saw, but didn't say anything. He returned to his shower. "We gotta ask the trainees how they do it!"

After their showers, they were slightly mellowed. The day had taken it out of them. The trainees came home and soon after, and dinner was served. The guys who worked with them talked about how fun it was, especially Marky and Vinny O, who pointed at Rory and mouthed, "YOU AND ME!"

Bravon asked his question, which got the guys worked up, "How the hell do you deal with getting so fucking horny around here?"

Clint answered first. "That is THE hardest part of training, and something you're gonna have to find out when you come back."

Bravon liked that answer. "So, YOU think I made it, and I'm coming back?!"

Clint tilted his head and shrugged.

Almost every guy at the table had a story about blue balls, and how hard it was to abstain. They snickered a lot. There was something they weren't telling the newbie's, but Marky did say, "Well, we DO get one day off a week." Clint gave him the "cut" sign, and nothing more was said about it.

After dinner, Scott and Eb went straight to bed. Clint walked Bravon and Rory up. He hung out in the bathroom with them, as they brushed their teeth.

Jeffry was not in the room, yet, when Rory and Bravon retired for the night.

They stripped down to their underwear and climbed in to bed. Neither one was sleepy, so they stared straight up at the ceiling.

Bravon's hand snuck over and brushed Rory's thigh. He pinched the head of Rory's erect penis with his thumb and forefinger.

"Oh!" Rory grabbed Bravon's wrist. "Wait! Stop!" He was surprised and excited, wishing they could act on the urges they both clearly had.

Bravon withdrew his hand, and said with a smile. "Just wanted to make sure you had one, too!"

Rory let out a hard sigh. "Oh, man! That just made it worse!"

"Wanna pinch mine, to get me back?" Bravon turned his head toward Rory.

Rory kept looking straight up at the ceiling. "No! No, I don't! If

I touch it, we're both in big trouble!"

"Oh, FUCK! How are we gonna get to sleep?" Bravon propped his head up on one hand. "For real. How bad would it actually be if we got each other off?" He knew they shouldn't, but felt it wouldn't hurt to ask.

"NO! Just lay down, and relax!" Rory looked him right in the eye and pointed his finger, directing him to lie back down.

"Aacch!" Bravon flopped onto his back, with his hands by his side.

Rory took a deep breath, and let it out slowly. "Just take a deep breath, and relax every part of your body.

Bravon followed Rory as he took another deep breath. They let it in through their nose, and out through their mouth, big and smooth.

Jeffry came in, and heard them both breathing loudly in the dark. He quietly closed the door behind him, and whispered harshly, "You two better not be doing what I think you're doing!"

Bravon and Rory couldn't help but laugh.

"No! We're just trying to relax so we can sleep!" Rory went back to his breathing exercises.

"We can't find a way to fucking calm ourselves down!" Bravon started breathing normally.

Jeffry stripped down, and plopped himself into bed. "Well, you should have done what I did, and got someone to help you out."

Rory and Bravon sat up. "What the hell? Whatta ya mean?"

"Mmmm." Jeffry stretched out and luxuriated on his bed, grinning like the Cheshire cat.

"Are you fucking with us? Who did you do it with?" Bravon nudged Rory and made a face.

"Oh, I'm not kidding. I'm not going to torture myself if I don't have to!" Jeffry pulled a pillow under his head and settled in to a sleeping position.

"With who?" Bravon really wanted to know.

"Oh, I'll never tell!" Jeffry's eyes were closed and he looked like he was drifting off.

"Aren't you worried about how it will affect your performance tomorrow?" Rory sounded like a Boy Scout.

"Oh, please!" Jeffry turned away from them, and his breathing slowed.

Rory and Bravon sunk back down.

Rory whispered. "Well, I ain't chancing it."

Bravon thought for a second, then said, "Yeah, me neither."

8 TRYOUTS, DAY 2

That whole next morning, as they got ready and rode out to the training facility, Jeffry was more relaxed than they had seen him. His attitude was much more carefree, and he was even able to share a couple of laughs with them.

Jake met them at the door, and walked them to locker room. The trainees had already changed and cleared out. There was a rack, with loads of gear on it, a lot of it pink. Next to the rack, was Bart Colt in his signature pro gear: Black Trunks, Brown boots with black laces, and brown leather wrist cuffs.

It was then that Rory noticed that Jake was wearing the same Brown leather wrist cuffs and boots, along with his black t-shirt and jeans. That was the gear they would wear when they were a tag team, along with a Cowboy hat and Brown leather chaps, which were ripped off before the match.

"Strip down, stow all your stuff in your lockers. Mr. Bart, here, will gear you guys up. Then, we'll meet in the interview pit." Jake turned and walked out.

Bart stepped forward. "Eb and Scott."

They walked over to him.

"Sizes?" Bart turned back to the rack and picked out their gear as they told him sizes. He handed them both tiny pink trunks and pink boots to match.

"Uh…" Eb and Scott held up the new gear as if they were objects they had never seen before.

"Just put it on. We'll answer all your questions later." Bart pointed at Jeffry. "Jeffry?"

Jeffry stepped forward as Eb and Scott took their gear back to their lockers.

Bart just looked at Jeffry and snapped, "Size?"

Jeffry stumbled on an "Oh" and "Uh", then answered.

Bart handed Jeffry similar gear to what he, himself, was wearing: black trunks, brown low boots, and big brown gauntlets for his wrists.

Jeffry made a questioning face, then wandered back to his locker.

Bart pointed at Eb and Scott. "Come on! Hurry up and change. I gotta check you out."

Eb and Scott ripped their underwear off, and helped each other get dressed. Jeffry also sped up his own process.

Bravon and Rory stepped in front of Bart, in their underwear. They looked at each other, then told Bart their sizes.

Bart handed them matching silver tag costumes. The trunks were very small, with bikini straps on the side. Rory gawked at his, with wide eyes.

Bravon held his up, and laughed. "Might not keep everything in."

"You guys got a problem?" Bart feigned annoyance.

"Nope!" "Nope!" Rory and Bravon hurried back to their lockers, and changed into their ridiculously small outfits.

In the Interview pit, there were two cameramen, two crew guys adjusting lights, and a big virtual backdrop of an arena full of fans.

Jake, Dyer Anderson, Bart Colt, and Max Gunn sat at a table, just behind the cameras. Bart and Dyer were completely suited up, pro trunks and all. Max wore regular, street clothes. They all had electronic and paper notebooks, and pens.

Jake directed the newbies to stand in a line, just outside the camera's view.

He had Scott and Eb come up, and talk about a match they were just about to have with Rory and Bravon.

Rory was impressed with the way Eb was able to convey arrogance and still be likable. For some reason, he thought Scott might freeze up, but he didn't. He was just animated enough, and came across as a gentleman.

Next, Rory and Bravon were brought up to tell their side. Bravon took the lead, and Rory was more than a little grateful. Nerves took him over. He spoke up when it was his turn, and tried to present his own personal twist on the Good Guy persona. He didn't feel great about his performance, but Jake said, "Good

Job".

Jeffry was brought up alone to talk about a match he would be having for the championship, against Bart Colt. He tapped into the cocky side of his personality and did well for the most part. Rory thought he went on a bit long, but it wasn't that bad.

Jake commended them all for doing well. The trainers went through their notes, compliments and criticisms. Rory was happy that he didn't have any more, or worse, than the other guys.

Dyer Anderson made an interesting comment that Rory didn't completely understand. The other Trainers agreed, and it sounded ultimately positive. Dyer told him that he was good, but he wasn't allowing himself to be completely vulnerable. He said that Rory had the potential to be the biggest "Good Guy" star of his generation, but he'd have to show more of what he really was. Max and Bart added that they could feel him "holding back".

Rory nodded, as if he understood, and thanked them for the praise, but he felt that he would have to talk to one of them privately to fully understand what they meant. He also didn't understand why *he* had the potential, more than the others. He saw things in Eb, Scott, even Jeffry, and especially Bravon that he admired, greatly.

Jake then directed each of the five to come up separately. He threw several different scenarios at them, and had them pretend to be in an interview for each. The trainers gave them notes, and ran them through certain parts a few times, until they were satisfied to move on.

Bravon and Scott got the note to "be yourself" and to "be more vulnerable". Scott asked what they meant, and they explained that he was putting on a bit of a façade, and that, possibly, he was embarrassed to show some side of his personality. They asked what his biggest fear would be, on camera. He answered, "I don't want to look stupid... or, you know... um... yeah, just ridiculous, or like an idiot."

The trainers laughed, and Max Gunn said, "Guess what! You WILL look stupid. You WILL look ridiculous, and you WILL look like an idiot." He moved his hand from himself, and pointed at the other three Pro Wrestlers at the table. "We ALL have looked like fucking douche bags, idiots, fags, assholes, little girls, pussies, and anything else you can think of."

Dyer Anderson agreed. "You are not going to be able to look like a really cool guy who is in control all the time, and make it in this business. You're gonna lose it. You're gonna cuss. You're gonna cry, and you're gonna look just plain stupid. But, whenever you do, and you're real, THAT'S when your audience loves you!"

All the trainers nodded. Rory was beginning to understand, and that scared the shit out of him. In fact, all the newbies were a bit shaken.

Bravon had an epiphany. He turned to Rory with a big smile, thinking Rory had one, too. Rory just let out a big sigh, and rested his hand on Bravon's shoulder, hoping his inner strength would rub off.

They continued on, and when it was Rory's turn, he worked hard to give them what they wanted. They said he was doing better, but that he was still holding back. After a few scenarios, they started asking him rapid-fire questions, and the last one was from Bart, "Why do you want to be a professional wrestler? Why are you here?"

At first, Rory was mad. "Cause this is all I've ever fucking wanted!" He went on to point at Dyer Anderson, and explained how his matches would excite him in so many ways, some of which he never told anyone. He talked about his admiration of Chris Enos, and how he practically worshipped him and hated him at the same time. Part of him wanted Dyer to dominate Chris Enos every time, because he was an egotistical, emotional bully, but another part of him was so passionately worked up when Chris was sexually sadistic. He looked directly at Dyer and said, "It made me want to do the same thing to you… then to Chris Enos."

Rory completely forgot himself. He couldn't believe he was saying these things, and his face became red-hot. His knees and hands trembled, and he thought he was all washed up. When he came to an end, all four trainers clapped. Jake shouted at Rory, "THAT'S what I'm talking about! THAT'S what it's all about!"

Rory looked at Dyer, who was giving him a particular smile he had never seen before. He quickly looked away.

Max Gunn excitedly interjected. "That passion is what your fans want to see! THEY can't climb into the ring, but YOU can, and they want to know what YOU are feeling when you're acting out THEIR fantasy, for real!"

Bart thumped his finger into the table to accentuate his point, "It's what is inside you! It's what you feel! It is always compelling, when it's real!"

Bravon hugged Rory when he returned to his seat on the sideline. "Dude! That was AWESOME!"

Eb agreed, and Scotty leaned across Eb to tell Rory, "I feel the SAME way!" He grabbed Rory's thigh and squeezed it. Unfortunately, Rory had no idea how he could ever recreate that speech or emotion.

All the guys did better after that point, though. They all told what they loved about wrestling, why they were there, and matches that were pivotal in their decisions to become wrestlers.

All the guys, except Jeffry, that is. For some reason, his on-camera arrogance turned into insecurity. His interviews seemed less impassioned, and more dramatic, for the worse. He talked about his tragedies and seemed to want to elicit sympathy.

Max Gunn said, without irony, "Maybe vulnerability doesn't work for some people." After he said it, he saw the humor in it, and laughed. The other trainers did, as well.

Jeffry didn't appreciate that.

Jake embellished, "Vulnerability is one thing, but you're treading into the territory of 'Too Much Information'. You should let your passion come through, but we don't want to hear about every bad thing that ever happened to you. That's for one of those women's, self-help shows!"

The trainers laughed, again.

"That's not cool! You asked for vulnerability, and then you laugh at me! What the fuck do you want from me???" Jeffry looked like he might be on the verge of tears.

"We just told you what we want from you!" Jake was ready to shut him down, again.

Dyer shook his head. "And, if you are afraid to get laughed at, you're in the wrong place!"

"But, you told me you want me to be vulnerable, and I am, and you just make fun of me!" Jeffry wasn't getting it.

"No! We are giving you notes. We are telling you what to do, and what not to do!" Jake was ready to stand up.

"And, I don't think anyone actually told YOU to be vulnerable. I thought you were doing great when you were acting like a cocky little shit." Bart glared at Jeffry, wondering why he was reacting like this.

Jeffry made a clicking noise with his mouth, sighed, rolled his eyes, and walked back to where his peers were sitting.

Jake stood up and pointed at Jeffry. "Attitude is good on camera, but NOT with us! Do you understand what I am saying?"

Jeffry made a noticeable attempt to improve his attitude before answering. "Yes."

There were a couple more tweaks the trainers gave the guys, then a tip from Jake, before they broke for lunch, "Don't eat too much, and relax. This last part of the tryouts is like a final exam, and it will take every bit of energy you have."

The newbie's followed Jake's instructions about eating, not because they wanted to, but because they were all agitated, aroused, keyed up, and jumpy. They didn't eat much, but they also weren't able to relax. Eb, Scott, Bravon, and Rory sat in a clump, going over their triumphs and pitfalls. Jeffry sat away from them, still stewing. Bravon and Rory thought about talking to him, but mostly they worked on getting their own heads in the game as much as possible.

Their 30-minute lunch seemed to fly by in five. Jake led them to a ring they hadn't been in, before. It was the sleekest, best-kept, and completely camera-ready. In fact, cameras were set up next to it, ready to go. The other three trainers sat on the ring apron, and talked quietly amongst themselves.

Jake explained that they were now each going to participate in one tag match, and one singles match, complete with an interview at the beginning and end. "These are real matches, just like you'll be competing in, if we choose you to join the federation. BUT, no biting, no injury, no blood, no eye gauging! Everyone understand?"

They all did.

"Good, cause anyone causing any real injury to another wrestler during tryouts will NOT be asked back... ever." Jake paused for effect.

Rory felt a lot warmer than usual, and moister. He thought everyone would notice that he was sweating from his head to his feet.

Jake announced the first match would be a tag, and they all assumed it would be Eb and Scott vs Rory and Bravon, since they had on tag team outfits. That was not they case. Jake announced that it would be Rory and Jeffry vs Bravon and Eb, with Scott as the ref. None of them saw that coming.

In the pre-match interview, Bravon stated that it would be a clean match, and that he was looking forward to facing his worthy opponents. Eb said the opposite. He talked about how sick he was of Rory thinking he was the greatest wrestler in the federation, and how he was going to take him down a notch. He also talked about how much he was looking forward to playing with "that little jobber, Jeffry".

When it was their turn, Rory applauded them for their talents. He hoped it would be a clean match, but that if Eb wanted to be shown why he was the greatest, he was only too happy to oblige. Rory was pretty happy with that.

Then, Jeffry started, and it was obvious Eb had gotten under his skin. He called Eb a liar, and said that no man had ever dominated him. He couldn't wait to make Eb "scream like a little girl!"

Rory was surprised, and found what Jeffry said to be amusing.

The trainers jumped up onto the ring apron, and leaned in a neutral corner.

Jake climbed up on the apron and made the announcements, as the guys climbed in and stood in their respective corners. Scott was center ring, not very confident in his role as Ref.

"In this corner, the reigning Tag Team Champs, Bravon the Brave, and the man who will be made to scream like a little girl, EB!" Jake said with a smirk on his face, and a tongue in his cheek.

The other trainers laughed.

"And, in this corner, Rory the Prettyboy, and toughest man in Pro Wrestling, today, little, tiny Jeffry!" Jake pointed at Scott.

"Call them center-ring. Check them over, and give them their instructions."

Scott meekly waved all the guys to join him. "Come on, guys."

He turned to Bravon, first, and lightly patted down the back of his trunks.

"Hold it!" Jake climbed through the ropes and walked over to center ring. He grabbed Bravon's butt cheek, and the other. "Like this!" Then, he hooked a finger into the top of Bravon's trunks, and pulled the waistband back so he could see. He exaggerated his movements, really craning his neck to look into Bravon's trunks. Then, he really exaggerated his commentary as ref, "What 'cha got in there? Is that ALL you?"

Scott smiled, and blushed. Bravon laughed, and leaned his body back a bit, giving Jake an unobstructed view of his junk.

Jake let go of Bravon's waistband, and it snapped back. He looked at Scott, "The ref is in control! He's just as important to the match as the wrestlers, if he's doing his job! You got it?"

"Yeah." Scott nodded.

Jake climbed back out of the ring, commenting to the other trainers, as he exited, "If *that's* all him, I'm pretty fucking impressed!"

Scott smacked Bravon's arm, "Lemme see your boots!"

Bravon lifted one, then the other for Scott, who checked them out, with a lot more authority, now.

Scott turned to Eb, and grabbed the back of his trunks,

hard, three times. He pat him down, then took a hold of the front of his trunks. Eb let out a quick giggle.

Scott's voice went deeper. He started enjoying his new role. He hooked a finger into the waistband of Eb's trunks, and pulled back. He looked in. "Ya got anything in there that's not you?"

Eb had to resist the urge to laugh. "Nope. All me."

Scott nodded. "Yup, that's about right, looks good... real good." That made the trainers chuckle.

Scott checked out Eb's boots, then turned to Rory, and gave him the same treatment. When he was done, Jeffry stepped forward and pulled his trunks down, exposing his penis and balls. He was pretty big, for such a small guy.

The trainers enjoyed that.

Scott was taken aback. "Ok, good." He forgot to check Jeffry's boots. Instead he went right into the instructions. "I want a good, clean fight. No blood. No biting. No injury. No eye gauging! Anyone caught doing any of these things will be immediately ejected from the facility! Got it?"

The guys weren't very committed to their answers. "Ok" "Mmhmm" "Yeah."

Scott smacked the two wrestles closest to him and yelled, "GOT IT?!?"

That caused the guys to snap to, "YES!" "ABSOLUTELY!" "SURE!" "GOT IT!"

"Good! Return to your corners and wait for the bell!" Scott

stood his ground, as the guys did what he said.

They conferred. Eb and Jeffry wanted to start the match.

Scott looked over to Jake, wondering who would call for the bell. Jake just nodded to Scott, so he brought his right hand up, then down with a snap, and said, "DING! DING!"

Eb walked out to center ring, extended a hand to Jeffry, and said, "Good luck, man, really!"

Jeffry smiled. He was touched. This was the one of the first times Eb had shown him some respect. He extended his hand, and took a step forward. He batted Eb's hand away, lunged in,GRABBED the bulge in Eb's trunks, and YANKED downward.

Eb held his crotch and fell to his knees.

Scott pushed Jeffry back and yelled, "HEY! NOT COOL! NO LOW BLOWS!"

Jake waved his hands, "HEY! I never said, 'No low blows' in my instructions!"

Scott looked over at him, confused. "But, you said no more of that during tryouts."

Jake nodded. "Sorry. You're right! Good job following directions! … Well, that's all over now. Nut shots are legal in these last matches, unless we state otherwise."

Jeffry was happy. He stepped around Scott, grabbed Eb by the hair, and pulled him to his feet. He whipped him into the ropes, and met him with a big knee to his midsection as he rebounded.

Eb flipped over, and crashed down to the mat on his back. He arched up and held his abs, in pain.

Scott was worried.

Jeffry pulled Eb back up to his feet, and scooped him up in a crotch and shoulder lift.

Everyone was surprised, and the trainers were more than a little impressed.

Jeffry slammed Eb down, center-ring, HARD!

"OOF." Eb was winded and embarrassed.

Jeffry jumped on top of Eb for the cover.

Scott was a bit hesitant, but also dropped down, to count out his boyfriend.

Jeffry yelled. "Come on, Ref! Count him out!"

Eb kicked out on the second count.

Jeffry bolted up to his knees, and yelled at Scott. "Come on! You gotta count faster than that!"

Scott stuck his finger in Jeffry's face. "My count was just fine!!!"

Jeffry pulled Eb back up to his feet, by his hair. Eb had a big fist waiting for him, and drove it in to Jeffry's gut. It wasn't his hardest, but Jeffry felt it. Again, he grabbed the front of Eb's trunks, and pulled him over to his corner.

Eb was forced to dance over on his tiptoes, as he held on to Jeffry's wrist.

Scott clenched his fists, wishing he could help.

Jeffry made the tag to Rory, then YANKED down on the front of Eb's trunks, once more.

"AGUUGHH!!" Eb fell to his knees, again.

Rory jumped in the ring, and his first instinct was to let Eb recover, but he could feel the trainers looking at him. He pulled Eb up, and clamped on a full nelson.

"Nnngghh" Eb tried to kick his feet and flail free.

Rory shook him like a rag doll, and faced him toward the trainers, hoping it made a good view for them.

Rory cranked the nelson HARD, forcing Eb's chin down into his chest. Then, Rory did what he would normally do in a match, and told the ref, "Ask him!"

Scott leaned in and put his hand on his boyfriend's side, "You ok, Eb?"

"Yeah, I'm ok, and no fucking way!" Eb spit the words out.

Rory spun around which caused Eb's feet to fly up, and then he let him go. Eb flew a few feet, crashed to the mat, and slid into a neutral corner. Rory followed, and proceeded to put Eb through a chain of his favorite moves. He slammed him, brought him down in a back breaker, and did a signature move he developed. He picked Eb up from the back breaker, jumped with him, then wrapped his legs around Eb's waist, mid-air. They both came crashing down to the mat, Eb's butt hitting first, and now Eb was trapped in Rory's steel-legged scissors.

"Ask him, Ref!" Rory said, as he gritted his teeth, and really clamped on the scissors.

"Fuck no! FUCK NO!" Eb was in pain, but he wasn't about to give up, either.

Rory felt he should let Jeffry have some more time in the ring. He pulled Eb up, and SHOT him into their corner, where Jeffry was waiting.

"UNGHH!!" Eb's back hit the ring post hard.

Rory walked over, and tagged Jeffry in.

Jeffry climbed to the top rope and on to Eb's shoulders, his bulge against the back of Eb's neck. He put his legs around Eb's neck, then down under his arms. He pushed himself forward, and down, and rolled on the canvas.

Eb followed after and flipped over onto his back.

Jeffry straddled Eb's head, facing toward Eb's feet. He pinned his arms down with his knees. As he lowered himself, his butt pushed Eb's face down.

Scott fought every urge he had to punch Jeffry in the head. He reluctantly lowered himself down for count.

Eb was able to grab Jeffry's legs and throw him off.

Jeffry flew back, and landed flat on his ass.

Scott was very happy.

Eb rolled to the ropes, pulled himself up and tried to get to the corner to tag in Bravon. Jeffry followed him, and Eb turned around just in time to take a kick to the abs. WHUMP!

Eb was on his feet, but doubled up, holding his stomach.

Jeffry whipped Eb into the ropes, and once again brought his knee up, to slam it into Eb's stomach.

Eb did the same thing, as he rebounded, and their knees slammed into each other.

Jeffry went down, like a ton of bricks and Eb fell on top of him.

Eb's hand just happened to be in Jeffry's crotch, so he YANKED a handful. "How do you like it?!"

"Uhnngg!" Jeffry didn't like it, but he didn't dislike it, either. His pained knee was a much bigger problem, at the moment.

Eb slid his arm under one of Jeffry's legs, pulled it up, and had him in a pinning predicament.

Scott happily dropped for the count, "ONE! TWO!"

Jeffry was able to kick out on the second slap of the mat.

Eb got to his knees, and CLAWED Jeffry's abs with both hands.

'AAAYEE YAAAH!!!" Jeffry didn't like that, and he hated it, too.

Eb stood up, and pulled Jeffry to his feet. BAM! He sent a very hard right punch to Jeffry's abs.

Jeffry fell to his knees, his mouth open, completely winded.

Eb pulled him back up to his feet, and scooped him up, by his crotch and shoulder.

He walked him over to his corner and slammed him down. BAM! He tagged his partner.

Bravon leapt in, taunted Rory, and showboated a bit, even though Jeffry was suffering from none of his handy work.

Eb climbed out, and held his aching balls.

Bravon pulled Jeffry up to his feet, picked him up, then brought him down over his knee. WHUMP! He held Jeffry there, really bending him into a backbreaker. "Ask him, Ref!"

Scott leaned in. "Jeffry. You ok to continue?"

"Unnghh." Jeffry answered, sounding more in pleasure than in pain.

Bravon really cranked on the pressure. "Come on! Give up, little man!"

Bravon was impressed at how much pain the little guy could take. He smiled, positioned his hand right above Jeffry's growing bulge and FLICKED it with his finger.

"Mmmnhhh" Jeffry moaned.

Bravon smiled, realizing that he was given the license to do whatever he wanted. Jeffry was now his own personal Jobber Toy.

Bravon had the trainer's full attention, so he did the first thing that came to mind. He pushed down on Jeffry's chin with one hand, and flexed his other arm at the Trainers.

He took Jeffry through a few moves and holds that were the most fun for him. He racked, slammed, and scissored him. He even carried him around in an upside-down, reverse bear hug.

Jeffry tried to fight back at every turn, but Bravon would just laugh and easily move on to the next humiliating hold.

Jeffry would not give up, and Bravon didn't want him to. After the upside-down bear hug, Bravon tried out a move he never had, before. He threw Jeffry down, face-first onto the canvas, and stepped on his thighs, facing his back. He leaned down, pulled up Jeffry's feet, and hooked them around his own calves.

Jeffry was flailing, and screaming, but there was no way he could possibly get away.

Bravon reveled in it, "Oh, yeah!" He leaned forward, and grabbed Jeffry's arms, just below the shoulder. He slid his hands down and clamped them around his prisoner's wrists. He jerked backwards, sat down, and rolled onto his back.

Jeffry was up in the air, in a suspended surfboard. He screamed out, "LET ME GOOOO!!!".

Scott asked him if he wanted to submit.

Jeffry just spat back, "FUCK YOU!"

That made the trainers laugh. Jake felt for the little guy. "Jeffry! If you're in pain, it's ok. We can stop the match!"

Again, Jeffry spat out, "FUCK YOU!"

That really amused the trainers.

The match continued.

Rory felt that he was far more aroused than he should have been. Part of him wanted Scott to be put in that hold, so he could do whatever he wanted. Another part wanted Bravon to use this hold on him, and that made him feel funny.

Bravon moved his legs up and down. "How you doin' up there, Jeffy?"

"AAAACHHHHHH!!" Jeffry's scream was a bit alarming.

Scott got in Jeffry's face. "Yeah, you ok to continue?"

"FUCK YOU!" He wasn't happy, but he also wasn't submitting.

This didn't feel like a real match to Bravon, and suddenly, it didn't seem all that fair. He brought his legs down, and let Jeffry go.

Jeffry plopped onto the canvas, then scrambled to the ropes.

Bravon got up, ready to pin Jeffry and end it.

Jeffry pulled himself out of the ring, and pointed up to the trainers, "WHAT THE HELL AM I SUPPOSED TO DO? THIS ISN'T FAIR! I'M JUST SUPPOSED TO BE HIS FUCKING JOBBER BOY, AND TAKE IT!?!?"

Jake and the trainers shook their heads. They had enough of Jeffry. "You coulda quit at any time..."

Bravon was mad. He stepped forward and calmly addressed Jake and the other trainers. "Actually, can we just take care of this?" He indicated Eb, Scott, and Rory. "Will you let us deal with Jeffry for a minute, then we can get back to the match?"

This was a pleasant surprise to Jake and the trainers, "Uh, yeah. Sure, be my guest."

Bravon quickly walked to the ropes where Jeffry was, and slid out. Scott and Eb followed, and Rory jumped down from the ring apron.

Jeffry put his hands up, and backed away. "Just leave me alone!"

Bravon got up next to him, put his arm around Jeffry's shoulder, and led him away from the ring. He leaned his head in close to Jeffry's.

Jeffry struggled for a second, but the other guys were around him.

"Listen. You came here to become a wrestler! I know you're having a hard time in this match, and I'm sorry that we are all a lot bigger than you. I KNOW you have it harder than we do, right now! I know if feels like shit, but YOU are doing good right now, EXCEPT for when you shoot off with that attitude of yours!"

Jeffry made a noise of annoyance.

Bravon kept going, "WE can help you through this, cause the FIVE of us are fucking good, and we can ALL make it! The ONLY thing that is different about you is your bad attitude!"

Rory grabbed Jeffry's shoulder. "All you have to do is get through the rest of the day. I'm seeing the trainers when you're wrestling, and they like what you're doing. Bravon is right. We will all help you, if you need it!"

Eb joined in, "Dude! I'm not as good as these guys! Didn't you see them working me over? But, hey go with it! If you lose, you lose, at least look good suffering!"

Scott nodded.

"And, if you get frustrated, DON'T take it out on the trainers! Put it into the match! Scream at your opponent! Fuck, do your dirty shit. They love it!" Bravon was now smiling, hoping they had convinced Jeffry.

Rory shook Jeffry's arm. "So, you ok? All you gotta do is just pull it together and come back to tryouts!"

Jeffry was pouting, but he nodded his head.

Bravon withdrew his arm, and held his hand in front of Jeffry, ready to shake. "Ok, man, take ten seconds, bring your attitude up, and come back to the ring!"

Jeffry weakly shook Bravon's hand, but Bravon gave it some vigorous up and down motion.

Rory patted Jeffry's back, Eb lightly punched his arm, and Scott patted his chest twice with his palm, then the four returned to the ring.

Bravon smiled as he climbed back into the ring, and announced to the trainers. "He's cool! Just needed a quick five."

The trainers were more than impressed with Bravon, and his three peers.

When Jeffry returned to the ring, Jake told him to lie down, center ring.

Jeffry's attitude almost forced him to question Jake, but he quelled it, and placed himself flat on his back.

Jake told Bravon to pin him. "That's the way this match was going to go, right?"

Bravon laid his body over Jeffry's awkwardly, not in any way he would ever cover his opponent in a match.

Dyer Anderson made a face. "Is that the way you would cover in a match?"

"Oh!" Bravon realized how stupid he was being, and he got into it. He PULLED up on Jeffry's leg, hooked it, and really leveraged his weight down.

Scott was one beat behind, but then snapped back into the mentality of the match, dropped down, and counted.

Jeffry struggled, but couldn't budge the much bigger man.

"ONE! TWO! THREE!" Scott leapt up and signaled for the bell, "DING! DING!"

Bravon stood up, with a goofy smile. Scott grabbed his right hand, hoisted it up in the air, and proclaimed him and Eb the winners. Eb was already in, congratulating Bravon.

Bravon was about to help Jeffry up, but Jake gave him a singsong reminder, "Inter-view!"

Rory jumped in the ring, helped his partner up, while Bravon and Eb jumped out, and began their after-match commentary.

Next up, Jake announced that all the trainers had talked about wanting to see a match between Rory and Scott, which made them both proud but tense.

They each gave Good-Guy pre-match interviews, except Scott said he would not let their friendship get in the way, and he would do anything to win.

Dyer Anderson stepped in the ring as the Ref.

Rory took the early advantage, but Scott was able to escape, then vice-versa. After some back and forth, Rory trapped Scott in a body scissor, facing his opponent. Scott squirmed and gripped Rory's ripped thighs. He couldn't break free, and couldn't reposition himself.

Dyer squatted next to them, his hand on Rory's shoulder. He pointed to the bulge in Rory's trunks, and said to Scott, "There it is! Grab it! Take the advantage!"

Rory's whole body turned red, and his trunks tented, beyond his control. He glared at Dyer with a look of incredulity. He wanted to wrap Dyer Anderson up in a hard, sweaty scissor, and make him beg. A strange, jumpy, sexual energy came over him.

Scott was also embarrassed. He had no intention of grabbing Rory's penis, but there it was, now hard and rubbing against his midsection.

Dyer kept talking them through it, "Come on, Scotty. Wanna gain control in this match? Grab it and pin this big, dumb, blond kid."

Rory's head was swimming. Why was he finding this all so arousing? All eyes were on him, and he had to put an end to it. He SQUEEZED harder. Scott moaned. Rory rose up on his arms then turned hard to his side, forcing Scott on his back, his shoulders down. Rory hooked one of Scott's legs, and kept his scissors tight.

Dyer was impressed. He dropped down for the count. Scott kicked out on "TWO!"

Scott was now in a sitting position, Rory's legs still tight around him. Scott took a queue from Rory, held on to the big blond boys legs, and threw his weight toward his opponent, which rolled Rory onto his back. Scott planted his legs down hard, and Rory was pinned.

Dyer counted, again, and Rory, also, kicked out on "TWO!"

As Rory kicked out, Scott was able to escape.

They both got back to their feet and circled. There was some more back and forth. Scott was able to slam Rory, but not able to secure a pin.

Finally, Rory put Scott through a pretty rough chain of moves that ended in a slam and a pin. Dyer dropped down, and began counting. Scott was struggling, but unable to kick out. Just before the third slap of the mat, Dyer very roughly PULLED Rory off of Scott, and stood up.

Jake yelled out, "THAT'S A DRAW!"

Rory was immediately up, and in Dyer's face. "WHAT THE FUCK??? I HAD HIM! WHY THE HELL DID YOU DO THAT?" The smile on Dyer's face threw Rory off. It had a strange calming effect on him.

Dyer grabbed Rory's shoulders. *"There it is, again!* This is the side of you we want to see more of!!! GOOD MATCH, PRETTY BOY!" He walked back to the trainers and they all talked quietly about Scott and Rory's performances.

Scott was still on the ground. Rory reached down to give him a hand, and help him to his feet.

Scott kept a hold of his hand, and pulled Rory into a hug. "Good match, man!"

Rory was still fired up. He put his arms around Scott and squeezed. "Yeah, man, TOUGH MATCH!"

Rory walked Scott back to the corner, where their peers were. Eb and Bravon hugged both of them, and congratulated them on a "tough fight".

Jake called Rory and Scott down, together, for their after-match interview.

Rory rested his left arm around Scott's neck, "I hope I never have to fight my friend, again, cause if he ever does get balls, and grabs mine, I think I'm toast!"

Scott laughed. "I would rather loose than resort to dirty tactics with my friends." He reached out his right hand and grabbed Rory's. "You are ALWAYS guaranteed a scientific, Gentleman's match against me!"

Jake leaned in to Max and whispered, "Kinda corny, but kinda real, right?"

Max agreed.

Next Jake had Bravon and Eb match up.

Bravon's interview was very much like Scott and Rory's. He talked about having to go up against a friend, and even though Eb was a good wrestler, he would easily beat him.

Eb, on the other hand, showed more of his blossoming heel mentality. He talked about knowing Bravon's weaknesses, how he would use them against him, and how he would not only pin Bravon, but he would get him to submit, as well.

When Rory heard that, he whispered to Scott, "Wow."

Scott put his hand on Rory's back and gave it a squeeze, "I know." The glint in Scott eyes, and the tiny curl at the end of his lips, told anyone exactly how Scott felt about Eb.

Bravon was a complete gentleman, starting the match. After the opening bell, he offered Eb a "good-luck" handshake. Eb smiled and accepted, but dodged it and feigned a lunge at Bravon's private region.

Bravon flinched.

Eb pointed at him with an evil grin on his face.

Bravon laughed, and Eb re-offered a handshake. Bravon took his hand, and Eb said, "Clean match, buddy!"

Bravon nodded, then turned to the trainers with a wink and snap, as if to say, "I got this."

When he turned back, in his continued circling, Eb had a dropkick all ready for him, which hit him dead-on in the chest, and sent him down.

Eb was up first. As Bravon scrambled to get to his feet, Eb was able to score another dropkick.

All the guys watching made an "Oooh!" sound.

Eb twisted in air, landed in a pushup position, and was up in a split second.

Bravon landed on his butt, and sat up dazed.

Eb had his knee in Bravon's back, in an instant, then grasped the bigger man's chin, and PULLED up hard.

"AAGHHH!" Bravon's hands went up. He worked to pull Eb's away.

"I couldn't wait until I got say this: ASK HIM REF!" Eb's smile stretched from ear to ear.

Dyer got in front of Bravon, and asked, in an almost comical manner, "You don't want to give up, yet, do you?"

Bravon yelled out, "NO!"

Eb kept a hold of Bravon's chin, and worked to get one of his arms, but was unable. Bravon was just too strong.

Eb kept one knee pressed against his opponent's spine, and SLAMMED the other into his lower back.

"AAAGAHOOOOONN!" Bravon yelled out.

"GIVE IT UP!" Eb was getting cocky.

Bravon got his feet up under him, reached back at the same time, and stood up. As he did, he caught Eb's head, then dropped down to one knee and flipped Eb over, in front of him.

Eb landed on his back. THUD!

Bravon inched forward, and pinned Eb's arms with his knees. His hands pushed down on Eb's chest, and he looked at Dyer, "Count him out."

Rory could see that Scott was uncomfortable, having to watch Eb being dominated.

Bravon flexed, and showboated.

Eb did something that Rory had never seen before. In less than a second, he planted one foot on the canvas, bringing that leg into a bent position, then PUSHED up on it, and let the other leg fly straight up and back.

WHACK! He hit Bravon right in the head with his boot.

Bravon's eyes crossed and he fell to the side.

Dyer wasn't even able to count to "ONE!"

Eb was up.

Dyer watched in awe, just like everyone else around the ring.

Eb rolled over, threw himself on top of Bravon, and hooked his leg for the pin.

Again Dyer dropped down, but Bravon easily kicked out on the first count, and PUSHED Eb off of him. Eb flew back into the ropes, but pulled himself out in no time.

As Bravon was getting up, so was Eb. He threw himself backward, into the ropes, and rebounded, intending to hit Bravon with another drop kick. This was one time too many. Bravon was ready for it, dodged it, and batted Eb's legs to one side.

Eb crashed down to the mat. Bravon jumped up and came down with a big leg drop across Eb's midsection. WHAMP! Then, pulled Eb between his legs and scissored him, HARD!

Eb grimaced, and struggled to regain his breath.

Bravon FLEXED the squeeze, then relaxed, needing a rest just as much as Eb.

Eb's body bounced very time he flexed. "UHNGH! UNGHH!" In between, he was able to squirm around so the two wrestlers were facing each other. He looked into Bravon's eyes with half a smile, and half a snarl.

Bravon didn't like that look. "ASK HIM, REF!"

Eb looked up at Mr. Anderson, "Hell no! ...I'm not a gentleman, like my boy Scotty. I WILL grab his nuts!" and with that, he clawed a big handful of Bravon's vulnerable balls.

"AYYY-YAAAH!!" Bravon threw his head back, and howled, but kept his tight scissors, like a vice around Eb.

"Now, you ask HIM, REF!" Eb was really cranking his arm, clawing that hand deep, and pulling back.

"NO!" Bravon flexed his muscular quads hoping to squeeze all the air out of Eb, but they both just kept making each other moan and grunt.

Rory leaned his shoulder into Scott's. "Damn, that's hot!"

Scott was breathing hard. "I know!"

Bravon tried to pull Eb's hand away, but couldn't.

Eb took his other hand, and felt around the front of Bravon's trunks. He grabbed Bravon's penis, and started pulling it the opposite direction he was pulling Bravon's balls.

"Wooooh!" Dyer Anderson drew in a long breath of air. "Oh, man! I'm sorry. I've had that done to me, before!" He pointed at Eb, and remarked to the other trainers, "This kid's been watching a lot of my matches!"

"AAAHHH...AHHHH!" Bravon couldn't believe this was happening. "Come on, man! Let go!"

"Give up, and I will!" Eb was ecstatic.

"NO!"

Rory was getting pretty turned on, so he positioned himself behind the ring post, grabbed the back of Scott's neck and shook him playfully. "Damn!"

Scott was also getting worked up. "He LOVES doing that!"

Bravon let his scissors relax. Eb broke them and was now on his knees. Bravon grabbed tightly onto Eb's wrists and did the same. He started to stand up, but Eb gave his dick and balls a quick yank, and Bravon fell back to his knees.

"COME ON!" Bravon was whining to Dyer, "STOP HIM!!"

Dyer held out his hands, "Do you give up?"

"NO!" Bravon was breathing hard. He wanted to work himself up into a rage, but the excruciating pain Eb was inflicting seriously deflated his fire. He reached out, grabbed Eb's balls, and YANKED straight down.

"UHNN!" Eb's smile screwed up into a twisted, joyful grimace.

While Eb was distracted for one second, Bravon got to his feet, holding tight onto Eb's wrists. Eb followed. Bravon gave Eb's balls an underhand SMACK!

Eb groaned and laughed at the same time, and he answered these actions with another yank on Bravon's private parts in opposite directions. Bravon yelled out, again, but then wrapped his arms around Eb and ran with him straight into the ring post, screaming like a kamikaze.

Eb's back hit hard, causing him to release his grip on Bravon's balls. Bravon fell to his hands and knees, right in front of Eb, who was holding on to the ropes and his aching back.

Bravon held his balls with one hand, and put the other on Eb's thigh. He looked up, anger finally flashing in his eyes. His hand slid up Eb's leg, and YANKED down on Eb's balls once more.

"UNGGGHH!!" Eb wasn't laughing anymore. He was dangling from the ropes by one arm, the other now holding his balls.

Bravon got to his feet, but was standing funny, his balls still on fire. He gave Eb a big CHOP across his pecs that caused him to bounce in the corner.

Scott gripped the ropes, wishing he could jump in and save Eb.

Bravon bent down, took hold of Eb's right boot and pulled it up and over the middle rope, then did the same to his left boot. He wrapped Eb's arms around the top rope, PULLED on them, and pushed his boot right into Eb's nuts.

Eb yelled out.

Bravon snarled at Eb, "How do YOU like it?"

Eb looked up at him, and through the twisted grimace of pain, he smiled at Bravon, "I LOVE it!"

Bravon shook his head. Dyer and the other trainers laughed.

Dyer stepped forward and smacked Bravon on the back. "Let him go!"

Bravon was dumbfounded. "WHAT?"

"He's in the corner. LET HIM GO!" Dyer wasn't playing with him. "How would you end this? I want to see what finisher you would use." Dyer said it very matter-of-factly, as if they were talking about something completely academic.

Dyer helped Eb get his legs out from the ropes, and his feet back down on the canvas. He asked Eb if he was ok to continue. Eb gave another short snort of a laugh, "Yes!" He held on to the ropes and stood up.

Bravon's whole attitude changed, and one would swear there was a twinkle in his eye. He turned to Eb, gave him another forearm SLASH across the chest, then immediately followed with a very hard, very quick PUNCH to Eb's gut.

"Oh!" Eb sunk to his knees.

Bravon took a hold of the back of Eb's neck and pushed his head straight down between his legs. He flexed his thighs around Eb's head, wrapped his arms around his torso and easily hoisted him up in an upside down bear hug.

Eb kicked his legs.

Bravon moved out to center ring, jumped up, kicked his legs out, and crashed down on his ass. Eb was driven down into the canvas in a very deep pile driver. He bounced down onto the canvas in front of Bravon, and was out like a light.

Bravon moved forward and hooked Eb's legs over his shoulders. He had Eb rolled up in a pin, with his feet planted behind him. It was unnecessary. Eb was coming to, but groggy as hell.

Dyer dropped down and counted him out, "ONE! TWO! THREE!"

Scott rushed into the ring to revive Eb and see if he was ok.

Bravon broke character and knelt down beside Eb.

Eb looked up at them, and mumbled. "Wha' happen?"

Dyer knelt down next to him, looked into his eyes then stated officially. "He's ok. Help him up, walk him around."

Scott and Bravon helped him to his feet. Dyer pulled Bravon back by the shoulders. "Not you." He pointed at Rory, "You help him."

Rory was already in the ring, standing by them. He took Bravon's place, and helped Scott carry Eb out of the ring.

Dyer turned Bravon toward the trainers, and the camera just beyond them. "Give your interview here." He mimicked an announcer. "Hey! That was a tough match. You were dominated in the beginning and almost made to submit."

"Uh… " Bravon was worried about Eb, but he told himself to snap back into the moment. "Uh, yeah. He's a really tough opponent. I made a rookie mistake, and took my attention off of him for a second. But, that's how good he is. He only needed that one second. It will NEVER happen again! I relied on my training and turned it around in the end."

"It looked less like training, that got you out of that tight spot, and more just total warrior mode!" Dyer was trying to compliment him.

"When I'm in a tight spot, I repeat my own personal mantra, in my head: 'I WANT IT TO KILL ME!', and that has pulled me out of every bad situation I've ever found myself in." Bravon stood up just a bit taller, and his aching balls ached just a little less.

The trainers laughed and Dyer screwed up his face. "O-K! That's fucking crazy. Remind me *never* to grab your nuts."

Bravon laughed.

Dyer ended the interview.

Bravon jumped out of the ring to check on Eb.

Scott and Rory had Eb propped in a chair, drinking water.

Bravon ambled over, still walking funny, but very concerned. "Hey, Eb, are you ok?"

Eb looked up with a smile, "Yeah! I'm fine. How's your junk?"

"Ah… still hurts like fucking hell. But, you're really ok? I'm sorry about..."

Eb sat up. "No! Don't be sorry! This is what we are here for! It was a fucking great match!"

"OK, GOOD! Cause that's what you get for what you did to my fucking dick and balls!" Bravon lightly rubbed his balls and clenched his teeth.

Eb reached out, "Want me to rub 'em for you?"

Bravon flinched back, and smacked Eb's hand away. "Keep your hands away from me!"

Next up, Jake called Jeffry outside the ring, to wait for his pre-match interview. He stood, looking over to his peers, wondering which one Jake would pit him against.

Bart Colt stepped in front of the camera, decked out in his gear. He talked about "teaching this stupid little rookie a lesson", and "ending his career before it even began!"

Jeffry gulped. He was seriously shaken at the thought of having to face the somewhat legendary Bart Colt. When he stepped in front of the camera, he turned it on, though. He stated that he would "throw the old man all over that ring", and he dared Bart to try and even last three minutes with him.

The trainers found his interview very entertaining.

In the ring, as Referee Dyer Anderson was giving them the once over, Bart took a finger and tapped it into Jeffry's forehead, "Don't grab my dick. Don't grab my balls. We want to see how you wrestle straight up. Got it?"

Jeffry backhanded Bart's finger away, "Whatever."

Dyer smirked. He liked that. He also liked what Bart was about to do to Jeffry.

At the bell, Bart locked up with him very quickly. He easily manhandled Jeffry into a chain of holds from a hammerlock to an over-the-knee back breaker, to a rack, and a slam from a gorilla press.

Bart leaned in the corner over by Jake and Max Gunn, chatting with them, giving Jeffry plenty of time to recover. When Jeffry finally got to his feet, Bart ran from across the ring, telegraphing a high drop kick. Jeffry easily dodged it, but Bart twisted on the way down, and landed in the push up position at Jeffry's feet. He grabbed Jeffry's boots and pulled them straight up. Jeffry landed flat on his ass.

Jeffry rolled to the ropes, and slid out, under the bottom one. He was red-faced and once again frustrated. He looked up at the trainers. Everyone could see he wanted to have another one of his outbursts, but he kept his mouth shut.

He jumped back up on the apron, and went to climb through the ropes. Bart was there to meet him, and he grabbed Jeffry's head to pull him through. As he did, Jeffry reached out and YANKED on Bart's balls.

"Oooh!" The trainers were on surprised. They knew Jeffry had just made a huge mistake.

Bart YANKED Jeffry through the ropes so hard, Jeffry fell face first onto the canvas. Bart bent down, PULLED him up to his feet by his hair, and YANNNKKKED Jeffry's balls down, very hard and very far.

"Nnnngg" Jeffry made a sound none of them had heard before. It was more internal than anything. He dropped to his knees and held his crotch.

"I told you not to do that!" Bart grabbed his own balls and yanked on 'em. "The HARDEST balls of steel you will ever tangle with!... Wanna see 'em up close?" Bart grabbed Jeffry's head, shoved his face into his balls of steel, rubbed it around, then pushed Jeffry's head away from him.

Jeffry looked up at Bart. He was pouting, but there was also a glimmer of something else. Perhaps it was respect, or maybe lust.

Bart looked down at Jeffry, "You can't be just a one-note guy. You can't just rely on low blows. You gotta be able to wrestle."

Jeffry nodded. "Ok." He wished they were having this match in private.

As Bart pulled him back up to his feet, again by the hair, Jeffry punched the older man's stomach as hard as he could.

"Uh." It didn't even slow Bart down. He put Jeffry through another series of punishing holds. Jeffry was now his plaything. He hardly resisted, and seemed to really enjoy the experience. His hands even felt along Bart's muscles, as he squeezed the air out of Jeffry in a bear hug.

Bart caught on. He saw that Jeffry would never submit, so he unceremoniously slammed and pinned him.

Dyer even counted slowly to give Jeffry a chance to fight back, but he was out. "Ding! Ding!"

Jeffry took his time getting up, and out of the ring, when Jake called him for his after-match interview. He looked completely relaxed, and unaware of the erection in his trunks. He applauded Bart on his win, but noted that he had "NOT ended this rookies career", then snapped "on the contrary!" and sauntered off camera.

Jake nodded, and pondered Jeffry's future in Pro Wrestling. After a few seconds he yelled out for the guys to "take a break", as he and the other trainers deliberated.

Bravon, Scott, Eb, and Rory gathered around Jeffry, next to the snack table. They all asked if he was ok, and told him they were impressed with his stamina.

Jeffry smiled, but said few words. He even remained silent as the other guys talked about their thoughts on whether they made it and if they would be invited back.

They were all pretty confident, but Eb noted that he wasn't as skilled as the other guys. He thought there was a good chance he might not make it.

Bravon and Rory both disagreed with him, and described how good his style, image, and charisma were. Rory said he thought Eb had the most realized persona of all of them. Bravon agreed and listed all the cool moves and holds Eb pulled out of his hat.

Jake came over to the snack table, followed by Dyer and

Bart. He congratulated them all on making it through tryouts. Then, he told them what would be happening, next. "Max is going to take you back to the house, eat dinner with you, then take you all to the airport in the morning. Don't get crazy, tonight. If you break any of the rules at the house, or do anything we don't like, we will NOT ask you back. Do you understand?"

They all did.

"Excellent. We'll be in touch with in the next week to let you know whether we will be working with you, or not." And, with that, Jake and Bart shook every newbie's hand, said 'good bye', and went to work with the trainees.

Dyer congratulated them, "You guys all did really well. I look forward to working with you." He turned to Rory. "Can I talk to you, for a minute?"

All the guys stared Rory. He was a bit rattled. "Uh, yeah, sure."

Dyer grabbed his shoulder, and led him away from the group. "So, Rory. I want to know how you see yourself in the wrestling business."

They stopped far out of earshot.

"Uh... well. Uh, It's all I've ever wanted to do." Rory's mind reeled. He could go on for hours on this subject.

"What are your goals, as a wrestler?" Dyer turned Rory around, so he couldn't see his mates.

"Um... I think the same as every guy: State Champ, American Champ, then World Champ." Rory stopped, to give Mr.

Anderson a chance to answer, laugh at him, or make fun of his grandiose answer.

Dyer just smiled, hoping Rory would expound.

"I want to... uh... wrestle guys like Bart, and Jake... Max... and...uh... you." Rory was embarrassed, but excited that one of his idols was asking him to open up about his biggest passion.

Dyer's smile widened when Rory mentioned that he wanted to wrestle him.

Rory had one more thing to say, "... and Chris Enos."

There it was. For some reason, unknown to Rory, that was just what Dyer wanted to hear. "Excellent. Well, I want to work with you, directly. If you are really interested in one day becoming the All World Champ, I want to help you get there. I feel you have a lot of potential. You have this 'Golden Boy' kind of thing going on." Dyer stopped, and waited for Rory to respond.

Rory's mouth hung open. He swallowed air. Fireworks went off in his head, and the whole world was screaming "TOUCH DOWN!" He just continued to stare at Dyer Anderson.

Dyer squeezed Rory's shoulder, "Well? Is that something you'd be interested in?"

Rory couldn't believe his mouth hadn't answered, yet. "YES! YES! Absolutely! Of course! ... Are you serious?"

Dyer nodded. "Never been more. Are YOU serious?"

Rory nodded violently. "Yes! ABSOLUTELY! OF COURSE!"

Dyer smiled, and grabbed Rory's right hand. "So, it's a

deal, then?"

Rory shook hard. "Oh, yeah! Oh, wow! This is awesome. So, I'm in! It's official? I'm in?"

"Oh, no! It's not official…" Dyer smiled, "but, yes, you are in."

Rory was stunned. He didn't understand. "Oh, uh…"

"Listen. I need you to keep it between us. Don't tell anyone. But, yes, you are in, and you will be OFFICIALLY notified next week. Does that make sense?" Dyer looked him right in the eye.

"Oh, yeah, of course. But, what about the other guys?" Rory went to turn back to see them.

Dyer pulled on Rory's shoulder, so his back was still to his fellow newbie's, "I need you NOT to tell them. Ok?"

"Oh, ok… but what about them? Did they make it?" Rory was sincerely concerned about them.

"Don't worry about them. And, DON'T tell them anything! Promise? I need you to assure me that you will NOT say a word!" Dyer grabbed Rory's right hand, again.

"Yeah, of course… but uh… I mean…" Rory didn't understand why he was being told, and they weren't.

"Ok, yeah. Most of them made it, and they will be told when the trainers are ready. So, you CAN'T say anything! Got it!" Dyer cocked his head to one side, "I need to be able to trust you."

Rory was worried about the other guys, but didn't push it,

"Oh, yeah, of course you can trust me."

"Ok, good. So when they ask you what we talked about, you tell them I just went over your strengths and weaknesses, and what you should work on. Ok?"

Rory nodded, again, "Ok, absolutely!"

Dyer gave him another vigorous shake and big smile, "Ok, good. I'll see you soon!"

Rory pumped Dyer's arm like he was pumping for water, "Thank you! Thank you so much!"

Dyer laughed, and pulled his arm back. "Ok, Rory, safe flight." He turned and walked over to join the other trainers.

When Rory got back to the other guys, Max was there. "Ok, guys, get changed up and out to the van in 15!"

Bravon grabbed Rory, wrapped his arm around him, and pulled him to the locker room. Scott and Eb rushed along, beside them. Jeffry strolled behind, not too interested.

"What was that all about? What did he say to you?" Bravon knew it was something really good.

Rory laughed. "He just said he wanted to give me some advice. He went over what I should work on, and stuff. You know, pointers."

Scott held on to Rory's arm. "So, did he tell you that you're in?"

Rory blushed, "Uh, no! Nothing like that."

Bravon thought there must be more to it. "Why did he want to talk to you, privately?"

"I don't know... I guess so he could speak freely. Uh... cause maybe he thought it'd be embarrassing in front of everyone?" Rory wasn't a great liar.

"You made it, for sure. Why would he *need* to pull you aside? Yeah! There's no doubt!" Scott was certain.

Eb nodded.

They took their time changing. All of them, except Rory, wanted the experience to last as long as possible, in case they weren't lucky enough to return.

Max rode back with them to the house, and waited for them downstairs as they showered quickly.

Dinner was set up outside by the pool, for just them, Max and Christopher, the house manager. The guys had tons of questions for both of them, and the first one was, "Do you know who made it?"

Max said, "Yup."

They all started screaming and yelling, and when they asked him to tell, Max said, "Nope." He smiled, and calmed them down. "We need to review, and you will ALL be notified next week... officially."

The newbie's all let out a disappointed sigh. Max held up one hand, and they knew to drop the subject.

They went on to talk about what it would be like if they were lucky enough to return. Max told them good and bad stories, which led the guys to asking him about this career, and other famous wrestlers. They wanted to know if Chris Enos was as big a "dick" as he was on TV. Max told them straight out, with no irony or sarcasm, "Absolutely. More so, even."

Max talked about his years as Champ, who he defeated, who he admired, who he trained, and more. He had great stories about Jake and Bart Colt, and Dyer Anderson, but nothing too bad, and all vanilla. He said that when they were chosen, got through training, and became working wrestlers, he'd tell them more juicy stories about their trainers, and himself. They had to earn it.

At the end of dinner Max warned them, again, to behave themselves in the house. They would be watched, closely. "Nothing is more important than your training, when you're here. If anything takes away from that, we remove it." He told them to relax, have a good time, but not to bother the trainees. They all have to get up early for another day of hard work.

The other guys had already come back, and Christopher excused himself to manage their dinner.

Max sat with them for a while, before also excusing himself. For a few minutes, the guys sat quietly, and stared at the pool, or up at the sky. Each knew what the other was thinking.

Rory smiled. "I can't wait to come back here!"

Scott jerked his head around, "So, Dyer Anderson DID tell you something!?"

Rory blushed, again, "NO! I'm just... you know, willing it to happen! I refuse to believe that I won't make it!" He hoped that sounded plausible.

Bravon nodded, "Oh yeah! Me too!" He looked at the other guys. "All of us! There is no reason to think any one of us didn't make it!"

Scott agreed. "Yeah! We ALL made it!"

Jeffry remained silent. He caught a couple of them looking over. Rory smiled, to make it seem like he wasn't thinking anything negative.

The trainees roared when the newbie's came in to the dining room, and congratulated them on getting through tryouts. Marky called them "Pussies". He and Vinny O said they couldn't wait to get their hands on them, *again*. Most of the other guys agreed with that, and pointed out whom they wanted most. Vinny O pointed at Rory and mouthed, "You're mine."

Clint raised his hand and yelled out, "Yeah, who here wants to work over Pretty Boy?!"

All the guys raised their hands. Red-faced, Rory laughed nervously, and had to adjust his trunks. The thought of wrestling all these guys was too much. He wished he could start right then, and there.

Bravon, Rory, Scott, and Eb sat down with them, and all got into loud, exited conversations. Jeffry disappeared.

Twenty minutes later, the guys started filing upstairs to relax, then retire for the night.

Ten minutes after that, Bravon, Scott, Eb, and Rory were in the Hot Tub.

Scott and Eb started out a respectable distance apart, but after settling in, they were right next to each other. Eb's arm was around Scott's shoulders and Scott's hand was on Eb's leg.

Eb caught a glance from Bravon, and asked him, "This doesn't bother you, does it?"

"Nah! No way. Why would it?" Bravon sincerely didn't care.

"So, you're totally straight, then, right?" Scott asked.

"Yup."

Scott looked at Rory, "And, you, Rory?"

"Oh, no. I'm into guys."

Eb laughed. "We kind of thought you guys might hook up."

Rory laughed.

Bravon looked at Rory. "For sure. Who WOULDN'T hook up with Pretty Boy, over here?"

Rory laughed, again, "Shut up!"

They all relaxed for a good, long while. Scott and Eb engaged in a little conversation about how each other were doing, then they engaged in a kiss.

Rory found it touching. They both seemed to really love each other.

After a few more minutes, they excused themselves, and returned to their room.

When they were out of earshot, Bravon moved next to Rory, and leaned in to him. "Ok, Rory! Tell me the truth! WHAT did Dyer Anderson say to you?"

"I told you…"

"Nah, nah, nah!" Bravon cut him off.

"No, really…"

"Rory!" Bravon grabbed his leg. "I know there's something you're not telling me!"

Rory wished Bravon wasn't straight. He felt he could really fall for him.

Rory let out a deep breath. He held up his hand, his pinky sticking out. "Ok, you gotta SWEAR NOT to tell ANYONE, EVER!"

Bravon wrapped his pinky around Rory's. "I swear!"

Rory whispered. "Ok, keep it quiet… Ok, I did get in!"

"Nice!" Bravon clasped Rory's hand. "Good going, man!"

"But! When I asked about you guys, all he said was 'Most of them got in', which I think means YOU for sure, right?" Rory turned to look at him. He didn't care that Bravon was straight. He wished he could kiss him. That would make the whole experience perfect.

"That's ALL he said, was 'Most'?" Bravon thought on it for a second. "Ok, we're not being uncool, or anything. We're just saying what we think. So, 'most', means Scott and me, for sure, right?" Bravon said with a questioning squint on his face.

"That's what I'm thinking. But, it could also mean Eb. He did a lot of really cool stuff in that ring! And, he's the best with interviews, I think." Rory matched Bravon's tone. "I really hope he makes it. I really do."

"Me too. That would FUCKING SUCK if he didn't make it." Bravon butted Rory's shoulder with his. "And, Jeffry? Are we just thinking 'no', for him?"

"Actually, when he didn't have the shitty attitude, I thought he was really entertaining!" Rory's hand made a flourish to emphasize "entertaining".

"For sure, but when you look at who is here, I don't think he fits in. I think they would deny him, only because he'd be too much drama, right?" Bravon looked Rory right in the eyes.

Rory agreed, "Yeah. Too much."

Bravon kept eye contact, and Rory became a little uneasy. He thought Bravon might actually kiss him. He wished it, actually.

Instead, Bravon butted him with his shoulder, again, and said, "So, FUCK! You made it! That is SO FUCKING AWESOME! Congratulations!"

"Shh! Keep it down! But, I really think you got in, too!" Rory couldn't stop smiling. It finally hit him. He HAD made it! He'd be back, and training as a real life Professional Wrestler.

Bravon whispered. "Ok, CONGRATULATIONS to me, too!"

Rory butted Bravon's shoulder, this time. "Yeah! Congratulations! But, you can't say anything, to anyone, ok?"

They sat silent for a while, then Bravon broke it. "So, tonight you'll help me out?"

Rory laughed it off, as a joke, even though he wished Bravon would force him, or trick him, into doing something he would regret.

They went inside and played video games until midnight. Christopher hung out with them for a little while, before sending them up to bed.

They brushed and flossed together, snuck by Jeffry, who was already asleep, then climbed into bed. Rory had never been so excited and relaxed at the same time.

They both stared up at the ceiling. Bravon comically mimicked the breathing exercises they did the might before. Rory imitated him, and they broke out laughing.

Jeffry made a noise and stirred, so they quieted down.

Bravon held Rory's hand in his, under the covers.

Rory's whole body came to attention, every part.

Bravon whispered, "Congratulations, Rory. We are going to have such a fucking good time together!"

Rory trembled, and whispered back, "Yeah, Congratulations, Bravon. I'm glad I met you!"

Bravon made an affirmative noise, "Mmm", then drifted off.

Rory was too stimulated to sleep. He took in the feel of Bravon's hand in his. He remembered Dyer Anderson's words. He fantasized about private matches with him, and time alone, so he could ask what is was like to have Rene Sebastian and Chris Enos work his penis over. All these thoughts just made him more excited.

Rory had to force himself down another line of thought. He tried to think about the athletic side of the training. It didn't help. Every time, it led to a sexual climax.

He tried to think about other hobbies. It didn't help. They all led back to what was causing his current erection. Then, he thought about his little brother, Reed, and how he couldn't wait to tell him about it. That morphed in to Chris Enos wrestling with his little brother. "STOP!" He yelled inside his own mind.

Nothing worked, so he let it all go. Chris Enos, his little brother, Bravon, Dyer Anderson, Scott, Eb, Marky, Vinny O, Max, Bart, Clint, and even Jeffry were all wrestling in his head. Symphonies, cloudbursts, puppies running wild, and all of a sudden, he was flying.

KNOCK! KNOCK! KNOCK! "Time to get up!"

Rory opened his eyes, and looked over at the door. It was morning, and Christopher was standing in the doorway. "Come on, guys, time to get ready!"

At the Airport, the guys said goodbye in the lounge, before

splitting up to catch their flights home.

Rory and Bravon hugged Scott and Eb. Rory, Eb, and Scott shook Jeffry's hand, but Bravon pulled him in for a hug. Jeffry resisted, but gave the faintest hint of a smile indicating that he might have actually liked it. The other guys all made a comical "Aw!" sound, and piled on, in a group hug.

"Alright, alright! Enough! I get the message!" Jeffry was mad at himself for smiling.

The guys held on for a few more minutes, uncontrollably laughing at Jeffry's screams for help.

Max broke it up. They all heaped their thanks on him, and shook his hand heartily. He said, "Goodbye" and was sure they could all be trusted to make their flights. He, also, had a flight to catch. He congratulated them, once more, and was gone.

Scott and Eb left to catch their flight, followed by Jeffry.

Bravon and Rory stood in front of their luggage. Rory kept his mouth shut, because his biggest urge was to gush about how much he liked Bravon.

Bravon gave him a big, goofy smile, then WRAPPED his arms around him, and kissed his cheek. "Aw! I'm gonna miss my little Rory!"

Rory melted in his arms.

9 RORY PEDERSEN

Back home, Rory stayed up late talking to his brother Reed, who was now 16 years old. At 5' 10", he was just a little bit shorter than Rory, and at 195 pounds, he was only about 5 pounds lighter. His face was rounder, and his neck and shoulders were broader. He was the young, redder, beefier version of Rory Pedersen. They were very close, and Reed also had become one of the best wrestlers on the high school team. Unlike Rory, though, he was on the Football Team, was more extroverted, and a bit of a smartass.

Rory told Reed every single detail about the Tryouts, except for his huge attraction to Bravon, the dirty tactics used in the matches, or anything about how aroused they made him. Reed knew that Rory dated Duane Birdsong when Rory was 16, and now, Mike Wall, but they never talked about it. They never talked about Reed's inclinations, either. Rory assumed he was straight, but he wondered sometimes, when they watched wrestling together. The thought of Reed's sexuality, at all, made him very uncomfortable.

When Rory told Reed about Dyer Anderson, his head almost exploded. He bounced around the room, and jumped on top of Rory, pinning his arms down. He yelled out, "YOU – HAVE – GOT – TO – BE - FUCKING – KIDDING – ME!!!" He made Rory tell every detail, three and four times over. He couldn't believe his own brother worked with Dyer Anderson, Jake and Bart Colt, and Max Gunn, and he was now going off to be a real-life pro wrestler.

Rory thought Reed might actually be more excited than he was.

When Reed stated he might try out for All Pro, when he turned 18, Rory had mixed feelings. He would love to have his brother follow in his footsteps. They would be an unstoppable tag team, but the thought of Reed being ringside while another man worked over his brother's genitals made Rory blush. Further speculation on the matter made him break out into a sweat, when it dawned on him that his brother might witness one of his uncontrollable erections.

After 3am, Rory finally fell asleep. At 9am, his communication device rang, and woke him up. He fumbled for it. It was Max Gunn. He snapped fully awake in that instant and turned on the voice-only option, as he was in his underwear, "Hello!"

"Rory! Hey, how are you doing?" Max sounded very happy.

"I'm great, thanks! How are you doing?" Rory tried to affect a refined tone.

"Great! Put me on visual. I want to see your face when I tell you why I called."

"Oh… but, uh…" Rory sat on the edge of the bed, trying to

figure out what to tell him he was doing.

"Shut up, I don't care if you were whacking off. It doesn't matter. Just do it!" Max snapped.

"Oh... Um, ok." Rory switched on the visual, and saw Max, in the back of a vehicle, wearing professional attire.

"Oh, look at you! Did I wake you up?" Max grinned.

"Uh, yeah, kinda." Rory rubbed his face.

"GOOD! So, the reason I'm calling is..." he paused, thinking he was building up anticipation, "All Worlds Pro Wrestling would like to officially invite you to the training camp, as a full-fledged trainee!"

"Nice!" Rory's heart soared. Even though he knew he had made it, hearing those 'Official Words' were still a huge thrill. "Thank you so much!"

"Damn it!!! Dyer told you, didn't he? He FUCKING swore to me that he didn't!" Max pounded something in front of him with his fist.

"Oh... no, no, he didn't!" Rory was still a bad liar.

"You are WAY too calm. No one has ever NOT jumped around when I told them that! Never!" Max gave Rory a scolding look.

"Uh, no! I really am surprised and excited! Thank you SO MUCH!" Rory bounced on his bed.

"Whatever! I'll deal with him, later! So, we want you here in 13 days. Is that doable?"

Max hadn't even finished the question when Rory answered, "YES! I can even come sooner, if you need me!"

Max laughed, "No, 13 days is good. Will we need to fly you out?"

"No, I'm gonna drive out, so I can have my own vehicle there."

"Ok, that's fine. We have some restrictions on personal vehicles, but I'll send you all of them. You'll have to sign, and return them before you leave your place of residence." Max went through all of the other formalities with Rory, then asked, "Do you have any questions?"

"Yeah! Bravon, Scott, and Eb made it?" Rory held one hand up, fingers crossed.

Max smiled, "I can not tell you that until I have officially notified them of our decision." He remembered he was mad, "Wait, Dyer didn't tell you?"

"No, he didn't tell me about them…" Rory stopped, mid sentence.

"A-HA! He DID tell you about yourself, then, didn't he?" Max pointed a finger directly at Rory.

"No! No! Uh…" Rory's face turned red.

Max laughed. "I'll tell the guys that they can contact you after I have told them."

"Ok, thanks! Thank you very much, Mr. Gunn!"

"Max. Call me Max, from now on, Rory. I'll send you your

pack ASAP. Let me know when you get it. I have other calls to make. I'll see you, soon, Rory!"

Max ended visuals right as Rory said "Thank you! Good bye!"

Rory jumped around his room, and threw on some gym shorts. He ran to Reed's room to tell him the good news.

When he got back to his room, he saw that Bravon had tried to contact him three times. He called back immediately.

"HEY!" Bravon also had had his shirt off, and had the biggest smile Rory had ever seen on a human being.

"SO?" It was obvious, but Rory wanted to hear him say it.

"Yup!! Max just called and confirmed!" Bravon howled. "AaaOOOO!!"

Rory jumped around the room, just like he had not done when Max called him. "THIS IS SO FUCKING AWESOME!!!!"

They yelled and screamed and carried on for ten straight minutes.

Rory asked, "Did he tell you about Scott and Eb? He wouldn't tell me."

"No, same here. He said he would have to talk to them, first, before he could say anything. I really hope Eb made it!" Bravon sat down.

Rory took a deep breath and did the same.

Rory tried to go back to sleep after he finished talking to

Bravon, but he couldn't. He tossed around in his bed, worrying about Eb and Scott. He looked up at his clock. 30 minutes had passed. If Scott and Eb got in, they SURELY would have called by now.

He wanted to call Bravon, but decided on calling to tell Mike.

Mike hooted and hollered. He was really excited for Rory. He almost lost his mind when Rory asked him if he'd drive out with him. Rory said he'd introduce him to all the guys, maybe even Dyer Anderson.

Mike demanded they see each right away, and started to talk about dirty things he wanted to do with Rory.

Rory was about to reciprocate when he received a call from Bravon. "I'm sorry, Mike! Um... uh, it's about training. I will call you right back!" He ended the call with Mike, and brought Bravon right up. "Hey! Any news?"

"NO! I can't take it, anymore, Let's call them!" Bravon was uncharacteristically flustered.

"Do you think we should? What if?" Rory didn't want to say it out loud.

"Yeah! What if? Then, what do we do?" Bravon thought for a second.

They went on, discussing what they should do about the situation for another five minutes.

Rory's face lit up. "It's Scott! Hold on! I'll network us!"

Rory brought Scott up. He and Eb were both on screen, looking rather deflated. "Hey guys! Bravon's on, too!" Rory split-screened them. He could see Bravon's expression change when he saw the state Eb and Scott were in.

"Hey! Guys! So, how's it going?" Bravon tried to keep an upbeat, happy tone in his voice.

Eb cleared his throat, "Well…. Scott got in." His voice cracked.

Rory was still hopeful. "That's awesome!"

"Yeah!" Bravon refused to believe Eb didn't make it.

"But…" Eb looked like his heart was broken.

Scott dropped his head down onto the desk. His shoulders were trembling.

Rory felt a pit in his gut. "But, what?"

"Yeah, but what?" Bravon held his breath.

Eb shook his head. It looked like his eyes were watering.

"Oh, fuck! Are you serious?! Why? How is that possible?" Bravon's hands went up.

Rory's heart sank, "Is there anything we can do?" He couldn't believe this had happened, "What exactly did he say? I mean, maybe we can…"

Eb looked right into the camera, "He said…." His voice broke, again. He was on the verge of tears.

Rory couldn't take it. He thought he might start crying, too.

Eb cleared his throat, and started again, "He said… that I was too fucking awesome, and THAT YOU DUMBASSES ARE GOING TO

HAVE TO SUCK MY DICK!"

Scott raised his head. His shoulders were still trembling, but because he couldn't stop laughing.

"I GOT IN, TOO, YOU ASS FUCKERS!!!" Eb threw up a double middle-finger salute to Bravon and Rory.

"WHAT?" Rory was up on his feet.

"THAT IS SO FUCKING AWESOME, YOU TOTAL FUCKING DOUCHEBAG!" Bravon was up, too. He and Rory both did a victory dance.

Scott was laughing, and Eb pushed his face up into the camera, "You two Ass Monkeys thought I didn't get in!"

"NO! We knew you'd get in!" Rory had never been so relieved in his whole life.

"What took you so long to call us???" Bravon sat down and gave them a dirty look.

Scott averted his eyes. Eb's eyebrows bounced. "Well, after we got our call, we had our own private, little celebration!"

Rory laughed.

Bravon rested his head on his hands and leaned in. "Really? What EXACTLY did you do? Come on, tell us everything!"

Scott laughed. Eb snapped his fingers and bobbled his head from side to side, as if he was one slick character, "Well, I WILL say this. It's probably not the way you think it is!"

Even Scott had a questioning look at that answer.

Eb threw his arm around Scott, "I mean, it's probably the opposite way you think it is."

"Hey!" Scott gave a funny, disapproving look.

The guys all yelled and screamed and talked about how amazing it was going to be. They reminisced about tryouts, even though it was only a couple days ago.

They were about to wrap up the call when Scott remembered, "Hey, have you guys heard about Jeffry, at all?"

"No! He didn't give me any of his contact info, at all." Rory answered.

"He didn't give it to any of us, did he?" Bravon wished he actually could reach out to Jeffry.

"No. I guess we'll just have to see when we get to training." Scott frowned.

There was an awkward pause. They screamed and yelled some more, then Eb ended the call by yelling into the camera, "I'M GONNA FUCK YOU TWO ASS-FUCKERS IN THE ASS SO FUCKING HARD WHEN I SEE YOU!"

All Worlds Pro Wrestling Trainee

Rory packed up his life, and spent as much time as he could with family and friends.

That night Mike took him out for a congratulatory dinner, and, of course, the evening wound up with them in bed... then in the shower, then on the bathroom floor, then in the tub, then back in bed.

They filled those two weeks with as many wrestling matches, for their Pure Pro Federation, as they could. The last two sessions were kind of sad. The guys were excited for Rory, but hated to see him go. Rory begged them to keep doing it, and said he would get involved whenever he could.

They all came over to Rory's house the day he and Mike left for the A.W.P.W. training facility in Las Vegas. Rory was really touched by the send-off. Some of the guys even cried! He couldn't believe it.

A few miles into their trip, it hit Rory, like a ton of bricks. He became choked up, and his eyes watered. Mike started to make fun of him, but he realized that he and Rory wouldn't see as much of each other in the coming years. He held Rory's hand, and they drove in silence for a few miles.

Then, Rory laughed, and their excitement snapped them back into the present. Mike talked about how much he envied Rory, not only for the wrestling, but for the amazing situation he would be in. He asked Rory if he thought about the sexual opportunities he would have.

Rory shrugged and shook his head. "Nah…"

Mike smacked Rory's chest with the back of his hand, "Who do you think you're talking to?"

Rory blushed.

Mike sighed, "I've been thinking about it, a lot." He grabbed Rory's hand, again. "I don't think it's fair for me to…" He had been contemplating this for a long time, and didn't realize how hard it would be for him.

Rory glanced over, quickly, then back at the road. "Oh, Mike. I don't..."

"Rory, let's be realistic, here." He squeezed Rory's hand. "I really don't want to be the guy who keeps you from doing what you've always wanted to do."

"Mike, stop! I love you..."

Mike leaned in and kissed Rory's neck.

Rory caressed Mike's head, while he kept one hand on the steering wheel.

"I know you do, but..." Mike looked out the window.

"I don't have to do that." Rory couldn't believe he was losing another amazing man, because their lives were going in different directions.

"Rory, we will be apart so much. I think it just makes sense." Mike pushed all the sadness out of him. He wanted it to be a completely positive experience for Rory.

"No, Mike..."

He cut Rory off, "Rory, if I was in your position, I would want to do THE SAME thing! I love you! I love you more than..." He looked out the window, again, and let out a hard breath.

"I don't want to make that kind of thing more important than you are, to me!" Rory knew Mike was right.

"You're not! I think we are just too young to exclude each

other from anything. If we were in the same city, it would be different, but you know what I'm saying is right." Mike rubbed Rory's stomach.

"I would just feel like shit doing anything with another guy…"

"DON'T! Cause it's totally fine! Do it! I have to tell you: I wanna do it when were up there! I wanna be with you! And, I love you, but I also wanna be in a fucking orgy with you, and Dyer Anderson, and Bart Colt!…." Mike had become animated and a lot louder.

Rory turned to look at him. He was shocked, but also aroused, and couldn't say anything for a few minutes.

Mike snorted, "I KNOW you want to do that, too!"

Rory blushed, and shook his head.

"You just have to realize that we both have conflicting feelings, inside, and that's all that's going on. Do you know what I mean?" Mike stared at him.

Rory nodded, shyly. He grabbed Mike's hand, and kissed it.

They were both silent for a few more miles.

Rory cleared his throat. "So, how is this going to work? I mean, if anything happened, YOU'RE the guy I'd want to share it with."

"Oh, hell yeah! I want to hear about everything!" Mike nodded.

Rory looked at him with wide eyes.

"I know it's weird, and kinda sounds sick, but that's how I'm gonna get through it. And, I'll be jealous, and I'll tell you, and we'll talk about it."

Rory had a realization, "It's true. It just hit me. You're gonna be with other guys, too…. And, It doesn't make sense, but I want to know about it!"

Mike nodded, harder, "See!"

"I know!" Rory pointed to his own head, "It makes sense in here…" His eyes watered, and he pointed to his chest, "…but, not in here."

Mike leaned over and kissed his cheek, and rubbed his chest. "I know. I know… But, you're not going to be living a normal life."

When they arrived at A.W.P.W. mansion, their energy shot through the roof. Mike couldn't believe it. He bounced in his seat, as they pulled through the gate, "Oh, my FUCKING God!"

Christopher met them at the front door. He cocked his head when he saw Mike, "Oh…wow, THIS is your friend?"

Rory wondered what that meant. Christopher shook both their hands, then led them up to Rory's room.

Bravon hadn't arrived, yet, but Scott and Eb had, and were already at the training facility. Rory hurried Mike, so they could get down there, too.

When they pulled up at the facility, Mike burst out of the car, and stared up at it. "It's massive!"

Inside, Mike's eyes popped out of his head. He stopped just inside the door, and covered his mouth with his hand, "I... I just fucking... I don't even know..."

Rory saw Jake and Bart, next to one of the rings. He pulled Mike over. Bart turned around, and greeted Rory with a smile, "Hey Rory! You're here!"

Mike's mouth dragged on the floor.

Rory shook Bart's hand and introduced them.

Bart grabbed Mike's hand and gave him a hearty, "Hello!"

Mike could barely speak. "Hello, sir."

Jake heard them, and turned around. "PRETTY BOY!" He grabbed Rory's shoulder with his left hand and Rory's right hand with his. He shook him with both, "You made it!"

Rory blushed, and introduced him to Mike, who did the same thing, "Hello, sir." Mike was having a hard time pretending he was not intimidated.

Jake smirked, and leaned in close to Rory, "HE'S your *friend?*... Is he ok?"

Rory nodded, "He's uh... a fan."

"Oh!" Jake smiled. "Good to meet you Mikey!"

Rory looked around and smiled. A lot of the same trainees were still there.

Clint was in a ring behind them. He yelled over, "Hey, Prettyboy's here!"

Rory and Mike turned around. Rory pointed at Clint. "Hey, Clint! How's it going?"

Clint was in his gray wrestling trunks and boots. Mike couldn't get over his unbelievably enormous chest and arms.

"RORY!" Scott ran over, and picked Rory up, followed by Eb, who messed up his hair. Rory hugged them as hard as he could.

He introduced them to Mike. Scott cocked his head sideways and Eb asked, "THIS is your friend?"

Rory wondered why three people, now, had asked that.

Scott took a hold of Rory's head and whispered in his ear, "Guess who's here, and asked about you!!!"

Rory's face scrunched up, "Who?"

"Dyer Anderson"

"He asked about me?"

Mike gave him a questioning look. Rory pulled him close and whispered, "Dyer Anderson's here."

Mike punched him in the arm, "Shut the fuck up!"

Just then, a big, meaty hand clamped around the top of Rory's head from behind. Mike's eyes bugged out, yet again, and he pointed, as if he had just seen a ghost.

Rory turned around, and it was Dyer Anderson. He blushed, and couldn't help but grin from ear to ear. "Hi!"

"Hey Rory! I'm glad you made it!" Dyer shook Rory's hand, then held it for a while.

It took Rory a moment and he clumsily turned and introduced Dyer to Mike.

Dyer gave Mike a curious look, "Hey, Mike. Good to meet you." And extended his hand for a shake.

Mike took it, and babbled, "Oh, yeah...uh. Hi."

Dyer didn't understand what he had just said, "Sorry, what?"

Mike lost control of himself, and completely geeked out, "You are fucking Dyer Anderson!"

Everybody laughed.

Dyer Anderson was amused. He had experienced this kind of reaction, before, "No, I'm not fucking him, anymore."

Everybody laughed, again.

He took Mike by the shoulder, and patted it, "Yeah, I am Dyer Anderson.... And, YOU are Rory's friend?" He asked with the same strange intonation Eb, Jake, and Christopher had.

"Yeah." Mike nodded.

"Yeah, he is. Why is that weird?" Rory really wanted to know.

"No! It's not weird. You guys just look good together. Like a tag team, or something." Dyer pointed a finger at Mike, "Are you trying out? Are you a wrestler?"

"Oh, no! I just drove out with Rory." Mike was flattered.

"He's a good wrestler, and WE actually *have* done some tag matches!" Rory was proud of everyone's reaction, now.

"Get out!" Dyer laughed. "You should try out, then."

Jake and Bart had been watching trainees in the ring, but talk of the tag team piqued their interest.

"Uh.. I don't know." Mike was now blushing.

"He's awesome! I have some great video on him!" Rory was beaming.

Jake pointed at Mike. "I knew I recognized you! You're on Rory's submission video!"

Rory was nodding wildly, "Yeah! He is!"

"From what I've seen, he's actually is pretty good!" Jake agreed.

Dyer pointed at Jake and Bart, then at Rory and Mike, "Don't you see it? Don't you think he should try out?"

Jake looked at Rory, "Put together a complete submission. I am definitely interested."

Bart thought it was interesting, "Yeah, I can see it."

"Oh... but, uh..." Mike stammered.

"You DON'T want to?" Dyer thought that would be unbelievable.

"He DOES want to!" Rory wasn't going to let Mike out of it.

"Yeah... I mean... but I'm in college... I'm on the football team." Mike gave Rory a look.

"That's cool. You can try out, and work around that stuff.

Football players make really good wrestlers." Bart turned around, figuring the deal was done.

Jake addressed Rory, Scott, and Eb, "I'll be with you guys in a minute. He turned back to the action in the ring.

Dyer looked at the two blond boys, again, and nodded his head, proud that he made it happen. He pulled out one of his devices, and made some notes, "Hold on, just gotta ..."

Scott and Eb pushed Rory, and grabbed Mike's arm, "You guys should TOTALLY be a tag team! You HAVE TO TRY OUT!"

Mike's head was spinning. His face was stretched out into a dumbfounded smile. He held his hands up to Rory, and spoke in a comical voice, "Wowdy! What the hell are you doing to me?"

Dyer Anderson looked up.

Scott asked, "Wowdy?"

Mike laughed.

Rory blushed, and waved his hands, "It's nothing. It's stupid!"

Dyer raised his eyebrows.

Mike smirked, "Aw, Woawy never told you about Wowdy?"

"Shut up!" Rory backhanded Mike's arm, and gave him a dirty look.

Eb laughed, "Woawy?"

Dyer still looked at Rory, with big questioning eyes.

Rory's face was really red, as he tried to explain. "It's just, uh, my little brother couldn't say, 'Rory', when he learned how to talk. He used to call me 'Wowdy', or 'Rowdy', so that's what my family calls me sometimes."

"Awww!" Dyer was smiling, with a pensive look on his face.

Scott jabbed Rory's arm, "That-is-awesome!"

"Biiig Wowdy!" Eb loved it.

"Uh... yeah, 'Rowdy'... something." Dyer had Rory's shoulder in his hand again.

Jake leaned back, and said, "Yeah, I heard that. Rowdy! Yeah, 'Rowdy Pedersen'? No! 'Rowdy', and some other last name. Something, kinda tough, or hard; something strong."

Bart agreed, "Yeah, the name "Rowdy" hasn't been used in a while."

"Nice! Rowdy!" Dyer nodded.

Rory looked at Mike. He thought he was mad at him, but that feeling had sort of melted away.

The guys got involved in other things. Mike stepped forward and nudged Rory. "I'm sorry."

Rory bit his lip and playfully pushed his fist into Mike's stomach.

Bravon arrived, and all hell broke loose. Scott, Eb, and Rory rushed him, and all three lifted him off his feet. They hugged him, and the four of them struggled a bit, in a sort of rugby scrum, then jumped up and down together.

After a few minutes, they settled down, and Rory introduced Bravon to Mike.

Bravon looked at Scott and Eb, and made thumb motion to Mike, "Did you guys already comment on them?... the two blonds?"

"Oh, yeah." Eb was over it.

"Yeah. Mike's even gonna try out!" Scott pointed at Mike.

"Oh, nice!" Bravon grabbed Mike's arm, and pulled him in for a hug. "Congratulations! Good luck, man!"

Jake, Bart, and Dyer came over.

"Ok, guys! We got some stuff to go over, then you can go back to the house!" Jake looked at Mike, "Oh, uh..."

"It's cool. I'll show him around." Bart put his hand on Mike's shoulder, and guided him away. Mike looked back at Rory, who just shrugged.

Jake began the orientation process.

Bart explained why they had to leave the group. "Sorry, there's just stuff we only want trainees to hear."

"Oh, ok." Mike understood.

Bart smiled, "So, I'll be one of the trainers working with you in tryouts."

"Oh... uh.. yeah, cool." Mike didn't know what to say.

"You ARE going to try out, right?" Bart said it as though Mike had no choice.

"Uh... yeah, I guess I have to, right?" Mike held his hands up.

"Yeah, you really DO have to. We can even get some video on you today and tomorrow." Bart put that to rest, and went on showing him the rest of the facility, as he would do with any future trainee.

THE END.

The Rowdy Armstrong Series.

ROWDY ARMSTRONG - Wrestling's New Golden Boy
1st Book in the Series

ROWDY ARMSTRONG - Pro Wrestling Rookie
2nd in the Series. (Out soon)

Other books by DAVID MONSTER,

SERVICE: A Love Story (1st in Series – Cover on next page)

Dude-on-Dude love story. "It's a fucking beautiful book!"

PARALLEL LINES - Commence Entropy (1st in Series)

The most desirable & celebrated woman on the planet finds she has everything she ever wanted, including the love of a devoted psychopath & a metaphysical link to a troubled teenage boy she will never meet.

SERVICE is a true-to-life love story of two young men:
George and Steven.

Half the story is told through excerpts from George's personal
Journal. He is poetic and brilliant, but often way off base. The
other half of the story is told through narrative – just the facts.

www.Facebook.com/ServiceTheBook

David Monster

ABOUT THE AUTHOR

David Monster is a Writer, Designer, and Filmmaker and has been working in the Entertainment Industry for decades and decades.

His first novel, *SERVICE, A Love Story*, received several 5 Star reviews. ReviewsByAmosLassen.com said, "This is a beautiful book... David Monster is someone to watch." The Web Series Pilot he wrote & directed called *R.A.D.MEN (2014)*, won awards on the Film Festival Circuit. In December of 2014, he released his second novel, PARALLEL LINES: Commence Entropy, a sexy Sci-Fi/Fantasy Thriller. One reviewer described it as "NOT 50 Shades of Gray, in an alternate dimension".

A devoted fan of vintage pop culture, David has spent 8 years researching and writing the most comprehensive resource available on Sex Symbols, called *BOMBSHELL: The Blonde Phenomenon of the 20th Century*, which will be published in 2016.

Facebook.com/RowdyArmstrong
Facebook.com/RowdyArmstrongWrestlingBook
Twitter.com/RowdyArmstrong
DavidMonster.com

Made in the USA
Middletown, DE
24 November 2017